Homme Fatale

A NOVEL

IN LIFE, AS IN FILM,
FIGHT FOR THE ROLE YOU WANT

JAYE VINER

Homme Fatale
Copyright © 2024 by Jaye Viner

All Rights Reserved.

Editor: Sarah McGuire
Cover Designer: Damonza Designs
Interior Book Formatting by: Authortree | https://www.authortree.co/

ISBN: 979-8-9878525-6-9

Jane of Battery Park

Elaborate Lives

Terrible Love

Casta Diva

The Afternoon Delight Shorts

Saucy Kaylee and her Stockbroker

Smart Jen and her Reality TV Star

Sweet Penny and her Tech Bro

Sour Marlee and her Sergeant

Homme Fatale

"I would recognise you in total darkness, were you mute and I
deaf. I would recognise you in another lifetime entirely, in
different bodies, different times. And I would love you in all of
this, until the very last star in the sky burnt out into oblivion."

Song of Achilles
Madeline Miller

"You've been neglecting me," said Quinn.

Lucas stirred as though from deep thought.

"It's fine," said Quinn. And it was, because now, once again the center of Lucas's meticulous gaze, he felt his skin crawling as though that gaze was a magnet and all Quinn's secrets were little shavings of metal being pulled to the surface so Lucas could pluck them out. *How can he be so much one thing and so much another?*

"Look at you." Lucas shook his head. "So inscrutable."

Quinn wasn't quite sure what inscrutable meant or if it was good or bad in this case, so he held his silence.

"What are you? I've had you in my house almost a month and you're as unknown to me now as you were then. Either I'm a terrible host or you're a very good puzzle."

"Do you like puzzles?" asked Quinn.

"Usually. But I like to feel that I'm making progress."

You are, thought Quinn. *I think about you when I'm trying to fall asleep at night. I think about you when I wake up. I feel sorry for you, you goddamn bastard.*

"Maybe you're blocked by something," said Quinn. "You're trying to see what Larisa sees instead of what could just be yours."

Warmth blushed bright and golden across Lucas's expression, a vibrant delight. "I want very much to know what you are to Larisa."

"I'm nothing special."

"That has been established. And yet." Lucas leaned forward in his chair. "You have witchcraft in your lips and galaxies in your eyes."

Content Warning

This book contains Male on Male sexual assault in Chapter 10. There are mentions of terrorist activity, people disappearing, and murder.

- Crazy in Love by Beyoncé
- You Can't Hide by CK9C
- Truth or Dare by Tyla
- Gimme More by Britney Spears
- U Don't have to Call by Usher
- LoveGame by Lady Gaga
- If I Ain't Got You by Alicia Keys

Chapter 1

Larisa on the Run

In the far distant past of that afternoon, Larisa had allowed Jaden to dress her for happy hour. At the time, it hadn't seemed significant. They were going to meet the other sisters at Cloud Nine. Larisa was going to tell them about her increasingly surreal life, meeting with an arms dealer in a country club, the dead body of a young woman in the backseat of the arms dealer's car. What she'd be wearing had seemed, perhaps for the first time in Larisa's life, inconsequential.

But a lot had happened since happy hour. There'd been the emergency call from Larisa's mother, then the rush to her parents' house to confront her wayward cousin Hannah, who'd escaped from Italy with a laptop stolen from Larisa's ex-boyfriend, also an arms dealer. Larisa's parents had learned all about his secret life, the life Larisa had been hiding from them, and then the cops had arrived to ask Larisa questions about the dead body she'd had nothing to do with.

And now, as she stair walked and skidded down the graded hill of chaparral and rocks behind her parents' house in Louboutin heels and a skirt that barely covered the lip of her butt, Larisa wished Jaden didn't still dress like she was twenty-one. She wished for a pair of sneakers to fall out of the sky. She wished she hadn't panicked and ran.

At the base of the hill, Larisa skirted along a fence, then came up to a neighborhood road. The heels came off. The dust and rocks had ruined their finish, but Larisa carried them with her because she found comfort in imagining there'd be a future where she'd see Jaden and be able to apologize for ruining her shoes.

"Now what?" Larisa asked herself as she followed the road past the houses mounted into the cliff to where it began to slope down toward WeHo. She had no phone, no car. The police were looking for her. Pam the local arms dealer was looking for her. Lucas the ex-boyfriend arms dealer was probably also looking for her. Or worse, he didn't have to look for her because he had Quinn and he believed Larisa would come for him.

A hedge fund bro yelled at her to get out of the road as he swerved by in his Tesla, leaving Larisa breathlessly leaning against someone's front gate, heart pounding with more fear than she could name. In the next moment, she thought, *How dare he?* And all the feelings and resentments and trapped nameless things she'd spent so many years trying to ignore welled up in a great roar that sounded more like a scream as she flung first one shoe, then the other at the disappearing car.

She'd have to buy Jaden a new pair of shoes. This thought sent a burst of hysterical laughter bubbling up and pouring out of Larisa's strained throat. Even with the allowance her father gave her and the fees she was collecting from her three clients, Larisa couldn't afford her own new pair of Louboutins, let alone a gift for her friend.

"Why don't we just call it what it is?" she muttered as she began to walk again, one hand braced against the hedge that bordered the road for support. "I'm a washed-up doctor who likes weird sex, has terrible taste in men, and has always exceeded her income."

She came to a stop at Sunset and Sunset. Traffic passed. Across the street, a new building was going up, replacing something that'd been older and possessed a soul filled with the blood, sweat, and tears of all the people who'd come to make it in that town. She wasn't exactly one of them, but it still felt like a personal loss, as though the construction team, the building developer, were all part of the greater problem lurking in her mind. Every time she tried to pin it down with a name it fractured into pieces.

Pam.

The police.

Hannah.

The CIA.

Lucas.

Quinn.

All Larisa's life, it felt like she'd always been fighting for the chance to make her own way. And here she was, almost thirty, with no prospects, and no closer to gaining that place of self-destiny than she'd been when she'd graduated from college.

That probably wasn't entirely true. But it felt true. As though she'd been predestined to forever be the lacky in someone else's grand plan. Whatever she did next, she wanted it to be something she chose for herself.

Her therapist, Dr. Bade, had an office in Beverly Hills. Larisa thought she could walk there without killing herself. It was early Friday evening so Dr. Bade wasn't likely to be there, but maybe there'd be a janitor or a security guard who could make a call for her. Larisa would tell her therapist everything and hope Dr. Bade would have an idea of what to do, or at least if nothing could be done, how she might come to terms with this mess that'd become her life. Larisa pointed herself west. No sooner had she taken her first step, than a black SUV careened out of the floor of traffic and pulled to a stop in the driveway of the Italian restaurant directly in front of her.

The door swung open to reveal a dim interior, a figure in profile. That Jackie O hairstyle could only be Pam.

Actually, it could've been any number of people, especially women of a certain age in the political sphere. But the only other person Larisa knew in that area of the world was Kahleah, and she wouldn't be caught dead letting someone else drive her around in a tinted SUV.

Larisa closed the distance between her and the door.

"You sent the police to my parents' house?"

"It was the fastest option," said Pam. "I didn't expect you to run."

"Clearly you did because here you are."

"I had *hoped* you wouldn't run. Running makes you look guilty as hell. You know that, right?"

"Remind me what you think I'm guilty of?"

"Just get in."

"I'd rather not."

"I can't be seen with you."

"Then I'll just be on my way." Larisa started to step around the SUV. Pam scooted across the bench and climbed out. "You've been lying to me, Larisa."

"The feeling is mutual."

"Are you working for Lucas?"

"No."

"But you've refused to cooperate with the CIA."

"You know what's funny? Every time we talk, you bring up the CIA. I'm beginning to feel you're a lot better friends than you want people to think."

"Are you in contact with Lucas directly?"

Larisa squinted into the last embers of the sunset. Palm trees, billboards for shows she'd probably never see, twin sets of red tail-lights all the way to the ocean. She couldn't remember the last time she'd been a pedestrian standing still with nowhere to go. As much as she wanted to take in the view and find some truth about the nature of being a lifelong Angeleno, the stillness bothered her internal balance. She was so tired, but still all she wanted was to go and go and go.

Chasing an impossible dream, she thought.

"Larisa? Now is the time for truth. I will have you arrested."

"I was just talking to him when your people came," said Larisa.

"Why?"

So I could hear Quinn's voice.

"I wanted him to hear about Ana from me."

"You told him I killed her."

"I told him she had an accident. Your security agent probably didn't even notice the signs? She was an addict."

At first Larisa thought Pam didn't believe her. But then Pam nodded, an increment of tension seeped out of her shoulders. "Does he believe you killed John?"

"We didn't talk about it."

"You should come stay with me until we know for sure."

Larisa shook her head. "I can't hide from him. He'll know something's wrong. I'm supposed to do something else."

"What do you mean?"

"Ana said there was another thing Lucas wanted me to do."

"What thing?"

"If you hadn't killed her, we could ask. And since you trashed my phone, I can't ask that way, so we'll have to wait and see."

"Then being arrested is your best cover. You wouldn't be able to communicate, and he couldn't expect you to run his errands."

"He'd come get me out. You want him in town?"

Pam made a face. "We'll move up our timetable then. Tell me about the winery you mentioned."

"Nothing about that has changed. It'll be too suspicious to move against it now. Have your people found anything at the club in Florence yet?"

Pam didn't answer, so Larisa turned and looked at her. "We're being honest with each other, right, Pam?"

"They're overdue for a report."

"How long has it been?"

"Twelve hours. But that doesn't mean anything. If they've made contact with Lucas's accountant, they wouldn't necessarily be able to get away to send a message."

"So it's still a waiting game."

"At twenty-four hours the B team goes in. We won't have to wait for long."

We, thought Larisa. She studied the woman beside her who looked like a regular person but did deals with terrorists with one hand and the CIA with the other. A woman who Larisa was certain hid a cutthroat thirst for power beneath that perfectly coifed hair. *You scare me just as much as he does,* thought Larisa. At least Lucas felt familiar enough to predict. Then again, Larisa couldn't remember the last time she'd accurately predicted something Lucas had done.

"So you think good things are happening." Larisa wanted it to be a question, but it came out like a statement, as though to make it easy for Pam to agree that everything with the plan to break into Lucas's finances and steal his account information was going swimmingly. Instead, Pam sighed. And in the volume of that nonverbal answer, Larisa couldn't help but add words that voiced her own feeling of bottomless dread.

"You think something's gone wrong," she said. "I feel it too." Even a twelve hour wait felt like too long. "You have a line to Agent Osna?"

Larisa watched Pam hesitate as she tried to decide what her answer should be. Instead of irritated, Larisa found the struggle strangely endearing. Here, they'd had this moment of bespoke honesty, and yet they were still lying to each other. Which was fine. Larisa wasn't about to say anything about Quinn being with Lucas. If Pam didn't want to admit her ties to the CIA, Larisa could accept that.

"I'm not sure you knew, but my cousin was playing spy at Lucas's villa. She just came back with a stolen laptop, and I told her I'd help her find someone who could use it." Larisa tried not to stare at Pam's face, as though every micro twitch of her expression could be written with meaning. And yet, this felt like a test of the boundaries of their partnership. If Pam said she could use the laptop herself, Larisa would know, once and for all, Pam was working outside of the government for her own aims and couldn't be trusted.

But Pam said, "I'll see what I can do." And for one brief moment, as twilight descended over the most famous street in the city, Larisa allowed herself to believe this was a sign of good things to come instead of focusing on the very real negative; nothing good in her life had ever come from the CIA.

Chapter 2

Osna Fails Her Again

CIA Agent Osna kept Larisa waiting until Tuesday, and then, instead of arranging for an inconspicuous place to meet, he came to the house to collect the laptop Hannah had stolen. This probably wasn't on purpose, as he looked just as haggard as Larisa felt, but he came at dinner time when her parents were both home and bustling around the kitchen preparing for what promised to be a painful family meal. Larisa was also in the kitchen, sitting at the island, getting in the way when Sarah, the house manager, showed him in.

"Larisa, he says you're expecting him." Sarah looked at Gunter, then at Suzette, apparently unsure if she should've made the unscheduled guest wait until after dinner. Larisa jumped off her stool.

"What the fuck, Osna? You can't be here."

"Larisa," breathed her mother.

"What? He deserves it."

"I'm here about the laptop."

"Oh. I'll go find Hannah," said Suzette.

"Would you like a drink?" asked Gunter. "Or a bite? We were just sitting down."

"No, Dad. He's not staying."

"I just need a few minutes with Larisa and Hannah."

Larisa stared at him. Not once in all the years she'd known him had Osna been this polite to her. When he shifted his gaze from Gunter to her, he almost looked like a regular person full of manners and consideration, which almost made her feel guilty for swearing at him.

"We can talk out here." Larisa opened the sliding door to the patio and left it open so Hannah could find them.

"Nice," said Osna as he surveyed the yard.

"You're working with Pam."

"My partner was." A pause, then a muttered. "God damn him."

"I heard what happened. I'm sorry."

Osna glared at her like he was going to say something biting, but the words came out soft. "He'd be alive if you'd agreed to help us."

There's no way to prove that's true, thought Larisa as she pushed down a rush of guilt she knew she didn't deserve.

"You gave Pam the information you've been withholding, didn't you?" he asked.

"I don't want to talk about this."

"Why her? She's a criminal, the same as he is."

"Exactly. She doesn't have rules the way you do. She knows how to cover her tracks."

"And yet, Lucas remains free."

"Not for long." Larisa nodded toward the door so Osna would turn to see Hannah standing there with the laptop clutched in both arms.

"This is Agent Osna," said Larisa. "He's with the CIA. Osna, this is my cousin Hannah who your Italian counterpart used, endangered, and manipulated so that she never felt risking her life was good enough."

"That's not true," said Hannah, eyes wide. "I mean yeah, it was scary. But I wanted to do it." She held out the laptop. "I took this from Lucas's dungeon."

Osna laughed. "See any rotting skeletons while you were down there?"

Hannah looked to Larisa as though she could decode if he was making a joke or not.

"Lucas has a sex room in the villa," said Larisa.

"But I didn't do anything sexual in it," said Hannah.

"What do you think is on this laptop?" asked Osna.

"Everything you need?"

"Or it could just be porn, right? Who keeps a laptop in a sex dungeon if not for porn?" Osna handed the laptop back to her. "Why don't you just hang on to it?"

Hannah's mouth dropped open.

"You're not even going to look at it?" asked Larisa.

"A sex dungeon laptop? I'm not a pervert like some people I know."

Larisa charged him. "Get out. Get out now!"

When he didn't move fast enough toward the door, she kicked his shins, and chased him through the kitchen, into the front of the house, and out the front door. "Don't ever come here again, asshole!"

Door slam, not as satisfying as she wanted. Even with the width of the house between them, Larisa could hear Hannah sobbing.

Thanks to Osna, dinner was even more painful than Larisa had expected.

First Hannah sobbing into her napkin. Then the pregnant silence decorated with the clinking of their silverware. Suzette's heavy sighing, which she probably didn't even realize she was doing. Gunter saying he would make some calls even though he had already run through his contact list trying to find someone who could help them navigate the situation. He was strongly against calling the public CIA tipline and telling the automated system Hannah had come home from Italy with a terrorist's laptop.

"Do you really think there's only porn on the laptop?" asked Hannah.

Suzette stopped chewing like the food in her mouth had suddenly turned rotten. Gunter cleared his throat. And then, almost on cue, they both looked at Larisa, the resident expert on explicit sexuality, but more importantly, expert on all things Lucas would or would not do.

"I don't know," said Larisa.

Hannah stared down at her plate. "I'm worthless."

"You're not worthless," cooed Suzette with more warmth than she'd ever given Larisa.

"We should watch a really great movie tonight to distract ourselves," said Gunter. "Hannah, do you want to pick?"

Quinn sending her home in his place was worthless, thought Larisa. *Now he's trapped there.*

"Movies remind me of Lucas now," said Hannah. "You know he hosts these film society meetings full of weird people who—"

"They're not weird," said Larisa too sharply. "They're just different than you." She stood up before Hannah started crying again. "I'm going back to my apartment. Which car can I take?"

"Oh honey, don't be like that," said Suzette.

"It's better to stay here," said Gunter. "You've had a shock. There's a lot up in the air."

"I'll just hire a car." Larisa realized this process required a smart phone. She stalked over to the secretary desk in the corner of the kitchen where Quinn's phone had been sitting since Hannah arrived. She took it, then the laptop from the island on her way out the door.

From the car, she called Sid to meet her at the apartment with the spare set of keys.

"How'd it go with the police?" he asked.

"The police? Oh, that was just a misunderstanding." She gave him the short version of Pam, and Osna, and the laptop.

They arrived at the apartment almost at the same time. Sid unlocked the door and stepped inside to hold it open. Larisa tried not to resent the way her white Persian kitten, Sabrina, came running to rub against Sid's legs.

"I'm sure she missed you." Sid swept Sabrina into his arms like it was no big deal to hold a cat and followed Larisa into the kitchen. Even though she knew Sid had been coming to feed

Sabrina, the apartment still smelled stale, the walls and ceiling too close. Larisa shrugged off the trapped feeling.

"So, I think I'm going to look at it. What do you think?"

"What do I think about what?"

"Turning on the laptop."

"You think it's rigged to explode or something?"

"Unlikely."

"Then I think it'd be fine?"

Larisa prowled through her kitchen cupboards without knowing what she was looking for. "It's probably porn. When I was with Lucas—" She stopped. Sid didn't need to know. No one needed to know. It was in the past. She'd moved on.

And yet, the story had dug in, was sitting there pressing at the edge of her mind.

"You ever date the wrong person, Sid?"

He laughed. "Doesn't everyone?"

"And you ignored the red flags for so long they stopped looking red?"

"Once or twice, yeah. But all before I met Quinn. After he was around, the bad ones stayed away. Or he drove them off. I dunno. What's that phrase? If your best friend isn't your partner, they choose your partner for you?"

"But you're single."

"When did I say that?"

"I just assumed—"

"Relax. I'm messing with you. Yeah. Solo for now. Too much going on to get involved like that."

"My friends didn't choose Lucas. But I suppose if they'd been more involved in my life that summer, they would have. He was exactly the kind of guy they—we—wanted. And he was all the things a man like that tends to come with under the surface." Larisa shivered as she thought of the men her sorority sisters had married. They weren't arms dealers, but Cade, Tate, and Adrian, were all carbon copies of that same masculine power that looked out on the world to see what he could conquer and call his own.

And she'd seen Krissy's more diminutive husband, Dev, watching them with envy more than once, which was almost worse than having it.

"So it didn't surprise me that he wanted to watch porn. Some of it I found exciting. It was easy to please him in the beginning. It felt like one of our special things, a way to explore. But then it became routine. A way to unwind from a long day instead of something we were doing together. The videos got darker, more about violence than desire. He started to act things out."

Larisa drummed her nails on the laptop lid, noticing she'd chipped a whole corner off her right pointer fingernail in her run from the police. "It's probably hard for you to understand, but there's a difference between a bondage scene that two people have planned, and a man coming upon his partner unexpectedly so he can feel like he's taking something from her."

"I actually don't find that hard to understand at all," said Sid. "Quinn taught me how it works. The bondage part, not the other thing."

"I told myself it was one of the things that came with a great man." Larisa brushed at tears that hadn't fallen from her eyes. "Anyway. I'm going to turn this thing on now. And if its porn I'm going to be really pissed off. And it's not going to seem like a reasonable response, right?"

"You think I care about reasonable responses?"

Larisa managed a laugh. "I guess not, but I do. When I write my memoir, the first twenty years are going to be called, 'Larisa Responds Reasonably in all Things.'"

"There's a loaded title."

She flipped open the lid of the laptop and pressed the power button.

"The funny thing is, now that I've been thinking about Lucas again, I'm still not sure I wouldn't go back to him if he asked me."

"Yeah?"

"And I hate that feeling. Because I don't want it. It was horrible. I didn't feel safe, I never knew what was coming. But it's like none of that matters because there's this hunger."

"When things were good, they were really good," said Sid.

Larisa nodded.

"Well, when you go to Italy, you won't be alone. So that's something. And you're not alone now."

The screen came to life. Larisa sucked in a breath and slowly let it out. She felt silly, bracing herself like the laptop could hurt her. What did she expect? For what felt like the umpteenth time, she tried to place a name on her fear.

The videos we used to watch.

Pictures of him with Quinn.

Pictures of him with me.

The desktop screen was a branded factory default with rows of file folders in a grid, no application shortcuts, not even for an internet browser.

"Strange names," said Sid.

"They're operas."

"Of course they are."

Larisa laughed. "You sound just like him."

"Hmm?"

"Quinn says it like that, 'Of course they are.'"

"Well, he gets it from me. Which one do you want to open?"

Larisa clicked on *Faust*. Inside the folder, a collection of spreadsheet files named by year. Larisa opened the most current.

"Is this the accounting you were talking about?"

"No," said Larisa, hardly daring to breathe as her eyes traveled down the list of names along the far-left column. "This is something else."

"I'm not great with numbers."

In all honesty, Larisa wasn't good with numbers either. But based on the trend of amounts and the cryptic notes tied to names she recognized, she could guess.

"This is Lucas's little black book. The people who owe him things. The things he owes to them."

Chapter 3

Lines Blurred

"I brought food," said Sid. He knocked on the apartment door, but then walked right in as though he lived there. Larisa supposed it was reasonable for him to feel that way. He'd been coming to see her every day since she'd left her parents. Sometimes she felt guilty about it, like a decent person would at least have asked what larger life Sid was missing out on while he sat around with her and watched her brain run through a rat maze of dead ends.

"Even when the world is ending, people take showers," he said.

Larisa pulled the end of her ponytail up to her nose and sniffed it. "I don't think that's true. At the end of the world, plumbing breaks."

"The shower still works. No excuses."

Larisa felt she had plenty of excuses. Besides, lots of people only showered every few days. And showering was a lot of work. Even pushing herself up off the couch to go to the kitchen, where Sid had laid out the food, felt like too much work, so she remained sitting on the couch, photo album open on her lap, the thumb drive, where she'd downloaded Lucas's black book ledger before the laptop's power ran out, on top. She still hadn't decided what to do with it.

Across from her, the little Christmas tree she and Quinn had purchased together was beginning to die. Every time Sabrina walked too close, it dropped half its needles. There were needles everywhere.

"What's the date today, Sid?"

"Twenty-third? Twenty-fourth?"

"Almost a month he's been gone. Did you know the only pictures I have of us together are from Jaden's wedding? We weren't even together then."

"But you wanted to be," said Sid.

"I was so afraid of wanting him."

Larisa pushed off the couch, clumsy as her muscles struggled to life. She made it far enough to lean out, snatch the present Quinn had wrapped for her, then fall back onto the couch.

"I'm going to open it."

"Now?"

"Why not? He might not come back."

She felt Sid go still behind her, arrested by the thought. Then he came around and sat down beside her on the couch. "He's coming back."

"There's no coming back from Lucas."

"That doesn't make any sense."

Larisa shrugged. She knew what she meant even if Sid didn't. Almost against her will she glanced over at the photo album that had been displaced to the coffee table when Sid sat down. That morning, she'd counted them. Thirty pages of sleeves, two photos on each page, a total of sixty frozen moments, not nearly enough to reflect the outsized space Lucas continued to occupy in her life. She tried to remember what she'd thought when she'd met Quinn for the first time at Club D. Lucas hadn't been in her mind then because she'd worked so hard to banish him. She'd been lonely in unnamable ways. She'd begun to believe that love was a thing that had also been banished, never to return. Quinn had surprised her. She'd never planned for him.

"Have you decided what you want to do with that?" Sid nodded at the thumb drive. Larisa tossed it to him so she could focus on Quinn's present. A square box, not very heavy, it gave a dull rattle when she shook it.

"This sounds like a puzzle," she said.

"Quinn would probably like to watch you open it."

She sighed and set the box on the coffee table. "Did he buy me a puzzle?"

"No idea."

"Liar."

"This thing feels like it will explode in my hands." Sid set the drive on the table. For a moment they both looked that direction, lost in thought.

"Well, obviously it's not going to the CIA. Osna had his chance."

"Do you think it's right to be petty when there's so much—"

"You didn't see him barge into my parents' house like he had a right to be there. He was horrible to Hannah. He's horrible all around."

"But he's also a good guy? Like in the cops and robber sense."

"You have any idea how flawed that narrative is considered now?"

"Well, you're not thinking about giving it to Pam, right?"

Larisa had, in fact, been thinking just that. Yesterday, or perhaps it'd been the day before, she'd thought, *If Pam calls with an update, I'll give it to her*. But Pam hadn't called. And the longer the silence stretched, the less Larisa felt confident she and Pam were on the same page. The scene they'd shared on the corner of Sunset had been aggressive, possibly like blackmail. But Larisa only remembered the timbre, not the content. She remembered that they'd agreed to go forward together, and that Pam was sending people to the Striped Blossom to look for Lucas's money.

It felt like weeks had passed.

In the movies, things happened faster. The dissonance made Larisa uncertain. She thought she might still be losing time even though everything felt clear, almost too sharp in her mind.

Sabrina prowled restlessly around the room. She hadn't liked being left alone and now that Larisa was spending almost all her time in the apartment, it felt like her cat was throwing daily tantrums as revenge. She'd knocked a miniature cactus pot off the kitchen windowsill. Now she hooked her paw into a dangling strand of the Christmas lights.

I could call again. Just hearing his voice would help.

Quinn's voice, she corrected her traitorous mind. *Not Lucas.*

"I don't think you should stay here alone," said Sid.

"I'm not going back to my parents."

"One of the sisters?"

Without her phone, Larisa had been cut off from the daily contact of the sisters' group chat. She hadn't seen any of them since they'd taken her to the Kahn estate on Friday evening. She remembered that she'd thought Kahleah was unusually quiet.

"If Lucas or Pam or the CIA or whoever come for me, they'll be able to find me at any of those places."

She thought it was strange how long the list of people who might 'come for her' had grown without her having any strong sense of why they would come for her. No one wanted the laptop, which seemed the most important thing.

And then, as though to undermine her fragile trust in the safety of her apartment, a knock sounded on the door. Sid grabbed her arm and began to pull her toward the bedroom.

"Sabrina!" she hissed.

"Forget the cat." Sid closed the door behind them.

"Assassins don't knock," she whispered.

"Quiet."

They stood together, straining to be still, as though even at this distance the sound of their breathing would alert the visitor to their presence. The knocking stopped. Then, a man's voice, "Hey Doc, you in there?"

Larisa laughed. "Open the door."

"Why?"

"It's Dansby."

"Dansby, the actor?"

Larisa pushed Sid aside and escaped from the bedroom, then raked her fingers through her hair and straightened her yoga shirt. She wasn't really dressed for public viewing, but Dansby would forgive her. She opened the door.

"Dansby. What on earth are you doing here?"

"Well, we promised we'd see each other."

"That's right."

"And your phone doesn't like my phone, or something, because all the messages I sent you didn't work."

"I broke my phone. It's been terrible. Do you want to come in?"

"Yeah, sure. Oh hi, Quinn's assistant."

"Hi, Quinn's actor."

Dansby grinned. "Oh right, he said that if I couldn't find Larisa, I should look for you next. But here you are together, awesome."

"Who said?" Sid renewed his earlier suspicion, casting a glance of warning toward Larisa.

"Quinn did. Like he didn't trust me to find the apartment or something." Dansby laughed.

"You saw Quinn?" asked Larisa. To keep herself from pouncing on him, she retreated to the kitchen and started her hot water pot.

"Barely. He only showed for one day of press, then the red carpet. But we had fun."

"London was this week?" Sid shook his head. "I completely lost track of that."

"The movie's doing really great, Doc. You should'a been there."

"How was Quinn?"

Dansby gave a laugh. This one felt more strategic than natural. Larisa thought it was a very actor thing to do, a symptom of media blitz brain, as though her question put Dansby unconsciously into interview mode. "Lively. In the moment, I was like, okay cool. But now I'm like, that was weird. He was probably on something. But maybe that's what he's decided to do so the reporters like him better? Anyway. He gave me some messages for you."

"Messages?" Larisa held on to the edge of the island as she watched Dansby fumble with his phone, too slow, so casual, as though he had no idea that she'd been waiting, living for exactly this.

"Alrighty. Yep, he said—well, here I'll just let you read it." Dansby handed her his phone. Sid came over to read over Larisa's shoulder.

"The sale is in process. Oh fuck."

"Got the accountants already, right?" said Sid.

Larisa read the next line about the accountant being sick. "That's probably Pam's doing. Sounds like it worked."

"But no name for the buyer? What can we do about that?"

"When did you see him?"

"Yesterday, London time?"

Larisa reached into her pocket for the phone Pam had given her.

"It could have happened already. We're too late," said Sid.

Dansby looked from one of them to the other. "Are you guys doing one of those global mystery games? Ya know, the clues are all around the world and you have to travel and eventually you find out some historical figure died at some random street in—" He stopped because Larisa had started crying.

Sid handed Dansby his phone and directed him toward the door. "It's good to see you. We should set up a lunch, yeah? Sometime soon?"

"That'd be good because I've been thinking about what the Doc said, and I think it would be really great to talk. I'm good, you know, but also not good?"

Their voices faded. Larisa heard the click of keys, the closing of the door. She braced her arms against the island and tried to pull herself back from wherever her mind had just flown, not a memory, or an idea, just a feeling that everything was collapsing in around her. *We're too late.*

She dialed Osna.

It went directly to voicemail.

She dialed again and left a message. "Tell me you didn't attack him." Which was just about the worst message to leave on the answering machine of a CIA agent, but she didn't care. As soon as she hung up, she dialed Pam. It also went directly to voicemail.

"Damn it!" Larisa ran back to her bedroom and dug around until she found her laptop in the sheets—she'd lulled herself to sleep the night before watching *Forensic Files*—then jabbed her finger at the power button. Nothing happened.

Dead. *Fuck.* Where was her power cord?

The door again. Sid returning alone. He carried a stack of mail and a package. "I checked your mail. He wouldn't stop talking."

"We would've heard about it if they'd attacked, right?"

"What're you talking about?"

"Our government. If someone assassinated Lucas, we'd have heard about it."

Sid stared at her. "That's a thing that might happen?"

"So they said."

Sid pulled out his phone. "There's nothing online. But I dunno. Italian news would say something maybe?"

"I can't do the math. What was the schedule for the premiere?"

"Press on Wednesday and Thursday, carpet Thursday night."

"This is Saturday, late Saturday there."

"So this information is way old," said Sid.

Larisa sucked in a breath and let it out. "No one is answering my calls. Do you think that means—"

"Hey look. This box came from London."

A mad rush to a kitchen drawer for the box cutter.

"Why would he have bothered with messages through Dansby if he was going to mail something?"

Larisa's burner phone vibrated with an incoming text, then a second.

P: We should talk.

P: Today.

The package was a new smart phone in its box, but the box had been opened and the phone inside had already been fitted with a protective case and activated. The lock screen image was the view from the Umbras balcony. Phone numbers had already been added to the contacts, her parents, her sisters, Quinn, Sid, her clients, Dansby.

"Wow," said Sid. "Am I impressed or really creeped out?"

As they watched, a handful of messages began to appear from a contact listed as Il Magnifico.

"Is that who I think it is?"

"Yeah."

"Ego much?"

"It's a reference to Lorenzo de' Medici," said Larisa.

"Are you arguing or supporting my point?"

Larisa opened the message app.

Il Magnifico: Vegas, Regis Grand. Make sure door #605 is open at 11 pm Sunday.

Il Magnifico: Tell me how it goes after.

Il Magnifico: It's okay about Ana. I understand.

Il Magnifico: But this is the chance to amend your error.

Il Magnifico: I'm in love with the noises he makes when he's in pain.

And then a video. The still cover image was too blurry to make out what she'd see if she hit play. Sid did it for her, then took the phone so she couldn't watch. It was enough to hear. Someone gagging, then stuttered moans mixed in, the mewing of a particular kind of agony that sounded enough like other sounds Quinn had made that she knew they were his. Then a cry.

"That sick fuck. That sick—" The front door of the apartment whooshed open, then slammed closed as Sid rushed out. Even with it closed, she could hear him shouting. There was a series of dull thuds. She thought he was hitting a tree or the cement retaining wall. It was strangely clarifying to hear him, as though Sid's expression of everything she wanted, but couldn't express, allowed her to feel. Which was probably what Lucas wanted, even if he hadn't realized it yet. Which meant, if she could find a way to do it, this would end.

Outside, the shouting had stopped. She walked to the small window beside her front door and saw that Dansby hadn't left, or perhaps he'd come back. Either way, he was now in the courtyard with Sid, the two of them sitting together on the bench on the far side of the orange tree. Maybe Sid was crying, or doing the Sid-equivalent of crying, and Dansby was rubbing his back.

All this time I've been playing to survive, thought Larisa. *I have to find a way to play to win.*

Four hours later, she was sitting at a West Hollywood jazz club across from Kahleah.

"I feel like we haven't done something like this in a long time," said Kahleah.

"Probably my fault," said Larisa.

"I feel like you have ulterior motives."

"I need to meet someone tonight and I didn't want to be alone." Larisa held her breath and waited for Kahleah to explode on her. Instead, Kahleah nodded.

"Do I get any more info than that?"

"Can we start drinking first?"

They ordered their first round from a waiter who was also tending the bar. Larisa watched Kahleah size him up as he walked away and smiled despite herself. "You've really gone off Cade, huh?"

"I'm allowed to look."

"Sure. But you haven't allowed yourself in years." Larisa made a gesture as though to illustrate a frame around her eyes. "Cade tunnel vision."

"You ever think about the fact that our definition of a successful relationship ends in death? Anything less than that is a failure."

"Your kids?"

"Tonight my kids don't exist." Kahleah slurped her drink, then leaned forward. "Now, tell me everything."

"I feel like we should talk about you."

"We should, but you haven't really earned that, so . . ."

Fair. But it still stung. An apology for Larisa's myriad short-comings in the friendship department seemed like it would come off as trivial, so instead she plunged in with her update. Pam on the corner of Sunset during the sunset. Osna that weekend. Quinn's message through Dansby. The phone Lucas had sent her with its cryptic messages and the video of Quinn in pain, which she absolutely would not think about because that was exactly what Lucas wanted.

"But he isn't dead?" asked Kahleah.

"I don't think so." *I would know.*

"So Quinn is probably okay too."

Maybe. Larisa forcibly swallowed down her drink, told herself it would be good for her to be a little loose.

"Any idea what you're supposed to do on this secret mission?" asked Kahleah.

"Make sure a door is open." Larisa held up the phone to show Kahleah the messages.

"And you're going to ask Pam for advice?"

"I just want to see what she's going to say. No details."

Kahleah snorted. "There's not much except the details."

"She hasn't given me any information in over a week."

The waiter was back with more drinks and a flirtatious smile. "You two waiting on dates?"

"No," said Kahleah.

"Yes," said Larisa.

"She doesn't know what she's talking about."

The waiter flashed his teeth even brighter. "Well, I'm just over there if you need anything."

Again, Kahleah watched him go. "I bet he thinks I'm too white for him."

"Or he noticed your wedding ring."

"That doesn't stop people these days if it ever did. Kahleah finished her drink and made a face like she didn't think she should have another. "You know, I don't have any Black friends?"

"What about—"

"College was a decade ago, Risa. Those girls all went off and started their lives without me."

For a moment, Larisa was confused, then she thought about the waiter. "You wish I was someone else so he'd see you with them instead of me?"

"Or something."

Fair, thought Larisa. *Complicated.*

"Am I at least allowed to ask how it's going with you and Cade?"

"How's it going? Hmm. I don't even know how to answer that. I asked him to get rid of the assistant. He said no. He needs her. I asked him to make sure to come home for dinner four nights a week and be at home until the kids are in bed. He did that, sorta. But what am I going to do? He knows he holds all the cards. And it just . . ." Kahleah scraped her future mayor's wife manicure along the table. "Some days I just want him to feel all the hurt." Kahleah glanced at Larisa. "I suppose you know something about that."

Yes and no, thought Larisa. It worried her that she'd never once felt the level of vengeful rage Kahleah was describing when she thought of Lucas.

"When we go to Italy—"

"She's here," said Kahleah. "What role am I playing?"

"Role? Just, I dunno."

"Come on. I need a role, like we did with the CIA guy." Kahleah's gaze cut to the bar, then back to Larisa.

"I think—"

There was Pam standing at the table looking like she'd just come from a White House press conference, pastel pumps, navy suit, even a lapel pin that looked vaguely patriotic. When she saw Larisa staring, she said, "I was just with the lawyer reading John's will."

"Weird," Kahleah deadpanned.

"It was. The legal complications of bringing him back to life will be . . . anyway."

Larisa reached over and turned off her pink phone. According to Sid, they could passively listen even if a line wasn't active, and she didn't want to have to do the mental gymnastics of assuming Lucas could be listening in.

"Nice phone," said Pam, as though it was just a compliment and not some kind of insult insinuating Larisa's reaction had been overly dramatic when Pam destroyed her old one.

Little does she know Lucas is so attentive he's sent me a new one. This thought, instead of disturbing her as it should have, gave Larisa a little step up of pride. Pam didn't have a man like that in her life. "What happened with your people at the club?"

"Ambushed," said Pam. "One was caught by the buyers. One disappeared two days ago. Are you here to complain I haven't called?"

"I heard that the gas was sold."

"From who?" Pam's eyes narrowed with zero-to-sixty suspicion.

"I have sources."

"The CIA? They know nothing."

"So the gas hasn't been sold?"

"The deal went wrong. I've sown enough doubt in Lucas's organization that every buyer has lukewarm feet. Discovering my agent scared them off."

"And then your agent died, right?" asked Kahleah.

"What is she doing here?"

"I'm her bodyguard," said Kahleah.

Pam emitted a soft laugh. "Your husband won't like you involved in this."

"What exactly am I involved in?" Kahleah batted her eyes at Pam, but Larisa could tell the comment had landed. Kahleah resumed drumming her nails on the table.

Then, as Pam said, "If you have sources, I need to know about them," Kahleah suddenly got up and sauntered down the length of the room to the bar.

"Did you get the accounts?" asked Larisa.

"It's in process."

"What exactly is 'in process'?"

"I think we've misunderstood each other." Pam leaned forward, just a little menacing, or at least as much as she allowed herself to look menacing in public. "I'm a professional. I know what I'm doing. You are neither of those things. I appreciate that you're anxious and you don't have a lot going on in your life, but you do not need to know."

"Leaving me out is a mistake. You're right, I'm not a professional. But I know Lucas. And I've watched previous versions of upstarts like you try to do exactly what you're doing. Guess what? They're all dead." *Except for that one guy who Lucas liked so he was allowed to retire to a resort and Lucas set him up as a day trader with a pet puma for company.* But Pam didn't need to know that.

"If you know so much, tell me about this man." Pam pulled out a tablet, powered it up, then turned it around for Larisa to see a grainy photo taken from a distance at the Striped Blossom. A group of men in a booth. Lucas, his right-hand man, Rifat. Three guys who looked like the mob. And Quinn with his head tucked down and pressed against Lucas's shoulder.

"Volpe Rossa," said Pam. "Apparently a middleman who's supposed to be dead. Lucas has made a pet out of him or something." Pam's upper lip curled with a prude's distain.

Larisa swallowed. "Sounds like you already know quite a lot."

"That's the story Lucas told to the Sforzas. But they didn't know that Rossa has been dead a month, after being caught skimming from the top. I know because he was reporting all the shipment movements to me. And then he went silent. So," Pam tapped her finger beside Quinn's head, "who is this man, and why would Lucas want the Sforzas to think he's a dead man?"

Volpe Rossa. The name was familiar, but Larisa couldn't place it. She thought Pam didn't have the whole picture if Lucas was playing with a false identity in the age of facial recognition.

He's made Quinn a target. Larisa clenched her jaw until pain shot up the side of her head. She'd have to be careful what she said.

"If you've undermined Lucas's reputation, he probably felt the need to compensate by showing off a conquered enemy."

"Fine, yes. But that's not what this is." Pam pointed to the pale blur of Quinn's hand on Lucas's thigh.

He's playing a role, thought Larisa even as worse thoughts flooded in, her darkest fears coming true. Because no one could resist Lucas for long, not when he wanted something. And Quinn was . . .

Quinn is . . .

. . . so soft.

It wasn't the right word, but she couldn't think clearly enough to find one that worked better. It didn't matter what word, because she knew it in her head, the essence of Quinn, his need, the desires he was just barely beginning to understand. Every part of him held up banner invitations that only someone like Lucas could see. Of course he'd gone in and sunk his teeth into every single one.

No one survives Lucas, she thought. And then it came to her, the same rush of violence she'd seen in Kahleah, the violence she should've felt toward Lucas.

I'm going to kill him.

"I want to end him," said Larisa. "Tell me that's what you want."

"I do," said Pam.

"He's asked me to do something for him. I'm going to do it, then I'm going to go over there and convince him he's won. What do you need?"

"His buyers," said Pam. "We can match them to the accounts and take it all away from him."

Larisa thought of the black book ledger, the numbers beside the names that she'd thought was some kind of code. *They're account numbers,* she thought.

"This man pretending to be Rossa can probably get them for you."

Larisa glanced toward the bar to keep herself from blurting out right there that she already had what Pam wanted. Kahleah had disappeared. The waiter was refilling his jar of orange slices, smiling to himself in that way that made Larisa want to cry.

"What are you doing for him?" asked Pam.

"It's just a trust exercise. He needs a door kept open at a hotel."

"You do it, and you'll be able to go back to him without suspicion," mused Pam. She apparently didn't know the CIA had been asking Larisa to facilitate this exact scenario for years. Pam definitely didn't know that Larisa had, once upon a time, tried it, and failed. Because she hadn't wanted Lucas to get hurt.

This time will be different.

"I'd like a knife," said Larisa.

"Guns are easier."

Larisa shook her head. "It has to be a knife. Tosca's kiss is the only way to go."

If Pam was confused by the opera reference, she quickly

moved on, began gathering herself to leave. "So, I'll get you a knife. Then you'll get me names." Pam paused. "Oh, and I was going to ask you about the vineyard. It's looking like there might not be a gas sale, but something that dangerous shouldn't be unaccounted for. Which one was it?"

"The Inverno vineyard in Orvieto."

"I'll send some people down there and see what I can find."

Then Pam left, and Larisa sat for a few minutes thinking only of Quinn's hand on Lucas's leg and all it might mean. She comforted herself with their plan. It felt good to have a plan. But then, as the rage spots began to die back from her vision and her blood began to cool, Larisa wondered why the accounts weren't enough. Osna had always acted like finding the money would be enough. Without money, Lucas wouldn't be able to run his organization. The CIA would be able to watch what went where and reveal the entire organization.

But Pam wanted names.

She didn't need names to stop Lucas. But she'd need them if she wanted to step in and take over his business. Larisa stabbed the plastic sword from her garnish at the impenetrable varnish of the table. *This was the first meeting we've had where she didn't mention the CIA.*

Which might mean nothing. But Larisa hadn't realized how she'd come to rely on her suspicion that Pam was working with Osna as a way to make herself feel safer working with her. *If they're not working together . . .*

Do I even know for sure it was Lucas's people who killed Osna's partner?

I'm finally taking action and everything feels wrong.

Kahleah rushed up to the table and dropped into her chair in a whoosh of fragrant air. "I did it."

"Did what?" asked Larisa, suddenly afraid Kahleah had somehow tracked Pam down a back alley and attacked her. But no, she was back in her regular life now, the non-spy, well-heeled housewives of LA life where her friend knew about the spy shit but didn't speak that language yet. So, process of elimination, the frighteningly unclear 'it' Kahleah referenced had to do with the hot bartender.

Kahleah's eyes sparkled. She looked ten years younger, energy juddering through her limbs so that she could hardly stay in her seat. "Is he at the bar?"

"Yes," said Larisa.

"Tell me if he leaves."

"I'm confused."

"So I've been reading this blog about feminine sexuality . . ."

Larisa nodded to give herself space to try and reorient her brain.

". . . and every blog post ends with a challenge for readers to take charge of themselves. So, I left the bartender a gift in the bathroom."

"Gift in the bathroom," Larisa repeated.

"My panties." Kahleah's eyes widened. "What do you think?"

Larisa still wasn't quite sure she was wholly understanding. "Well, I think it depends which panties."

"The pink ones with the lace Jaden gave us for the wedding."

"Don't they have champaign glasses and two wedding rings on them?"

Kahleah started to giggle. Larisa also started to laugh, mostly from disbelief. But then she saw movement out of the corner of her eye. The bartender had left his station and was moving down the hall to the bathroom.

"I can't believe you."

"I know!"

"What do you want to happen here?"

"No idea." Kahleah was seized by another fit of giggles. "Oh my God, this is so weird. I think this is you and your weird life. It's unhinged me. I'm even thinking I should come with you to Vegas."

"You don't have to do that."

"I know, but it might be fun. And I'm in this too deep now.

I'll be sitting at home tearing my hair out if I'm not at the scene. Besides, it's Vegas, baby. We could go wild."

Larisa wished she had it in her to go wild. The funny thing about her life was anyone on the outside would've said she was already wild, that her very public dating, her sexuality, her general lifestyle all reflected a release from the boundaries that governed other people. But none of it was true. Inside, she was this coiled bundle of frightened rabbit nerves flinching at every perceived movement because it felt like she lived in a world full of things that wanted to devour her.

How would I go wild? thought Larisa. *I'd contact all the people in Lucas's little black book and tell them he's never paying them back.*

A silly thought.

An absolutely outrageous thing to do.

And yet, the more she thought about it, the more it sounded like a good idea.

The Open Door

"Can I admit something terrible right now?" asked Kahleah.

Larisa was halfway down the hallway. She turned to look back. "This is exciting."

Eyes wide, Kahleah nodded. "I feel like we're doing something illegal, and I like it."

They'd been trolling the hallways of the Regis Grand Hotel for almost an hour looking for the door Larisa was supposed to make sure was open at eleven that night. They'd been yelled at on the loading dock for getting in the way. They'd been shooed out of a security hallway by a guard who'd taken his job very seriously until he'd recognized Larisa, said, "Hey, you're that slutty shrink," then had the nerve to ask for her autograph. Larisa, always wanting to make people happy, gave him her autograph and a lipstick kiss pressed into the paper.

"I'm doing something illegal and its exciting."

"Not *very* illegal," said Larisa. "Not like that time we—"

"Don't even. Our phones are probably listening to us right now."

"If you'd wanted to avoid pseudo criminal activity, you should've stayed at home," said Larisa.

"The last thing I wanted to do was stay home. You always get to have all the fun."

Larisa glared at her.

"Okay, not fun, exactly. But isn't there some kind of

psychology about our need for danger and how people have so much anxiety because we don't have any natural predators anymore?"

"If you feel like danger is missing in your life, you could try skydiving or something more than panties in the bathroom."

"It worked, didn't it?"

"I still can't believe you did that." Larisa squinted at the faint paint stencil number on the next doorframe. "We're getting closer."

"Weird. I feel like we're in the middle of the basement or something. Wouldn't it make sense if it's an exterior door?"

"You think I'm supposed to let someone in?"

"What else?"

Larisa shrugged. She'd been trying not to think about it. Lucas had given her this job. It was a simple job. She was going to do it and redeem herself of Ana, and of lying to him about Senator Hagan, and for loving Quinn. It wouldn't be enough, but maybe it would buy enough time for Pam to do her thing, then maybe the CIA would arrest Lucas, and then—

"This is hopeless."

"You just said we're close."

"I mean the rest of it. Nothing I do is going to change Lucas. The CIA isn't going to arrest him. Even if they did, don't you think he could find a way to do everything he's been doing from jail? This is never going to end."

Kahleah closed the distance between them and rubbed Larisa's arm. "Don't say that. He's just a man. There are ways to deal with men."

"Would you actually leave Cade?"

"Who knows."

"I think you know," said Larisa. "You were glowing after we left the club last night."

Kahleah gave her a sideways glance. "The universe punishes middle-aged women who have a good enough life but think the grass is greener."

"We're not middle aged." Larisa pointed at the door label. "The numbers stop here. Dead end." She pressed her ear to the wall to listen. "This might be a street wall. Or I'm just imagining it."

Kahleah tested the nearest door to see if it would open. When it didn't, she went to the other side of the hallway. "This one's open. Stairwell."

They stood side by side looking for an obvious direction. "These stairs are weird."

"Yeah, but why?"

"Not full stories between the landings?"

"We were on street level before."

"But not necessarily street level now." Larisa started down the steps, turned the corner of the landing. "Here's our door." Larisa pressed on the security bar and pushed the door open. "Alleyway and small loading zone." She released the door and stepped back inside, then joined Kahleah sitting on the steps.

"This feels easy."

"Don't say that until it's over."

"All I want is for it to be over."

"What's the 'it'?"

Larisa wanted to say *my connection with Lucas,* but the first thought that came to mind was Quinn. She wanted him back home, furious with her for lying to him. She wanted the chance to make it right, to learn how to be in a real relationship that was forgiving and healthy and full of trust instead of unending layers of strategic lies.

"Did you trust Cade before all this stuff with the secretary started?"

"She's an aid not a secretary."

Larisa rolled her eyes.

"I felt he was predictable in a way that I could work with," said Kahleah. "And he was stable."

"But now he's not."

"I didn't sign on for politics. Honestly, this trip is the first time I've ever walked out on him, left him to manage the kids on his own with no plan, no staff—it felt good. I thought, I could just keep driving. I could go wherever I want and start over and never have to worry about accidently saying 'fuck,' or showing my slip, or being too Black for Congress ever again."

"But you'd miss him."

"I miss the old him every day. The old us." She paused as though they were both thinking about better days. "Promise me that after you do this little thing with the door, we're going out dancing tonight?"

"You're not afraid of getting caught on camera?"

"Well, yeah. That's why I brought masks and feather boas."

Larisa laughed, then stopped. "The last time I was wearing a mask, Quinn asked me out. He had this whole speech about who we could be to each other and why we were different from everyone else and why it would work even if no one understood it." Larisa's voice caught. "He said he wanted to protect me."

"Seems like that's what he's gone off to do."

"Then why does it feel so horrible?"

"Woah, let's not fall apart at the scene of your future crime." Kahleah got to her feet and pulled Larisa up with her. "You can cry up in the room. Take a hot bath, get your face on, and then you're gonna do this. And you're not gonna fall apart because we're in Vegas, baby."

The strange thing about carrying out her little task for Lucas with Kahleah as her partner was that it didn't feel dangerous. The whole time they were getting dressed, Kahleah carried on as though they were getting ready for a night out. Music playing from her little portable speaker, dancing in the bathroom, joking about gray hair and Spanx, and laughing that the other sisters didn't have any idea where they were or what they were doing.

Even when they left their room and wove their way back down to the back staircase and the door Larisa needed to have open by eleven, it felt almost too much like a lark, like Larisa was getting away with something, when instead she should have been punishing herself for once again falling into Lucas's honeytrap.

They were walking too fast, so they paused to play some slots in the hotel casino. Kahleah kept leaning into Larisa, tickling her with the feather boa she wore, touching her almost like it meant something. Larisa knew from experience it didn't. But this guise of flirtation also added to the feeling that she needed to be wary even though she couldn't quite keep herself there. It was too easy to pretend they were having fun and let the rest go.

At ten till eleven, Larisa left Kahleah and retraced the winding path of their afternoon to the obscure back of the building stairwell with the door that opened into the alleyway. She did not think about why Lucas needed the door to be opened at this time, or who was going to pass through, or what would happen if she were caught.

She simply did. It was the next step to getting Quinn back. And that was all she wanted.

We'll have a house with a pool and a rock garden, she thought. *And Quinn will make his office in the pool shed so he doesn't get distracted when he's working. And I'll make sure he eats and remind him to fight for what he wants, and sometimes he'll finish early and sneak into the house where I've fallen asleep with Sabrina and he'll—*

A knock sounded on the other side of the door. Larisa pushed it open. Two men dressed as plumbers walked through and began to noisily stomp up the stairs in their heavy plumber boots. She stood at the door until she couldn't hear them anymore. And then she went back the way she had come.

"All done?" asked Kahleah. "Just like that?"

Larisa nodded. She could hardly believe it herself.

"Then it's party time."

There might have been a moment when Larisa worried about

what she'd just done. But it didn't feel real enough to be worthy of dread. And in the next blink, Kahleah was waving her boa and dancing across the casino and Larisa was following her, exhilarated by a feeling of triumph she hadn't earned. They spent a roll of quarters in the casino, pregaming with dirty martinis, then took the escalators up to the hotel lobby. The wail of ambulance sirens drifted in from the street. Not an unusual sound, but it struck Larisa cold. Some unconscious part of her had been waiting for this, the other half of the yin and yang of her choices. The pleasant buzz of her martini dissolved. She began to run.

Outside, a crowd had gathered, their necks all crunched at acute angles as they looked up at the sky. Larisa pushed her way through them until she could see what they were looking at. High above, on the floor where the size of the windows changed from single occupancy rooms to suites, a window was missing. A man dangled from the opening, his body against the window on the floor below. Blood dripped from his arms and legs and other places hidden by his clothes.

"Larisa, is that—" Kahleah didn't finish her sentence as Larisa grabbed her and dragged her back inside.

"We need to leave."

Impossible to take the stairs all the way up to their room, but the elevator felt like a trap. Larisa watched the floor numbers drift past with a particular kind of hatred that later she would recognize as self-loathing. A week after Ana's death and here she was again at the scene of a murder, an accomplice.

"Fuck."

"But maybe it's—"

"Lucas said tonight was my opportunity to make things right." Larisa slammed her fist against the gold tinted mirror of the elevator wall. "I didn't think he meant literally. How could he know Hagan was here?"

"That security guard from this afternoon can place you," said Kahleah.

"I know."

"Does that mean—"

"I don't know."

Finally on their floor. The two of them walking because running would look suspicious. In their room, shoving things in their overnight bags. They put on sneakers. Out again in ten minutes. No waiting for the elevator this time. They took the stairs, running now that there were no security cameras. Parking lot. Kahleah's car.

More torturous waiting. A line had formed at the exit to the parking garage as traffic was diverted around a police barricade in front of the building.

"Why hasn't someone gotten him down yet?" asked Kahleah. "He could still be alive."

"The point might not be for him to be dead." Larisa pulled her burner phone from her purse. "Maybe Lucas wanted to point to the CIA faking Hagan's death. Maybe it's useful for him to reveal a dirty politician."

"Do you think many of them are?"

"What?" Larisa tried to look up the building as the car crawled past.

"Dirty."

"I think it's the nature of the job." Larisa powered up the phone.

"What are you doing?"

"Calling Pam."

"Are you serious?"

"She should know."

"Larisa de France-Kahn, don't you dare." Kahleah leaned over and slapped the phone away. "At least wait until we're out of the city." She began to cry. "This is going to be us, isn't it? Someday some woman is going to call me and tell me that Cade is hanging off the side of a building."

"Don't be dramatic. When was the last time a US politician got caught doing anything worse than sending dick pics to minors?"

Kahleah forced a laugh through her tears.

"Seriously, this is all Lucas."

All Lucas, Larisa told herself over and over. *He's won again.*

As soon as the city lights faded, Kahleah pulled over and put on her hazards. She called Cade.

"Have you seen the news? Well, turn it on. Senator Hagan's alive."

Larisa couldn't help but smile at her friend; even in distress, she remembered to pretend she thought Hagan had died in a drunken accident over New Year's. Kahleah got out of the car and began to pace the shoulder. Not the greatest idea, but there was so little traffic it seemed safe enough. Larisa also got out. She walked around and leaned against the back of the car, burner in hand.

What if it had been Quinn? Larisa stuffed her fist into her mouth and bit down until she tasted blood. When the wave that threatened to drown her passed, she pulled up Pam's number. Just as she was about to dial, the phone came alive with an incoming call.

"Hello?"

"You're up late."

Larisa wasn't sure if Pam said this out of consideration or if she was making an accusation. Larisa decided not to answer.

"I called to say we found what we were looking for."

Larisa's grip cinched around the phone, sending an angry line of pain down her arm.

"It was where you said it would be. Osna owes you an apology."

"He won't see it that way." Larisa swallowed. "Any problems?"

"They weren't expecting it. Buyers were even in town."

"So, good all around?"

"Lucas won't be able to function after this. With the money gone and his prize stolen, no one will trust him. It's over."

Too late, thought Larisa.

"I'm sensing a distinct lack of enthusiasm."

"Something has happened here."

"Here where?"

"Vegas."

A long silence that told Larisa Pam had known her husband was hiding in Vegas. When Pam spoke again all friendliness had gone out of her voice. "What did you do?"

Tears burned Larisa's eyes. She was going to confess. She couldn't bear not to. In her shame, the only thing she could do was wallow in her guilt and hope Pam would see some of the truth. Larisa hadn't meant for anyone to get hurt. She'd just thought it was a test of loyalty.

Had she really thought that?

On the dark sliver of road behind them, the night suddenly cut through with flashing red and white lights. *They've found me.*

Larisa didn't think, at least not in a way she was aware of, she simply did. Phone off, dropped into the brush down the shoulder of the road. She turned and shouted at Kahleah, "You have to go. Go now before they're close enough to see your plates."

Kahleah was so startled she dropped her phone, losing precious seconds as she scrambled to pick it up, then hesitated as though there were other options than leaving Larisa behind.

"Go!"

Kahleah jumped into the car and peeled out.

Then Larisa waited, alone, the cold desert night stabbing through her thin dress.

No more games, she told herself.

Chapter 5

Larisa in Jail

On that lonely shoulder of Nevada highway, Larisa vowed she would cooperate with the police. For once in her life, she would trust in honesty and take whatever came. Because she deserved it. Because she was tired of trying to figure things out on her own. Nothing she'd done had worked and people had died because of it. So she surrendered to people who looked like Las Vegas police. She sat in a cell in county lockup with two drunk women and a hooker, who must have been arrested for something else because prostitution was legal in Nevada, and by the time they called her for questions, she knew everything she wanted to say.

But then Agent Osna walked into the interrogation room with that smirk on his face.

The handcuffs attaching her to the table had been one thing before he arrived, then something else as he sat down and glanced at them just long enough to make his point. He finally had Larisa right where he wanted her and there was nothing she could do about it. Larisa felt her cheeks burning, part from that damning shame, and part from rage. Her eyes tracked him as he sat down, doing her best not to wither under that knowing look.

"So," he said.

"So," she answered. "I believe I have the right to a lawyer."

"Not today."

Larisa had assumed as much. All she knew about police she'd learned in the movies, but if Osna was here, it meant this wasn't just police following up on a murder. The case had already been elevated and attached to Lucas's file. She wasn't sure Osna could legally hold her without due process, as he'd threatened on more than one occasion, but she also didn't have the energy to fight him.

"How long have you been working for Lucas?"

"I think the better question is, why did Lucas know where Hagan was hiding? This is on you. All I did was open a door."

"Why?"

You couldn't possibly begin to understand.

"Larisa, this is the end of the road. You were recognized at the scene of a crime. The detective in charge is standing outside waiting to get his claws in you. Once that happens, I can't do anything to help."

Larisa smiled at the thought of him helping her. And then the tears started. No one had ever been there to help her. She'd made it this far on her alone, and she could own the failures, but really, she'd never felt like there were many options. Osna certainly had never been her friend.

I hope Kahleah made it home okay.

"How exactly would you help?"

"You have a history of mental instability. You became fixated on Hagan after he rejected you sexually. You're unwell."

Despite herself, Larisa smiled again. An old story still so easy to tell. "I think I'll just tell the truth."

"What truth is that?" he asked, still wearing the smirk.

"I've been working as a consultant for the CIA trying to take down an arms dealer who wanted Hagan assassinated for supporting a competitor, and the CIA dragged their heels so long people got killed. Not just Hagan."

The corner of Osna's jaw twitched. "You have no idea what you're playing with."

Larisa gave him a long, hard stare. She was so very tired of his bullshit. It wasn't even worth arguing at this point. Ana was dead. Hagan was dead. At least one of Pam's people sent to

Italy was missing, presumed dead. And Osna's partner was dead.

"When was the last time you spoke to our mutual friend?"

Osna didn't miss a beat. "We have no mutual friends."

Are we being recorded or is Osna really not going to admit it?

Then a pang of doubt. *What if they weren't ever working together? Pam just wanted me to think they were.* A deep fatigue washed over her, so sudden and so powerful her eyes drifted closed. For a moment, she thought she might fall asleep sitting there handcuffed to the table. The feeling passed. She opened her eyes and leveled her gaze at him.

"Alright, Osna. No more games. What do you want to know?"

"The location of the nerve gas, his accounts, his network, everything." Osna leaned forward as though daring her to claim she could deliver all that.

"And if you get it, you arrest him? Full weight of American imperial justice, and all that?"

"Of course."

She didn't believe him for a minute, but this was the end of the road. The handcuffs told her she might not have another chance. If she was going to be locked in a cell, she didn't want to sit there and think about the things she'd chosen not to say.

"The gas is being stored in a winery in Orvieto. I believe the buyers are there and a deal's being made or has already been made. Pam Hagan has gained access to Lucas's accounts and has been redirecting funds to the point where he will not be able to do business." She took a breath. *No going back.* "And I have a list of his contacts including legal names, aliases, phone numbers, and how much money he owes them."

Osna's skin had turned a kind of papery white as the blood drained from his face. Larisa couldn't help but feel some satisfaction at his shock. All these years taunting her, he'd never really believed she knew anything. The irony was that most of what she knew had come from Pam, and if Pam had been lying to her, all she had was a list of names from the laptop. She decided not to tell Osna that she'd spent Saturday night calling them, helping along the rumors Pam had seeded that Lucas was no longer good for his debts.

The silence lengthened. Osna was so very pale he could have passed for a vampire. Larisa wasn't even sure he was breathing. *This is more than just the facts,* thought Larisa. *He was working with Pam. But she didn't tell him about the gas or the accounts.*

So now he's thinking how he helped a terrorist, believing it was going to be a good thing for the country, and she betrayed him.

"Excuse me," said Osna. He got up so quickly his chair flew out behind him. The door slammed after him, a ringing silence that faded too slowly.

Larisa looked down at her cuffed wrists and prayed no one had leaked her name to the press. If her parents—

No, she wasn't going to think about that.

She laid her head on the desk and twisted around so she could paw through her hair with her right hand, find one of the bobby pins Kahleah had placed there, and use it to unlock the cuffs. If she was going to sit in this cold, little room, at least she'd make herself comfortable. The detective investigating Hagan's murder probably wouldn't mind. Unlike Osna, most men didn't see Larisa as a threat.

Time passed. No detective came. There was no clock in the room, not even a one-way window to knock on. She tried to remember the date, to estimate hours and days that had passed, but everything since New Years felt slippery. Quinn had been gone a month. The film had released in the UK. Which meant the next major date on the calendar she hadn't consulted in weeks was Lucas's birthday. *At least Quinn will be with him,* she thought. Lucas hated to be alone on his birthday. When the cold began to seep into her toes, she got up and tried the door. Locked of course.

I've done what I could. Larisa prayed it was enough.

Something funny happened to time when it did not exist. The rules that normally kept her thoughts in order became less and less relevant. At first, Larisa hung on to the assumption that someone would come for her sooner than later. Then she attached herself to the belief that she was an important part of the murder investigation of a US senator, so they couldn't just forget about her. And then it began to feel plausible that she wasn't actually part of the investigation and Osna had arrested her as some separate thing, and no one else knew she was there, and no lacky had been assigned to bring her water, or assign her an arrest number, or anything that would mark her presence in the system, which meant no one was coming for her.

She pounded on the pressed-iron door, her shouts echoing back at her like she was in a cave.

And in the midst of all this, her thoughts collapsing upon each other like so many cascading dominos, a spotlight of clarity. How easily the squad cars had found her on the highway. Almost as though they'd been waiting for her. Tracking her.

Did Lucas have people in the police? Maybe. But more likely he'd just given the right people a tip, which meant he'd wanted her arrested. He wanted her here where she'd be cut off, unable to do anything.

He knows I've been helping Pam.

He's punishing me.

But neither thought felt quite like the truth. Everything about Lucas was close contact and high drama. If he wanted her to suffer, he'd also want to see it.

He's coming for me.

Her thoughts quieted. This little room was not a prison, but protection. He was sparing her the general holding cell and all that might happen there with other prisoners and the guards. Most likely, he'd also managed to keep her name out of the records. She hadn't been fingerprinted or photographed when they'd brought her in. But then, she thought it didn't make sense how Osna had found her if she wasn't on record. He certainly wouldn't be part of Lucas's plan.

Unless . . .

Larisa shook her head. It didn't make sense, but she also didn't care. Osna would do whatever he wanted and there was nothing she could do about it. Best case, he finally did his job and acted on the information she'd provided. Worst case, he was just as dirty as his partner and had gone to Lucas to tell him Larisa betrayed him. Even that possibility no longer felt like much of a threat. Lucas was coming for her, which meant she'd see Quinn. No more hiding, no more lies, no more games.

Or perhaps there would be games. After all that had happened, their main problem remained. She thought of the knife Pam was supposed to give her after Larisa returned from Vegas.

There are knives everywhere at Umbras, thought Larisa. If Osna hadn't done his job by the time she arrived, she'd do it herself.

She wouldn't hesitate.

She wouldn't look Lucas in the eye until he was dying.

She would make sure he knew she didn't love him anymore.

Vengeful thoughts that didn't match the steadily growing warmth in her gut as she also thought, *He's coming for me.*

Bright sun flashed across Larisa's vision as she stepped out of the jailhouse. She held her hand up to shield her eyes. When she lowered it, Rifat stood before her, thick eyebrows drawn down, deep shadows under his eyes, but still looking like the overgrown teddy bear who had more than once snuck her snacks from the kitchen in the middle of the night, kept her company through jet lag, and been the silent witness when Lucas had gone too far.

In two steps she was with him, arms around his shoulders in a tight hug. After a beat of hesitation, he hugged her back. And then he was grinning that giant grin she remembered so well and laughing at the tears in his eyes that were also in hers.

"It's good to see you," she said.

"I thought you'd be mad."

"Never at you."

He wiped at his face. "Come on, let's get out of here before someone sees."

A hired car was waiting, a giant SUV with tinted windows and seats that were the equivalent of living room recliners. Rifat used a scanner on his phone, Larisa assumed to check for bugs, then gave her the okay sign. "We're good to talk."

Larisa turned off her phone. Rifat turned off his. Larisa opened her mouth and realized she didn't know what to say. The release of honesty she'd had with Osna couldn't happen here. As much as she loved Rifat, his loyalty was to Lucas. Anything she said could, and probably would be, repeated.

What role am I supposed to play here?

He's orchestrated both my arrest and my rescue.

I'm not supposed to know anything about gas or the CIA or Pam.

Larisa tried to fix these boundaries in her head.

"How is he?" she asked.

"Honestly? Horrible." Rifat shook his head. "I just want you to know that this wasn't my idea, and I don't support bringing you in now. It's too dangerous."

Larisa's throat constricted so sharply she struggled to swallow. "Dangerous?"

"Deals falling through, people making threats. The head of our point person in London arrived in a box last week."

"Literally?"

"Things have been going badly, and people are making straw about it."

Some of that came from me, thought Larisa. In all her phone calls to Lucas's contacts, she hadn't thought any of them would resort to violence. Amazing now to think she could still be that naïve.

"So, we're going to the airstrip, and I'm supposed to bring you home. But I'm willing to say you escaped or whatever. That's what I'd do if I were you. It feels like something big is going to happen."

"He hasn't canceled his birthday?"

"Still on for tomorrow night."

"Chocolate or vanilla?"

"Both, in Italian rum cake."

Larisa arched a surprised eyebrow. "Dinner?"

"TBD."

Larisa's surprise deepened.

"He wants you to decide."

"Rifat—"

"I know. But I'm not saying you have to come. I've got Francie's write up on the plane, if you just look at it and pick something, he'd be happy."

Larisa turned to the window so she could pretend to be alone with her thoughts. It felt so nice to think Lucas needed her for something. She knew that's exactly why he'd held off planning his birthday dinner. Maybe it was a sham assignment; she couldn't imagine the war he'd have staged with Francie holding off deciding on the dinner menu until the last minute. But the pull of it, that need of his, the way she knew so well what would be perfect for him, brought to life an ache she'd been pushing to the back of her mind for a long time. And after all, it was a nice thing to plan your own birthday, but an even better thing if someone you loved planned it for you. When she'd decided to return to Italy, Larisa had known she'd be with her sisters who would have protected her from this pull. Instead, here she was alone, in the middle of the Nevada desert, faced with an impossible choice.

Quinn was on the other side of that choice.

So in the end, it wasn't a choice at all.

The Striped Blossom

Florence, Italy
Two Weeks Earlier

In the kitchen that had become his home, Quinn stood at the island counter beside Francie, the chef for Villa d'Umbras. The two of them watched as their visitor, a Florentine pâtissier of some renown, laid out dishes of chocolate and vanilla pastry filling beside a dozen small spoons. Technically, Quinn was just an observer in this very important taste testing. But he'd been sitting in the breakfast nook since lunch and Francie had invited him over to participate.

Francie and the pâtissier chatted in Italian, probably talking shop, as the work of setting out and labeling the different fillings took place. But once they were ready, the conversation died back, and a serious mood settled over the kitchen as Francie dipped a spoon into the first chocolate ganache, abandoned the spoon, then selected a new spoon to try the second.

The pâtissier motioned for Quinn to take up a spoon and also try.

"I'm not really an expert," he said.

The pâtissier smiled in the way that was becoming familiar, the Italian version of, 'I most likely speak English but don't feel like it right now.'

Quinn tasted a few of the chocolate fillings, then the first vanilla. To him, they were all great.

"You three look very secretive in here."

Quinn started up as Lucas oozed into the room, hands behind his back, sashaying from side to side as though to try to see over Francie's wide shoulders.

"Fuori!" barked Francie. "Fuori ora."

Lucas stopped his advance. "Don't worry. You can keep your secrets. I'm just here to steal Quinn away from you."

The way he said it, that slight softening of his voice like he had a secret of his own, made heat rise on Quinn's face. He didn't know what Francie thought of him, but he didn't want it to be whatever Lucas was insinuating. He didn't want her to be reminded that he was damaged, that his hips still felt like they'd been locked into the wrong position, and as a result the pain wasn't limited to his entrance, or the too-small tunnel the Commissario had forced to expand.

Once they were in the hallway away from Francie's kitchen, Lucas smirked at him. "I can smell the chocolate all the way upstairs. Don't you think she knows that?"

"This is a house full of performance and shadows," said Quinn.

"Quite right." Lucas laughed. "Did you give your opinion?"

"On?"

"My birthday cake."

Quinn hadn't known there'd been a particular occasion being planned. Lucas's extravagant dining habits meant specialists of all kinds visited the villa and presented Francie with options even for a common dinner party.

"Your birthday."

"Don't look so shocked. Everyone has one. It's a bit off yet. Lots happening before you and I have the luxury of thinking about cake."

They'd been walking along the main hallway of Lucas's villa where Quinn had been living for the past month, and now came to a stop in front of Quinn's bedroom door. Lucas opened it as though it was his own room and showed Quinn inside.

"Tonight, for instance, we are taking some very important guests out on the town. Dinner at il Palagio, then the club for dessert." Lucas gave him a sly grin as he opened the doors of the armoire and stuck his head into the darkness. "Which presents a difficulty for the wardrobe. Il Palagio is formal in a traditional sense, the club is something else. And, of course, we must consider that if I'm going to be looking at you all night you should be wearing something I want to look at."

Quinn was currently wearing the lounge clothes Larisa had bought him for their Christmas trip, which weren't quite warm enough for the villa. Most days, when Lucas would allow it, he'd wrap himself in a shawl from the kitchen. Now, he gripped the shawl a little tighter at his chest.

"I'm not great with important guests."

"Nonsense." Lucas's head reappeared. He began pulling clothes out of the armoire. "You're very important. All you have to do is look beautiful and do what I say."

"Everything you say?" asked Quinn, feeling the words weighted down with extra meaning.

"Everything."

And what happens if I don't?

Lucas carried a white suit over to the bathroom and hung it on the hook behind the door. As he moved, Quinn moved with him, making sure never to have his back to Lucas.

"That look, get it off your face right now. You can't bring it to dinner."

Quinn made a half-hearted attempt to look less nervous, but Lucas just shook his head. "We haven't spoken about my work, so I understand this is surprising to you. But tonight is very important. I need these people to think I have something they want."

"A sexy hooker can't do that for you?"

"No." Lucas edged closer. "You know why not? Because you make me feel powerful. And if I feel powerful, they're going to pick up on that. All you have to do is fawn."

"I've never fawned."

"Tonight you will. Get dressed."

"Lucas, I'm not—"

"Did I give you permission to argue?"

Quinn snapped his jaw shut, but it was too late. Lucas was upon him, backing him up against the very same wall he'd been trapped against his first night in Italy when Lucas had almost strangled him. This time, Lucas grabbed a fistful of Quinn's hair and jerked his head back.

"Let me be clear. From the moment we enter that restaurant, every single thought, every breath you take, will be for me. And if it isn't, if I don't get what I want out of tonight, what happened with the Commissario will be a pleasant dream. I will feed you to vultures who specialize in stuffing soft little creatures like yourself. I will watch them fuck every hole you have and some new ones they'll make. And then, if there's anything left of you, it will be my turn." He leaned in, pulled Quinn's head to one side so he could trace a hot, wet line up Quinn's neck with his tongue. "I know you don't want that." A pause, as though Lucas had lost control of his voice, somehow moved by the fact that he knew Quinn didn't want him. Then he recovered, speaking vengeance into Quinn's ear with a hiss. "Once I'm inside you, I never come out. What would Larisa think about that?"

The grip relaxed. Lucas stepped back, raked a hand through his hair that had fallen slightly out of place. "Now, get dressed. Don't wear anything except what I've provided."

Quinn's knees were shaking so badly he barely made it into the bathroom and closed the door before he collapsed against it. Hard, cold tile, the solid wood of the door. One full breath, then another. The fear faded into the background of the perpetual numbness that had kept him company since the rape. He wasn't sure it was healthy, but it was a relief, to be able to pin it back, to center his mind around what was important.

This is it, thought Quinn. The clarity in his mind seemed at odds with his body in full catastrophe mode, shaking with unspent adrenaline. He'd never thought it would be like this, a sharp split between warring factions, the delirious push and pull between what he wanted to happen and what terrified him. It was too much to understand, but he didn't need to. It was clear he'd passed some test. Lucas was taking him to an important dinner where Quinn would have access to privileged information. With any luck it would be information he could take to the CIA, something that would link Lucas to the weapons he sold so he would be taken into custody and spend the rest of his life behind bars far, far away from Larisa and Quinn.

Slowly, Quinn pulled himself up to his feet and began to get dressed. The pants Lucas had chosen were cut skinny and almost obscenely tight. The shirt that went under the jacket was a transparent argyle button-down that tickled his nipples. Not a shirt Quinn would ever choose for himself, but he was surprised by the effect of the fragile black lines against the sharp white, his pale skin and stark chest hair shining through the shirt, making the effect even more dramatic.

Quinn faced the mirror and tried to make his face do something that could pass as fawning. "You're so full of shit," he muttered. But then he thought about Lucas pressing him up against the wall, the shocking pain as his hair was yanked upward. A twinge of heat rippled through Quinn's groin. He touched his neck where Lucas had licked him as though with a demon's burning tongue. In the mirror, his face softened, his gaze took on the faraway look of a dreamer lost in his own fantasies.

You're wrong, he thought. *I do want you. I just want a version of you that doesn't exist.*

Il Palagio turned out to be the very fancy restaurant attached to the Four Seasons hotel of Florence. Quinn caught the briefest glimpse of the elegant dining room as they hurried past it, across the hotel's beautiful central lobby—this was a palazzo, thought

Quinn as he recognized the architecture—and down a corridor into a private room that felt like a miniature church with frescos on the walls, crosshatched lattice windows, and a single table set with five chairs.

Lucas was moving so fast, he almost crashed into the sommelier who emerged from behind the bar to ask about the evening's menu.

"I already settled this. The Camarcanda for the first course and the 1893."

"But this is the order I have for—"

"It's the wrong order. Who would serve a sparkling wine for a first course? No one. If that was your idea, you can just leave."

The sommelier started back, glanced at Lucas's assistant, Rifat, then at Quinn as though hoping someone else was in charge. Unconcerned by the man's distress, Rifat went over to the table and began pulling out, then tucking in each chair. He looked under the tablecloth, then started poking at the runner of greenery and candles like a kid looking for Easter eggs.

So it was up to Quinn to mediate. He ducked in between Lucas and the sommelier. "You're stressing me out."

"He's incompetent."

Quinn grabbed Lucas's flying hand and held it in both of his. "It's fine. Look, he's going to switch it out. You've made your point."

"Everything has to be right, or they'll spook."

"Who?"

"The guests!"

"Everything looks good here," said Rifat. "I'll go check the perimeter." He glanced to Quinn as though to check if he was okay. Quinn wasn't sure if the answer was yes, but he nodded. Then he and Lucas were alone in the little room, with the fanciest table spread Quinn had ever seen and a stressed out arms dealer.

"This place looks like it has history," said Quinn.

"Everything here has history," snapped Lucas. But then he took a breath, let his eyes wander as though seeing the place for the first time. "This hotel was combined from the Gherardesca Palazzo and a convent. It belonged to a cardinal who became a pope. This was his chapel I think."

"You think?" Quinn teased.

"I'm eighty-nine percent certain this was a chapel and it's reasonable to assume it was used by the cardinal when this was his home."

"It's beautiful."

"Yes." Lucas tilted his head to look up at the fresco on the ceiling, then blew a kiss to the mythic, half-naked figure above. "Bring me luck."

"What's so important about this dinner?" asked Quinn.

"Everything."

"It's not like you to be vague. Even your threats are strangely specific."

Lucas stared at him for a moment, then coughed out a laugh. "Look at you, making a joke."

"I was just thinking the more I know, the more I'll be able to help?" Quinn held his breath. It felt so very obvious that he was fishing for information.

"You know some of my work deals with the darker side of politics."

Quinn resisted the instinct to lean in as though Lucas was telling him a secret he'd long wanted to hear.

"The less you know, the safer you'll be."

Not the answer Quinn wanted. He scrambled to keep the conversation going. The sommelier had returned and was noisily rearranging his cart. In a moment, Lucas was sure to go over and supervise him.

Hannah had said someone was coming about the nerve gas Lucas was selling. A family, like the mob. Quinn couldn't remember. But it gave him an idea.

"Should I be worried? In political thrillers, the slice on the side is always expendable."

Lucas had been glaring at the sommelier, but now his gaze

shifted back to Quinn, turned into something softer. "You're not expendable. Larisa would have me drawn and quartered if anything happened to you."

Larisa, thought Quinn. *She's alright.*

But it struck him as strange that Lucas would so violently threaten him at the villa and just an hour later promise that Quinn wouldn't be hurt because Larisa would come for vengeance.

He thinks he's allowed to do whatever he wants to me, thought Quinn. *But no one else can.*

Hurried footsteps in the hall. And then Rifat, a little out of breath. "They're here."

Lucas snapped his fingers at the sommelier. "You, out. Stand at the door and greet them, don't let anyone disturb us once they're inside. Rifat?"

Rifat was already taking the sommelier's place at the bar.

"Kneel," said Lucas. It took Quinn a moment to realize he was being instructed. He looked down at the stone tile floor. He'd taken a pain killer, but it would still be difficult to get himself up off the floor in his tight pants once he was down there.

"Kneel." Iron seeped into Lucas's voice and Quinn found himself obeying without another thought. The pants fairly creaked with strain as he got down on his knees.

Above Quinn's head, a tinkling. Then Lucas's hands reached down and clasped a cold band around Quinn's neck. A dog collar made of diamonds with a matching leash attached to the hook. Quinn shivered.

"Your name is Volpe Rossa."

"What?"

"Don't question me, just listen. Volpe Rossa. You used to be a powerful man. Now you're my slave."

"I don't think—"

Lucas slapped him across the face so hard the leash pulled taut as Quinn fell sideways. He was just pulling himself upright as footsteps again sounded in the hallway. A moment later, three pairs of black suit shoes filled his vision.

The shoes belonged to two brothers and their cousin. Freddo Sforza, Gino Sforza, and Paulio Sforza. They spoke English like they'd just walked off the set of a Scorsese film. They walked like bulldozers. Two of them passed Quinn without notice, but the third stopped close enough that if Quinn had leaned forward, he could have scratched his nose on the shiny fabric of the man's not-tight pants.

"Who is this?"

"You don't know him?" asked Lucas.

"Should I?"

Lucas nudged Quinn with his foot. "Tell him the great name you once carried."

Panic staked through Quinn's heart. He wasn't an actor, and even if he was, he hadn't been prepped. Was he supposed to fake an accent? Was he Italian or Spanish or something else?

Lucas dug his foot into Quinn's hip where it hadn't stopped aching for days.

"Volpe Rossa," said Quinn as though full of shame.

"Louder."

"Volpe Rossa."

"And what are you now?" asked Lucas.

"Slave," said Quinn softly.

"I had heard Rossa was taking cuts off the top," said whatever Sforza. "You're lenient. I would've choked him with his balls."

"There's still time for that." Lucas tugged on the leash and Quinn felt he had no choice but to crawl on his hands and knees to the table. There, Lucas removed a chair from the circle and made space for Quinn to sit beside his feet on the floor. The men took their seats. Rifat poured the wine. A moment later, three waiters materialized and delivered the first course. Seafood by the smell of it.

Quinn felt he would be okay not eating. The stress of this bizarre pantomime had tied his stomach into knots. But then, just as he was settling into the misery of his pants pinching off circulation in his joints, Lucas dropped his hand down to Quinn's eye level and motioned for him to rise.

Tall on his knees, Quinn's shoulders just cleared the surface of the table. He wanted to look around, to mark the faces of each Sforza, but instead, he trained his gaze forward, as though his mind had been beaten out of him.

"Are you hungry?" asked Lucas.

"Yes." Quinn lifted his eyes to Lucas, unable to keep the pleading out of them. *Please don't feed me. I don't want this.*

Lucas reached over to the plate that had been left at Quinn's place setting, plucked a white fleshed slice of something from it, and dangled it in the air. Sauce dripped down onto Quinn's face. He opened his mouth, chasing the thing as Lucas danced it through the air before finally allowing it to drop into Quinn's throat, where it slid down so smoothly he almost choked.

"Impressive feat to turn a man into a dog," said one Sforza.

"But more dangerous than killing him," said another. "It sends a message to others who would cross you."

"I know exactly what message I'm sending," said Lucas.

"And Agent Smith? Has he received the message?"

The air in the chapel turned frosty.

"Competition is good for business," said Lucas.

"Even when the competition is working with the American government?"

"I fail to see what that has to do with our working relationship."

A Sforza slammed down his hand so hard the silverware rattled. "A quarter of your organization defected to him, and you pretend it was nothing?"

"It's been taken care of."

"The same way the senator was taken care of?" asked another Sforza.

"How dead did you want him?" asked Lucas.

"We've heard he isn't dead."

"Rumors Agent Smith is using to undermine us. Apparently it's working."

"Even we are not immune to rumor when this much is at stake," said peacemaker Sforza. "This food is excellent." A pause for chewing. Beneath the table, Quinn felt his ears burning as his mind rushed to pull together pieces of the puzzle. John Hagan was a California senator, very much alive last Quinn had known. Agent Smith was a character in *The Matrix*, a great alias for whatever rival arms dealer had shaken things up. He was probably the reason Lucas had been so distracted since New Year's. And Volpe Rossa was a middleman in their business who'd been caught cheating. And now Lucas was pretending to use him to send a message.

Quinn breathed a little easier, understanding that when Lucas had said, *You at my side will make me feel powerful,* he hadn't meant the level of fawning infatuation Quinn had assumed. Still, the situation felt precarious.

Is this the kind of dinner where if things go south, they draw guns on each other?

As a slice on the side, he might hope to survive a shootout by hiding under the table, but as Volpe Rossa, he would certainly be executed if Lucas wasn't there to protect him.

Suffocated with my own balls, thought Quinn. It was a night for strangely specific threats of violence.

"You have nothing to worry about," said Lucas.

"Of course we know that," said the first Sforza. "Or we wouldn't be here enjoying wonderful northern hospitality."

"There is one thing I'm curious about," said another. "Your cache had to move? Why?"

"I move it every few years," said Lucas.

"It wasn't discovered?"

"Tourists," said Lucas airily as he plucked another piece of fish from Quinn's plate and dropped it on the floor. Quinn picked it up and studied it before putting it on his tongue and quietly savoring the way it seemed to become a liquid in his mouth.

"Tourists!" said the peacemaker Sforza. "They've completely overrun us in Sicily. Let me tell you this story."

Then they talked. And they talked. The brothers interrupting each other, the cousin saying his side always did things better. Trouble with tourists, trouble with wives, trouble with local rivals, including one mob boss who was making a run for the Italian presidency and the Sforzas couldn't decide if they should support him or set up a rival campaign. They asked Lucas for his opinions about politics and going legitimate. They drank a great deal of wine.

Four courses passed. When Quinn's legs fell asleep, he managed to prop himself up against the leg of Lucas's chair. He ate the sumptuous scraps Lucas dropped for him. He forgot to be afraid.

There was a certain kind of genius in Lucas's plan for Quinn to play the disgraced Volpe Rossa. It meant Quinn never raised his eyes high enough to see any of the Sforza men's faces, so he couldn't be called as a witness to identify them. And they never directly saw his face, so if they ever encountered the real Volpe Rossa (assuming he was still alive) they wouldn't immediately discount Quinn as an impersonator.

Even when they moved to the club and everyone was seated together in a round couch booth, the lighting was limited enough that as long as Quinn kept his chin tucked against his chest, he knew he'd never be recognized.

But wouldn't it be useful to be able to identify them? he thought.

Too dangerous. He was going to stick to Larisa's plan for self-preservation, don't do anything or gather any knowledge that put a target on his back. So he settled into the couch, his body turned slightly into Lucas, and tried to be as invisible as possible.

A waiter wearing dangerously tall heels and a leather bondage corset served them drinks that had been apparently ordered ahead of time. The Sforzas didn't reach for theirs until Lucas had taken a sip of his.

"You come here often?" asked the leader Sforza.

"I own it," said Lucas.

"I like it," said the peacemaker Sforza. "What did you do to fix the smell? Sex clubs always have that smell."

"The ventilation system in here is separate from the ventilation in the private rooms."

Quinn heard pride in his voice, almost like he'd brought them here to show off.

"I can arrange anything you like."

"We're here for business," said the cousin Sforza.

"But when the business is finished," murmured the peacemaker. The way his voice moved as he spoke, Quinn thought he was probably watching someone walk by and thinking of what he might like to do with them.

"Are we decided there's business to conduct?" asked the leader Sforza.

"What reservations remain?" asked Lucas.

"I want assurances that working with you will not lead people to us. The Agent Smith problem—"

"Has been handled," said Lucas.

Quinn felt eyes on him, but he couldn't tell whose or from what direction.

"Send the Volpa Rossa to the bar," said the leader Sforza. "I want something fresh." He dropped his drink on the floor where it crashed so loudly Quinn jumped.

"Go," said Lucas. "Don't come back until I summon you."

He'd only been on the couch for a few minutes, but Quinn hadn't noticed how quickly he'd lost feeling in his legs. When he tried to stand, they nearly gave out beneath him, and he had to brace against the couch to keep from collapsing to the floor.

Behind him, one of the Sforza's snickered. Another said, "He shouldn't still have feet."

Across the aisle and through an open seating area, Quinn made his way to the bar, then turned so he was partially facing back the way he'd come, ready to see Lucas call him back.

"Cosa Vuoi?" asked the bartender, a young man wearing heavy eyeliner and a red body harness.

"Sparkling water?" asked Quinn.

The bartender made a face but sidled away toward the cooler.

A man stepped up to the bar beside Quinn. He was older than what Quinn expected at a sex club, dressed in street clothes and wearing a messenger cap low over his eyes like he didn't want to be recognized.

"Why'd they send you away?"

Warning prickled over Quinn's skin. He started to back up, but the man moved on to him, hooked his foot behind Quinn's ankle, slipped an arm under his jacket, and grasped his waist.

"Don't panic."

"Who are you?"

"Hannah said you got her out."

The CIA handler. He shoved the man back. "Where the fuck do you get off?"

"Sorry?"

"She had no business doing what she was doing. And all you did was push her."

The bartender returned with Quinn's water. He exchanged a brief spat of Italian with the handler, then disappeared again.

"What did your people find on the laptop?" asked Quinn.

"It takes time."

"Well tell them to hurry up. I want to go home."

In the booth across the room, one of the Sforzas was waving his hand in that very Italian way, illustrating a point as Lucas listened, apparently calm, though Quinn knew it was just a façade.

"Do you have backup?" asked Quinn. "You could take him tonight. His buyers are sitting right there." Quinn wondered how the whole club wasn't aware that a deal was going down for something bad. Two of the three Sforza's kept scanning the room like they expected to be attacked.

"It's not enough," said the handler. "We need a money transfer, manifests, delivery."

Quinn slowly translated each of those words into something that made sense. "You're not going to stop the gas sale. You're going to watch it happen, then hope you can grab it after?"

"Who are the buyers?"

"Sforza," said Quinn.

"Go back to them."

"Not until he asks for me."

The handler gave him a look like Quinn was a coward, which just made him more angry. "I'm not working for you."

"Is it true he uses this club as a front for his accounting firm?"

"Why would I know anything about that?" snapped Quinn, but his mind took up the idea and began to chew on it. He'd had his eyes on the ground since arriving, all of his concentration focused on following Lucas as he held Quinn's leash, trying not to follow too closely and trip.

Now he took in the room. The industrial style décor with walls of metal bars dividing up the space. Signs branded with the two curves of a rounded backside with text printed for the bathrooms, for room and equipment rentals. He located the bouncers, but no one who looked like a host walking the room to help anyone who needed it. In that way, Club D in LA was better than this one. It wasn't as atmospheric, one never stopped feeling like they were in a warehouse, but it knew how to make people feel comfortable.

This club assumed its clienteles came with a certain familiarity with the lifestyle. It wasn't a place people showed up without a plan. It also wasn't particularly crowded. The thrumming club beat and the low lighting made it feel busy, but Quinn counted only a dozen people in the main room with most of the booths empty.

"Did you need a special invitation to come here?"

"Yes, why do you ask?"

"How did you get it?" Quinn strained his eyes to try and

make out the faces of the other customers. If his hunch was correct, they were all connected to Lucas and his work. This wasn't a sex club, it was an office. A door opened and he half expected Winter Duryea to walk through. Instead, it was the nervous blonde he'd met at the villa, the one who'd supposedly come for a bondage session with Lucas but hadn't known about Lexan canes. Tonight, she wore a black leather dress and the same boots. Her hair pulled up in a severe bun. She carried a tablet across the room to Lucas.

He watched Lucas turn the tablet on, press some buttons, then pass it across the table to the Sforzas. *There's the physical proof.*

"Do you have backup?"

"I'm not authorized to make any arrests," said the handler.

"They're using a tablet. It probably has all the evidence you need—don't turn around!"

The woman had continued walking through the club. She was stopped by two men at a far table. A casual conversation, chatty, smiles. But then she pulled out her phone and began looking something up for them.

"Just to your left, see that woman?"

The handler turned his head.

"She's probably doing the money."

"That sweet thing?" the handler laughed.

Quinn swept his gaze back to Lucas's booth and froze. Two of the Sforzas were looking at the tablet, but the cousin had his head up, eyes pointed straight at Quinn.

"We've been noticed," said Quinn. "You need to leave."

Instead of leaving, the handler moved back into Quinn's personal space, reached under his jacket and began to massage his nipple.

It didn't shock him as much as he felt it should. Mostly, Quinn just felt a new layer of fatigue sink over him. *Do I just give off an 'it's okay to fuck with me' vibe?*

"What do you know about her?" asked the handler.

"You don't get it. You're not blending in."

"This is my city. You're an American." The handler moved even closer. "Work for me and I'll teach you."

The suspicious Sforza was still watching. Quinn waved for the bartender and asked for a bottle of grappa and five glasses. As soon as they were delivered, he pulled out of the handler's grasp and returned to the booth. Lucas hadn't summoned him, but he sure as hell wasn't going to be killed by suspicious mobsters who already believed his alter ego should be cold in a shallow grave.

The Sforza watched him the whole time with such intensity that when Quinn lowered his eyes to resume his Volpe Rossa persona, it felt dangerous not to be able to see what might be coming for him.

"I'm sorry," he whispered to Lucas as he set down the tray with the grappa and resumed his position on the couch.

"What's wrong, Slave? Didn't like the attention?" asked the Sforza who'd been watching.

This got Lucas's attention. He had been leaning across the table, talking about something on the tablet. Now he sat back. "What attention?"

"The local at the bar."

Quinn felt Lucas turn to look. "Him? He's security," said Lucas.

"This all seems to be in order," said the Sforza with the tablet. "Exactly what we wanted, isn't it, Freddo?"

This was a hint for the other Sforza to stop being difficult and agree to the deal, but Quinn knew from the stillness of the silence that answered it wouldn't be that easy.

"What about the one at that table?"

"I assure you, everything is fine," said Lucas.

"He looks familiar." The suspicious Sforza got up and left the booth.

More silence. In his narrow, downward angle of vision, Quinn could see the rounded edge of the couch bench, the smooth line of Lucas's right thigh. He wished Lucas would touch him. Or at least reach out and pull the dangling leash into his lap, something that would help him know Lucas was still thinking of him and would protect him if something went wrong.

Did this ever happen to Larisa?

The thought was horrible to consider. Even worse knowing Larisa would have trusted Lucas more than Quinn did. She would have loved him.

"Give me Rossa and you have a deal," said the leader Sforza.

No.

Lucas didn't so much as flinch. When he spoke, Quinn thought he heard a smile in his voice, one of those cold smiles that made Quinn feel small. He doubted it would have the same effect on Italian mobsters.

"I'll give him to you in a month when I'm done with him."

"As long as he lives, your organization is compromised."

"You think he's still cheating me? The thought wouldn't enter his mind. He's terrified of his own shadow."

"I don't believe it."

"If I ask, he will give you the best blowjob you've ever had."

The peacemaker Sforza laughed.

"Agreed. And if I'm unsatisfied, he dies here in your very safe, private club."

No.

"Fine." Lucas snapped his fingers in front of Quinn's face. "Do it." The command was an iron rod against Quinn's back. He slid off the couch and crawled around the table, not breathing, hardly thinking. It didn't feel real, this thing he had to do, and do well or else he was going to die. And what could Lucas do to stop it?

Quinn had never given a blowjob. There'd only been a handful of situations when he'd found himself in the position of it possibly happening, and every time he'd been the one in the chair sitting back, letting soft lips take him in and bring him to conclusion. Now, his racing mind tried to remember how it was done, how to avoid teeth, how not to choke. But most importantly, he was thinking, *surrender, surrender, surrender.* Because he could not, at any point in whatever happened next, reveal that Lucas had yet to break him.

Someone, probably Rifat, pulled the table back so Quinn had enough space to position himself between the Sforza's legs. A bushy, black-haired ball sack pushed out from the open fly of his pants, the limp penis resting on top of it not the least bit interested in what was happening.

Lots of people do this, Quinn told himself as he debated how he would get the thing in his mouth. *Just do it and survive.*

Lucas will be pleased.

He hated how that last damning thought was the one that had him leaning forward, ready to put a stranger's genitals in his mouth. He was stopped short by the sound of a blade being unsheathed and the sudden vision of his ashen face staring back at him from the reflection of a knife that would have made Daniel Bowie's look like a toothpick.

"You bite me, I bite back," said Sforza.

The blade retracted out of view, but it had done its work. Everything that hadn't felt real, that had allowed him to somehow keep Lucas's command in his mind and follow it, had exploded into a thousand shards of all too sharp reality. Quinn's stomach clenched and roiled. It only took leaning a few inches toward his destination for the smell to send that roil surging upward, acid burning his throat, making him want to cough at the same time he was certain he would regurgitate his minuscule dinner.

Still, he was going to do it. He wouldn't fail, not with Lucas counting on him.

Quinn was just opening his mouth, closing his eyes against the flesh coming into focus before him, when Sforza palmed the back of Quinn's head and mashed his face into his groin. He pushed it one way and then the other, as he said, "All in."

In a panic Quinn's hands came up from the floor, floundered to find something to push back against. As he struggled, Sforza's other hand came into the mix and scooped his balls into Quinn's mouth.

"Not so tame are you?"

Quinn was choking, but he still managed to calm himself and refocus. Balls. Tongue. Hair on tongue. The smell. The penis limp across his face a breath away from stabbing him in the eye if he managed to coax it to life.

Spots blinked in and out of his vision. Skin. Cloth. The point of that blade, as though it hovered just to the side of his head waiting to strike. He tried not to think about anything except working his mouth. The muscles were already straining with the size pushed into him. They didn't want to work. He felt paralyzed, but he knew he wasn't because Sforza's breathing had begun to deepen, his hips twitching with threatened thrusts.

And then, without warning, though the people not with their faces in someone's crotch would have seen it coming, he felt the concussion of a body colliding with the table behind him. Quinn was so startled he bit down to close his mouth. He was saved from disaster by the startled Sforza who shoved him back and kicked him to the side.

"What is this?"

"He was taking pictures of us," said the suspicious cousin.

"I'm doing a thesis," murmured the person who'd hit the table. American English, a voice high-pitched with panic.

From where he'd fallen against the couch, Quinn could see a little bit of the man's face under his arm, blood pouring out of his nose, remarkably muscular for a graduate student. Not that Quinn believed in stereotypes, but typecasting was part of his job, and he knew right away the guy should have chosen a different cover story.

"You know this man?" asked the lead Sforza.

Lucas shook his head.

"Kill him."

"No," said Lucas. "We need to know what he's doing here."

"I told you, I'm—"

The curious cousin slammed his fist into the man's face.

From out of the shadows, the two bouncers from the door emerged and pushed the cousin aside. They handcuffed the man, put a bag over his head, and led him away as though they took care of unwelcome spies every night.

"It seems our concerns were founded." The lead Sforza was standing and, with him, his brother. "We are no longer interested."

"Don't be a coward, Freddo," said Lucas. "I'm the only one who can give you what you want. It's the best way to announce yourself to the world in a way that they take you seriously."

"Do not tell me about my work," said Freddo. "There's blood in the water here and the sharks have come. I will not feed them."

They walked out.

For a moment, Quinn thought Lucas would go after them and make one more appeal, but he stayed sitting with Rifat beside him. Across the room the bartender was watching. The two genial men who'd talked up the blonde were watching. As far as Quinn could tell, the CIA handler was gone.

"Do you want me to—" Rifat began.

"No," snapped Lucas.

"Do you think they'll—"

"Just be quiet and let me think."

Rifat sealed his lips. But he only sat still for a moment before he scooted across the bench and bent over Quinn. "You okay?" He pulled Quinn up onto the couch, gave him a pat on the back. "You did good."

It was a nice thing to say, but it only counted if it came from Lucas, and Quinn knew that was too much to hope for. He poured himself a shot of grappa and swished its fire all around his mouth. The second shot he poured down his face. When that wasn't enough, he began to rub it into his skin using the motions that had become familiar now that moisturizer was a daily part of his life. His skin burned. Still, he could smell Sforza's balls through the alcohol fumes.

The next morning, just like every other morning since he'd arrived, Quinn was startled from sleep by music playing over the villa's sound system. Lucas had chosen an overly cheerful, French pop album, as though he needed to prove to everyone that nothing was wrong.

Chapter 7

London

The first day after the failed Sforza meeting passed, then the second. On the surface, everything in the villa remained as it had been before. Music to start the day, breakfast with Lucas, conversations about art, opera, cinema, storytelling in general. Then Quinn would be sent off on his own to read or write.

But even if the schedule remained the same, the feel of it had become something entirely different. Lucas's interrogations of the knowledge Quinn was supposed to have absorbed became shorter, his lackluster answers suddenly sufficient enough for Lucas to wave a dismissive hand and move on.

On the evening of the first day, as they sat in the library together reading, Quinn had been angry. He'd wanted Lucas to acknowledge what he'd been put through, or at least thank him for doing a good job. By the second day, Lucas's tyrannical hold over the villa had become so obviously fragile Quinn found himself wanting to break through the façade and put his arms around Lucas, to force him to recognize that things were not okay. Instead, Quinn kept his hands and his thoughts to himself. He watched Lucas's distraction and told himself he was doing enough just being there. Soon Lucas would figure out a solution to his problem. They would go back to the way they had been.

An absurd thought. One that did not at all match the other thoughts squirreling around Quinn's head about how he had to get out and go home before things got worse. He'd thought that

Lucas's main opponent was the CIA, but now Quinn understood what he was sure Larisa realized before she also began looking for her escape route. Lucas attracted violence, and anyone with him would sooner or later be collateral damage.

By now the CIA have searched the laptop Hannah stole. They'll have found what they need. Why haven't they come for him?

That afternoon, Lucas was in his office and Quinn was sitting in his chair near the door, scribbling half-nonsense notes about his sea people story—free associating, as Lucas called it—when a blond woman in black leather walked up the stairs from the first floor of the palazzo and walked around the balcony toward him. Not the same blond woman from before, but still not a true submissive arriving for a bondage session as she was pretending. She pulled nervously at her sleeves as she came to a stop before the double-sided wood doors of Lucas's office.

"Is this where I'm supposed to be?" she asked. A slight accent, similar to the previous woman. In fact, they looked remarkably similar. Quinn wasn't sure if he was blinded by some blond woman bias or if it was reasonable to think the two were related. If so, the other one had the fashion sense. This woman let her hair hang around her face, ignored, unadorned. The leather corset under her black jacket was a poor fit. Her fishnet tights smelled like their packaging.

"You new?" he stood up and offered his hand. "I'm Quinn."

"Eeva."

He nodded to her purse, which looked too much like a laptop bag to be anything except a laptop bag. "Those the updated files?"

Eeva's face contorted. She looked like she would burst into tears. "I'm sorry."

"Crying on your first solo trip? That's no good. What's wrong?"

"Janne's sick. She showed me how to do the transfers. But there were so many steps. I'm not used to burying transactions that far down. I couldn't—"

Quinn's mind raced to fill in the gaps of what she wasn't

saying. *Burying transactions? Money transfers? Was this to do with the stolen laptop?* he wondered. *Or something to do with the failed sale?*

From within the office, Lucas's voice rose loud enough they could hear him clearly through the doors. "Get them back to the table. The goddamn clock is ticking." The apparent end of the call was punctuated by a dull thud that Quinn thought was probably the phone hitting the wall.

"He'll understand," said Quinn without confidence.

"That's not everything." Eeva sniffled, then, in a hushed voice rimmed with horror, she said, "I think I lost some of the money."

"Which money?"

"The Sforza security deposit."

Footsteps. Quinn pulled her into his arms and gave her a hug, made it look good, as Rifat opened the office door. For a moment he looked suspicious, then he focused on Eeva.

"What's wrong?"

"She's worried she might be sick like the other one." Quinn held out Eeva's hand which was trembling. "I'm not sure she's up for much flogging today."

Rifat looked like he wanted to argue. But Quinn had invoked the charade of Lucas's bondage sessions and Rifat didn't have permission to violate it by insisting Eeva come to her session. He retreated back into the office and closed the door.

"You're new to this, aren't you?"

"I used to work at a bank," said Eeva. "I thought this would be easier, small operation, less bureaucracy." She shook her head.

"You don't owe him anything," Quinn whispered. "Wherever you came from, go back. Start over. This isn't for you."

He wanted to ask her about the money and where she thought it had gone, but Rifat had returned. "Go home and rest. We'll reschedule."

Eeva practically ran around the balcony and down the stairs. Rifat stood beside Quinn at the railing and watched her go.

"I think the least sexy thing I've ever seen is a crying girl," said Quinn.

Rifat grunted.

"Anything good on the Sforzas?"

Rifat shook his head.

"What about that guy they caught? Was he really . . ." Quinn couldn't remember what he was supposed to know or not know so he just let silence fill in his question.

"A rival government agent," said Rifat. "We're not sure who." Rifat wiped his meaty hand across his face. "You should convince him not to go to London. I can take you, no problem. He has things to do."

London, thought Quinn. "Is that happening already?" A rush of thoughts swamped Quinn's brain. His movie was releasing in London. The studio, Sid, Eddie, and Dansby his irritating star. His work. His life.

"Started today actually," said Rifat. "But don't worry. I told them you'd be late."

"Late for the press?" Quinn could barely form the words. "That's a breach of contract."

"Like I said, it's handled. You'll leave when he's ready unless you can convince him to stay."

"You're communicating with the studio?"

"Obviously."

"I have an assistant."

"Well, he's not here, is he?"

Quinn retreated to his chair and stared down at his journal so Rifat wouldn't be able to see his distress. Panic seemed to be an ever-present state of being for Quinn these days, but this felt like a new level, not just a psychological shock, but something in his head so entirely unprepared for realizing Rifat had been communicating as his official representative to the studio and perhaps other people who knew him back home. It felt like a new level of violation.

"You've spoken to Larisa also?"

"Of course not." Rifat squinted at him. "You still haven't talked to her?"

"I did last week, just briefly when she called Lucas."

"She called? I didn't know that." Rifat glanced toward the office doors and studied them like they hid a puzzle.

"Did the studio invite her to the premiere?"

"Lucas is your plus one," said Rifat. "That's what he wanted when they asked. Now . . . well, he shouldn't be wasting his time. And it's too much exposure."

Too much exposure.

A common phrase. Easily understood in terms of visibility and the desire to avoid it. But in this context, with Lucas as the subject, it took on a new connotation. Why would an anonymous citizen like Lucas want to avoid exposure? If someone wanted to come after him.

"I could say I'm sick."

"The accountant's already sick."

"Maybe I got it from her?"

Rifat rolled his eyes. He was just about to reply when the doors burst open and Lucas emerged. He glanced from one to the other and grinned. "You must be waiting for me. Everything packed?"

"Yes, sir," said Rifat.

"Plane ready?"

"Of course."

"Then what are we waiting for?"

An hour later they were boarding Lucas's jet. Quinn settled into one of the armchairs and accepted a sparkling water from the steward thinking Lucas would join him. But Lucas kept on walking and took a seat at the back.

From the seat across the aisle, Rifat caught Quinn looking. "I told you he's stressed. Don't take it personally."

Everything's personal now. He was so close. He knew on some level, Lucas wanted him. He knew if he could just push a little closer, he'd be able to get what he needed to cast Lucas from his life forever.

"Do you think he would've let Sforza kill me?" asked Quinn.

Rifat made a face. "Are you still thinking about that?" His tone made it sound like Quinn was hanging on to nothing, but his face said something else. The night at the club had shaken Rifat. Which probably meant he believed Quinn could have ended up bleeding out on the floor at Lucas's feet and he still would have tried to close the deal.

"Look," said Rifat. "I know you're here for Larisa. It was a nice idea in theory to try to get between them, cut her lose or whatever. I was cheering for you, I really was. But it might be time to think about the middle ground, you know?"

What middle ground?

"If you leave now before he's attached, it will be better for everyone."

Attached. Rifat was saying he thought Lucas might be becoming attached. *To me.*

As the pilot's voice came over the speakers to announce take off, Quinn left his seat, hurried down the aisle and slid into the seat opposite Lucas. He was looking out the window. When Quinn arrived, he didn't turn, didn't so much as blink. His hair showed permanent furrows from raking his hands through it, but this only added to his mystique, the svelte masculine power projected from his fine jaw, the sharp edge of his shoulders, the brooding that made Quinn itch to reach over, take Lucas's hand, and pull him into his lap.

Which he definitely wouldn't do.

But still.

This was what Larisa saw, thought Quinn. It wasn't about the sex, or the excitement of a different life, it was the silence of Lucas drowning in himself, looking like he needed to be saved. As someone who frequently felt like a lost cause, Quinn knew Larisa would have done anything to be the person Lucas needed. He hadn't ever stopped needing her, which was probably why she'd found it so hard to break free.

"You've been neglecting me," said Quinn.

Lucas stirred as though from deep thought.

"It's fine," said Quinn. And it was, because now, once again the center of Lucas's meticulous gaze, he felt his skin crawling as though that gaze was a magnet and all Quinn's secrets were little shavings of metal being pulled to the surface so Lucas could pluck them out. *How can he be so much one thing and so much another?*

"Look at you." Lucas shook his head. "So inscrutable."

Quinn wasn't quite sure what inscrutable meant or if it was good or bad in this case, so he held his silence.

"What are you? I've had you in my house almost a month and you're as unknown to me now as you were then. Either I'm a terrible host or you're a very good puzzle."

"Do you like puzzles?" asked Quinn.

"Usually. But I like to feel that I'm making progress."

You are, thought Quinn. *I think about you when I'm trying to fall asleep at night. I think about you when I wake up. I feel sorry for you, you goddamn bastard.*

"Maybe you're blocked by something," said Quinn. "You're trying to see what Larisa sees instead of what could just be yours."

Warmth blushed bright and golden across Lucas's expression, a vibrant delight. "I want very much to know what you are to Larisa."

"I'm nothing special."

"That has been established. And yet." Lucas leaned forward in his chair. "You have witchcraft in your lips and galaxies in your eyes."

Quinn didn't lean forward even though it felt like the right thing to do. He didn't want to be too encouraging to this new version of vulnerable Lucas. It felt like whiplash watching him shift guises. "I think she would say I am her favorite pufferfish. So ugly I'm cute and then, when you blow me up, I stab you."

Lucas didn't laugh. The joke seemed to have opposite the

intended effect. He turned sober. His golden light dimmed. "Have you missed her? Don't retract. Answer. I deserve to know where I stand. What was it like hearing her voice on the phone?"

Where he stands?

"You can be honest," said Lucas.

Quinn reached for his water and too late realized he'd left it at his previous seat. He needed an answer that was plausible but also the answer Lucas wanted to hear. What had he decided about Quinn over their weeks together? What kinds of feelings did Quinn's behavior support? He'd been so focused on responding correctly whenever Lucas approached him, or touched him, or looked at him, he hadn't been thinking about how it added up. Everything since Hannah had left seemed to make what had come before meaningless. Even the idea of Larisa in this space, the invisible third point of their triangle, seemed a distant phantom.

"I miss the idea of her," said Quinn. "We set up a relationship that did all the things we needed it to do. She wasn't single anymore. My name was attached to a celebrity. Her dad set me up with a couple meetings. I loved how it felt to be out with her in LA, you know?"

Lucas pursed his lips. "No. I don't."

"But being here, it's like time has been suspended. I barely think about work, the future. This is the first true vacation from trying to make my life the way I want it that I've ever had. It's weird. I'm excited for London, but it also means returning to real life and all that work putting myself out there, chasing the next thing, trying to be charming so people will want to work with me."

The irritation on Lucas's face deepened. Quinn watched his jaw move back and forth as though he was grinding his teeth or chewing a particularly unpalatable piece of food. Finally, he said, "Go back to your seat. When we land, we'll have dinner at the hotel, and I'll expect you to be able to keep me interested for at least an hour."

"You don't like that answer?" asked Quinn, surprised by the

creeping desperation he felt to make things right. Now he did reach for Lucas's hand. "Talk to me."

But Lucas brushed him off, turned back to the window and gazed out into the clouds as though Quinn didn't exist.

Quinn spent the rest of the flight thinking of things to say during dinner, but in the end nothing worked. Pulling obscure historical facts out of his head, manifesting a strong opinion about Dickens, being able to work in a quote from Kant while commenting on the lackluster service of the hotel's restaurant all failed to draw Lucas's full attention.

That night, Quinn lay in bed in his suite bedroom listening to the soft murmur of Lucas and Rifat in the living room and couldn't help but feel that everything he'd worked for was slipping away just at the moment when it had felt within reach. He cursed the skittish Sforzas, and the CIA, and whoever that spy writing the dissertation had been working for.

Tomorrow, I'll be back with my crew, thought Quinn. There would be plenty of opportunities to slip away. Eddie, his producer, would help him. He could borrow a phone. Larisa would meet him at the airport. The more he thought about it, the easier it sounded. Just walk away. Give up the foolish plan. Let the CIA do their job, eventually Lucas would be gone. Quinn fell asleep having decided the next day would be his last with Lucas.

When he walked into the suite's central room for breakfast the next morning, Lucas was on the phone pacing by the window. "It's all been settled. Get the paperwork signed. Take the deposit so we can transfer it to the Sforzas. Perfect, that's great. Thanks."

There's a new buyer, thought Quinn. And he was the only one who knew.

Lucas turned from the window and looked surprised to see him.

"Good news?" asked Quinn.

"Excellent news."

"So you'll be your regular grouch today?" asked Quinn.

"Is that what you think of me?"

Quinn shrugged. "Well, it doesn't matter to me. I'll be in interviews all day. You can grouch all you want. Did Rifat talk you out of the red carpet yet?"

"You're trying to get rid of me."

"He voiced some concern about visibility, and I think he's right."

"I pay Rifat to worry, not you."

"But what happened this weekend. The spy—"

"No one is going to attack me at a film premiere." He gave Quinn a cold smile. "In fact, until this deal goes through tonight, the safest place for me is at your side."

This turned out to mean that Lucas would accompany Quinn to all his interviews, standing by the sideline like a clingy girlfriend while Quinn talked to the press. The first part of the morning, it was just the two of them in a hotel room that looked like the one from the press junket scenes in *Notting Hill*, with reporters circulating in and out every fifteen minutes.

After that, Quinn was directed to a larger room set up with lights and stage chairs. Before he could think about how Lucas might act in a room with more people, Dansby arrived with an actual clingy girlfriend and entire posse of attendants, and Quinn felt a weight he hadn't known he'd been holding drop through the bottom of his stomach.

In three steps he crossed the room and threw his arms around his actor. It wasn't just a hug; it was a homecoming, the first grasp of true peace Quinn had felt in weeks. He held on until Dansby began to laugh.

"Hey to you too. Good you finally showed up."

The cast had done a full day of press without him, probably with no explanation. All because of Lucas.

Behind Dansby's shoulder, Quinn saw Lucas shooting

daggers at him. And in that moment, a scene clicked into place, a way to push Lucas that last step into Quinn's Venus flytrap arms.

He whispered in Dansby's ear, "Your girlfriend is hot." But he did it while eyeing Lucas, a look that promised disobedience.

The first interview was Dansby, Quinn, and the other lead of the film, a veteran star named Vince. Because this was the actors' second day of press, they were tired of talking, which gave Quinn extra space to play things up. Every answer he mentioned Dansby. Once or twice, he reached over and tapped Dansby on the knee. And Dansby played right along, leaning in, giving Quinn long, knowing looks, and uncomfortable, embarrassed laughter when Quinn gave an answer he found too revealing. To people who didn't know them, it might have been nothing. But at the end Vince muttered, "You two are making the extras jealous."

Quinn made sure they ran late so there wasn't time to check in with the 'extras.' As they transitioned to the second interview, Quinn didn't so much as glance in Lucas's direction. He could feel him, a column of fire in a sweater stitched like a Shakespearian doublet, standing next to Dansby's coffee addict girlfriend. *It can't be this easy,* thought Quinn. He didn't have time to unpack what 'this' was. Some halfway genius plan to warp, confuse, unhinge, make Lucas feel as unmoored as Quinn felt. It didn't matter as long as it looked disobedient.

Because that's what gets to him, thought Quinn. *He doesn't want a submissive. He wants something to conquer.*

"What would you say is your best personality trait?" the reporter asked Vince.

"My attention to detail."

The reporter turned to Quinn.

"If I say what I think is my best, you all will judge me," said Quinn. "But I can say for sure that Dansby's best trait is that everyone loves him."

"Aww," said the reporter. "Dansby, is that true?"

"Well, I was going to say, my sense of humor? But sure. I like being liked. And Quinn likes for everyone to think he's right."

"Morning person or night person?" asked the reporter.

This time, Quinn didn't wait for Vince. He pointed accusingly at Dansby. "Morning person."

"There is no time of day that meets fully with Quinn's expectations," said Dansby.

"Favorite comfort food?"

"Mashed potatoes for him," said Quinn. He wasn't even sure he knew this. It was just a guess pulled out of thin air. But Dansby didn't say he was wrong.

"Baking soda crackers for him," said Dansby.

"Worst habit."

Quinn looked at Dansby and Dansby looked at him. They both dissolved into a fit of giggles. To Quinn's left, Vince just shook his head. "Are you two high?"

Quinn certainly felt a certain kind of high, like he was releasing pressure after too long holding his breath. Never would he have envisioned a moment when looking at Dansby and seeing that knowing in his eyes, would solicit laughter. And yet it happened. And it felt amazing.

For this second group interview, the chairs had been adjusted to accommodate two cameras, one for the three of them and one for the reporter. Instead of standing on the sidelines in Quinn's peripheral vision, as he had during the first interview, Lucas was almost directly ahead of him. If Quinn didn't stare directly into the reporter's eyes, he could see Lucas just to the right. Lucas was not amused.

Make it worse, thought Quinn, too high on his success to think about consequences.

As soon as the interview finished, Quinn grabbed Dansby's arm and pulled him into the en suite bathroom.

"Wow, so are we really doing this?"

Quinn flipped the lock on the door, then turned to Dansby. He had his hand on his belt ready to unbuckle. "You really want to?"

For a moment, in that giddy afterglow of Lucas's jealousy,

Quinn was flattered. Then he saw the flutter of muscles twitch across Dansby's face as he battled back whatever he really felt. Quinn pushed Dansby against the back wall and lowered his voice. "Just listen. I need you to give Larisa a message. Do you have your phone?" Quinn felt Dansby's pockets, pulled out his phone, and handed it to him. "Tell her the sale's in process. There's going to be a deposit tonight. What are you staring at? Write it down."

Dansby's head bent over his phone, typed a text message to Larisa's number, then held it up for Quinn to see.

"Good. Send it."

The phone made a little chime.

"Next, tell her the accountants are out of a bondage club, The Striped Blossom. One of them is sick. No one with experience is in charge right now. There's space for a plant."

"A plant," repeated Dansby. "Huh. The first message bounced. Did she change her number?"

Quinn sucked in a breath. He'd forgotten Larisa's phone had been off when he'd tried to call her. What number had she used to call Lucas if not her cell?

"You're going to have to find her first thing when you get back. This is her address." Quinn took the phone and began to type. "This is her parents' address. This is Sid's number. Remember Sid?"

"Card shark," muttered Dansby, as though he nursed a grudge.

"He'll help you find her. Have her tell Osna he needs to stop sitting on his hands. Things are happening now. Look at me. You do not tell anyone about this. You do not want them to know. Not your parents, not your girlfriend, not a random stranger who approaches you on the plane home. Understand?"

"Maybe?"

A knock sounded on the door. "You two okay in there?"

Dansby grinned. "That's my girlfriend. I'll see you tonight?"

"Where we'll pretend this didn't happen," said Quinn.

"Now I'm a real spy, huh?"

"You're just passing secret lovers' messages," said Quinn. "Don't tell anyone."

Dansby mimed pulling a zipper across his lips, which was not at all reassuring, but also so like Dansby that Quinn told himself if there was a god who looked out for simple people, Dansby would be fine. He waited a few minutes to gather himself after Dansby left. What waited for him on the other side of the door wasn't going to be easy.

Make him love you. Get what you need. Get out.

Quinn opened the door and nearly fell back. Lucas stood directly on the other side, apparently on the verge of barging through. He pushed past Quinn into the bathroom, slammed the door behind him.

"Strip."

"What?"

"Strip now. Everything off."

A command as equally undeniable as it was frightening. How thick were the walls? How many people just on the other side of the door had heard Lucas? Still, Quinn didn't hesitate. Breathless seconds later he stood before Lucas in his briefs and socks.

"Everything," said Lucas.

No sooner had Quinn dropped his briefs than Lucas advanced on him, circled him. "What were you doing with him?"

"What do you think?"

Lucas slapped him. Not hard, but it was enough to be shocking.

"We didn't do anything. It was just a show."

"What?"

"I did it for you." Quinn ducked his head, a penitent submissive. "I thought you'd like it."

"Why would I like watching you flirt with another man?"

"Larisa—" Quinn stopped, acting as though he'd forced himself to cut off a too revealing thought.

"Larisa what?"

"I'm sorry. I shouldn't have assumed."

"Finish your thought."

"She likes to watch me with other people. And I thought after what happened with the Commissario . . ." Quinn paused as a memory rose up unbidden of that night in Lucas's dungeon, the quiet satisfaction in his expression as he'd watched Quinn struggle to comply with the police chief's desires.

He held his breath, kept his head down even though every part of him was braced for another blow. There was a bulge tenting the front of Lucas's slacks, but Quinn wasn't sure if this was a good sign or bad.

Once he's been inside me, everything will change.

You're doing this for Larisa.

For your future.

"If I want to watch you like that, I will instruct you," said Lucas.

"I won't do it again."

"Let's make sure of that. Come."

Quinn reached for his clothes, but Lucas kicked them away. Before Quinn could protest, Lucas had braced his hand at the back of Quinn's neck and was pushing him ahead of him out the door.

The room was empty except for a technician packing up the lights. He glanced up, then quickly looked away as Lucas directed Quinn through the room and out into the hallway. Empty, but it didn't relieve the feeling of wanting to melt into a puddle and die.

"I have wasted my entire fucking morning watching you undress an actor with your fucking eyes."

Quinn stumbled on nothing and realized his feet were leaving him, his extremity senses shutting down. They were almost to the stairs, no, Lucas was turning. They were taking the elevator.

"As though I mean nothing to you. As though everything you've learned has changed nothing."

Lucas leaned against him to push the up button. The erection remained, but Quinn no longer felt like it was something Lucas would want to satisfy. He'd never sounded so angry. Quinn's eyes skittered to the left and right watching for feet. *Please let no one come. Please let no one come.*

"I have dedicated every waking moment of my leisure time to making you into someone worthy of your art. And as soon as you're back in your world, what do you do? You throw it away to be one of the *guys*."

The elevator dinged open. A well-dressed woman and a man fell silent as Quinn and Lucas joined them. No eye contact, but the walls of the elevator were mirrors. It was impossible for them not to see.

"I'm sorry," Quinn muttered under his breath, half to them and half to Lucas. He stared down at the feet he couldn't feel, wanting to melt, to die, to be anywhere but there.

"Don't fucking apologize," said Lucas, shaking him.

Two floors, and they arrived. The short private hallway, then into the suite. Lucas didn't release his grip on Quinn's neck.

Rifat startled up in surprise as they came through the central room, then passed into Lucas's bedroom without a word of explanation. Another slammed door. Three people in his entire adult life had seen Quinn naked. In the past five minutes that number had more than doubled. And now Quinn stood before Lucas, fully exposed for the first time. It was a little misleading to say Quinn stood. He was out of breath, skin aflame with shame, hands on his knees as he tried to keep himself upright. Lucas stood before him with much better posture, but equally out of breath.

"What do you want from me?" asked Quinn. "I can't be Larisa. I'm just me. No one has ever really wanted me for me." *Except her.*

Lucas moved closer. With a surprisingly delicate touch, he rested a finger under Quinn's chin and used it to lift his head. "I do want you."

A ripple of electricity brought Quinn's body to his attention, blood pulsing, a new awareness of the limbs that had been drifting away from him.

"Are you going to fuck me now?" asked Quinn.

"Is that what you want?"

"Yes," breathed Quinn, and it felt true.

"That's unfortunate for you. I'm not in the habit of rewarding bad behavior."

"So what then?"

"You'll be punished. And then we'll see if I'm feeling charitable."

Small Ball in a Tight Space

If I'm feeling charitable, Lucas had said.

Even with the insult souring the promise, Quinn felt a rising of hope arch through his chest. He was to be punished and all that came with it, an intimate meditation, consideration, an act focused on him.

That hope broadened when Lucas returned to the bedroom with a black vinyl bag from which he brought a harness and cuff set. *You planned for this,* thought Quinn. But what mattered more was the second thought, *Even when you seemed so far away and distracted, you were thinking of me.*

"Not much of a punishment," Quinn couldn't help but say as he stood at attention and allowed Lucas to fasten a black leather belt around his waist, cuff his wrists, then pull them back to hook them to the belt.

Lucas only grunted in response. His movements were brusque and efficient, no extraneous touches, no hint of desire or any of the tenderness he'd briefly revealed minutes earlier when he'd said, *I do want you.*

It had felt like a direct line to only a few possible acts, but now, without notice, his mood had shifted, and Quinn couldn't tell anything about what to expect. He tested the hooks that held the cuffs to the belt and found he could twist his fingers around to free himself if it came to that.

It won't, he thought. *Lucas would be so disappointed with me.*

Lucas led Quinn over to the bed. "Lie down."

Quinn began to lay down on his back.

"Other way," said Lucas, not even looking at him.

A frission of something that might have been disappointment, or the threat of oncoming disappointment, brushed against Quinn's hope. "You don't want to look at me?"

"Doesn't work like that."

If Lucas had bothered to look at him, Quinn might have tried to tease out a protest. But he could already feel his ego eroding under Lucas's impatient disinterest, as though he was doing Quinn a favor and he better not push his luck. So Quinn lay down on his belly and turned his face to the side so he could breathe. In this position, he could just barely see Lucas, but only when he was standing a few feet back from the bed. Lucas didn't stay there for very long. Quinn heard him opening zippers, handling things that clinked together. A tantalizing noise that made Quinn's mind leap from one imagined method of punishment to another.

He planned for this, Quinn thought again. *He wants me.*

Such was the power of that thought, the supposed realization of what he'd been trying for since he made his daring plunge at Christmas, that Quinn didn't ask himself if this was what he wanted, to be pinned down and laid bare before a man he couldn't trust, to know that whatever was about to happen was entirely outside of his control and a violation of every one of the rules he and Larisa had established for their own bondage play.

A line of silver crossed his field of vision, a stainless steel hook with a ball the size of a jawbreaker attached to the end.

"Open your mouth," said Lucas.

Quinn opened and Lucas pushed the end of the hook in, rolled it roughly around Quinn's tongue, knocked it against his teeth, then pulled it out again.

"You done this before?" asked Lucas.

"No."

"Of course not. Larisa doesn't like this sort of thing."

Quinn wondered, *What sort of thing?* And then the thought, and all others that came with it, left his mind, as he felt Lucas part his ass cheek and press the ball through Quinn's entrance. It was a small thing and yet the weight of it, how quickly it sank into him, made Quinn jerk against his cuffs. Lucas pushed it in farther until Quinn felt the cold line of the hook resting against his skin. He felt the flick of a nylon rope, the hook shifting as Lucas secured it to the belt. Each shift couldn't have been more than millimeters, but they rippled through him in tidal waves.

If he'd been on his side, it would have been easier to breathe. He'd be able to see Lucas as he worked, and Lucas, in turn, would be able to see Quinn's appreciation. As it was, he felt he should say something. But everything he thought felt inadequate. And then, just as he was opening his mouth, Lucas left him.

Not just left the bed, left the room. Quinn heard the door click closed. The silence instantly dreadful as it sank through Quinn that this was not at all what he'd thought it would be. Somewhere within that sinking dread rose his old shame, as potent as rejection, as damning as the worst personal failure. It mocked the pleasure he felt. Even worse, he realized how much of a fool he'd been, thinking Lucas would want to share something so intimate with him.

He won't get away with it. Quinn tried to flick open the hooks that attached the cuffs to the belt and found that, lying on his belly, the angle had changed. He couldn't manipulate the hooks the way he could standing up. And standing up, he realized, was impossible with the hook inside him. Even the slight movements of his hands trying to free himself jostled the hook enough that the shockwaves left him breathless. Already he was on the edge of an orgasm without the promise of release. That small ball with its oversized weight held him captive, anything more than a twitch would set off the earthquake that would ruin him.

And when it did, there would be no one to see it.

But there, the click of the door. A smell that made Quinn think of Christmas, though he struggled to understand why. *Christmas mass, candlelight mass, melting candles—hot wax.* Lucas carried a bowl of liquid wax over to the bed and set it down on the table directly in front of Quinn's face.

"What's that?" asked Quinn, praying it wasn't meant to go inside him. He'd read something about hot wax and renaissance era torture techniques. Lucas had said punishment. It would be Quinn's fault to assume he'd meant the pleasurable kind instead of the literal kind.

"Wax," said Lucas without an ounce of irony.

Quinn made an effort to twist himself so he could see better and immediately gave it up as the thing inside him ping ponged against his too sensitive walls.

"Your red carpet outfit is backless," said Lucas as he stepped out of view, opened another bag.

"Like a dress?" Quinn asked, heat warm with a fresh flush of humiliation; he didn't understand where this was going.

"Not a dress. But this"—Lucas brushed his hand along Quinn's back—"is unacceptable."

Still, understanding eluded Quinn. He strained to see what Lucas was doing. There was movement in the air above him. He thought Lucas was setting objects out on the bed along his side.

"I've decided to restrain your legs," said Lucas. "Do you have a preference?"

Do I have a preference? Some small creature in the back of Quinn's brain was waving its arms and screaming at him to find a way to get away. Instead, Quinn found himself saying, "Whatever you want."

Lucas huffed out a puff of air that sounded like he'd wasted his time asking because Quinn gave the expected answer, an answer that felt like failure. But there was no way for him to know what a better answer would be. And it wasn't like he was in a position to say, *Please tie them to the belt,* because a hog-tie position would ruin his circulation and he had no idea how long he was meant to stay restrained. And he couldn't say, *Don't restrain them,* because he didn't know why Lucas had decided on that additional step in the first place.

Scrambling, he managed to say, "Why restrain them?"

Hands on his feet rough and impersonal, the light zinging sound of the nylon drawing into knots, the loose ends dancing over the backs of his thighs.

"I don't trust you to stay still, and that will ruin the pull."

Ruin the pull.

The rope bound Quinn's feet together at the ankles and his knees, which felt too tight and gave a new edge to that sinking dread that was beginning to make him feel sick. There was also some unfamiliar weight placed across his ankles, not heavy enough that he couldn't lift them, but substantial enough that it took effort, and effort clenched the raw walls of his insides around that ball; he wouldn't be doing that.

Just keep as still as possible, Quinn was thinking as Lucas came back into view and leaned down to stir the wax.

"Shall we take a picture for Larisa?"

No, thought Quinn, but Lucas wasn't looking for an answer. He picked up a phone with a bright pink protective cover, not a phone Quinn had seen Lucas holding before.

"I can't imagine you've had a wax before, have you?" Lucas didn't wait for Quinn to answer. "Rifat packed a razor, but I've decided this is more wholistic. When you see that actor tonight, I'll be at your side and in your mind."

Aren't you already in my mind? thought Quinn while the rest of him panicked. Lucas was correct, he had no experience with waxing, but he'd heard it was painful.

"I forgot. One more thing. We don't want the neighbors complaining about the noise." Lucas walked away and came back with a bit gag, the kind usually cushioned with a washcloth until the wearer became used to it.

There was no washcloth. Lucas pushed the bit between Quinn's teeth and fastened it behind his head, painfully fastening some of Quinn's hair into the buckle in the process.

"There." For a moment Lucas looked down at him, an inscrutable expression that if Quinn had still been delusional, he might have interpreted as fondness, if not tenderness. But now, he could only see it as a passing, almost clinical, interest, as though this was all an elaborate test to see how far Lucas could push before Quinn panicked and asserted himself.

You have no idea what I'm capable of, thought Quinn, glaring up at him. Most likely the glare, the half of it Lucas could see, was diluted as Quinn's racing mind had gone back to the reason he'd given for the gag. Because Lucas didn't want the neighbors complaining. Because he expected Quinn to make noise.

The shutter sound on the phone clicked for an overhead shot. Lucas held the phone down by Quinn's face and took another. Quinn tried to tell him not to send anything to Larisa, but all that came out of his mouth was an incoherent gurgle, too wet, desperate sounding. He resolved he would be quiet. He would not react. But now Lucas was propping the phone up against the lamp, positioned so Quinn's face was likely in the camera frame.

"Now we are ready." He picked up the jar of wax, stirred it, then disappeared from Quinn's sight. A moment later, sticky heat touched down on his right shoulder and began to spread. The first touch had felt hot enough to burn, but it cooled quickly. By the time the paper was being pressed down over it, a pleasant warmth soothed his muscles. For a moment.

In that moment, Lucas looked down on him. Quinn couldn't imagine he liked what he saw. He seemed to be going through the motions of some required ceremony, as though Quinn had forced this extra work on to him instead of choosing it. But then Lucas cupped the seat of Quinn's ass, pressing ever so slightly on the hook. Quinn moaned.

"You're ready," said Lucas.

Quinn had never thought before how moans could come from the throat instead of the mouth. The erotic act of moaning, a gift of sound to a partner to demonstrate pleasure, or something that came from the pleasure itself, had always seemed to him a mouth action. But with his mouth held open, his tongue pinned down, he became aware of his throat and the way it acted on its own regardless of what he wanted.

The moans became a cry when the paper was ripped from his back. Then a series of smaller concussions that mimicked the aftershocks, the gasping breaths, the blinking dark spots of fear as his body told him this was the end, the end, the end, run.

But he couldn't run. Every explosion cost him as his arms jerked sharply upward in a vain attempt to protect himself, and in the process yanked the hook upward over and over. In between pulls of the paper, Quinn was trembling, which meant the ball inside him never stayed still. It pressed against him here, brushed that raw nerve there, muscles straining with contraction as his entire body seized in pain, clenched around the ball and set fire to a part of him he'd never known existed, blood surging, a chaos of mixed signals trapped between careening panic and bliss, all trapped beneath a blanket of pain as his back seared itself through layers of skin that only existed in his mind.

When it was over, Lucas offered no comforting words, no balm, not even a Tylenol. He picked up the pink phone and ended the video he'd presumably been recording. Then he released Quinn's legs, his wrists, and lastly, the hook, pulled out of him without care. If there had been anything left in him, Quinn would have cried out again. Instead, he merely lurched as though he'd been stabbed, the ripples of feeling falling on exhausted nerves and aching bones.

Lucas removed the gag, but for several horrific moments Quinn's mouth remained open, frozen in place. He tried to move his head to a different side and found that even the slightest shift sent pain shooting down his jaw and neck.

Just as Quinn thought it would be alright to just lie still until it felt safe to try to move, Lucas commanded him to get up. "Go wash yourself," he said.

Impossible.

But Lucas was asking. Not asking, *commanding.* Quinn forced his right arm out of the right angle it'd been restrained in, then tried and failed to push himself up. Pain everywhere. Not the good kind. The kind that felt like something was broken. Lucas grabbed him and pulled him to the edge of the bed. Quinn fell, landing so hard on the floor he was sure if he hadn't been broken before, now something had shattered. White heat blanched across his vision.

"Move," said Lucas. Something—the nylon rope—flicked across Quinn's back with just enough force that he contorted himself to avoid it. On hands and knees, he crawled around the end of the bed and began to move toward the bathroom. Even in agony, Quinn was aware of Lucas's eyes watching him from behind, seeing his blood-thickened balls between his legs, the movement of him, the exposure.

But there was nothing in Lucas's voice as he again commanded Quinn, "Move." He flicked the rope across Quinn's raw skin. His palms and knees scraped over the unforgiving carpet as he scrambled across what felt like the unending floor until he reached the cold tile of the bathroom where Lucas stepped ahead of him and turned on the shower.

"Wash yourself."

When Quinn hesitated, Lucas pushed him into the shower. The water burned Quinn's skin, wrenching more cries from his lacerated throat. Lucas threw a wash towel at him. It was only muscle memory that allowed Quinn to find the soap, to put it to his skin. He was surprised to find semen splattered across his lower belly. Enough that he realized he'd come more than once during the session.

Calling it a session didn't feel right. The last thing he wanted was to associate what had just happened with the scenes he and

Larisa played out. He looked up and saw Lucas watching him, so cold, almost disinterested.

"Did you enjoy that?" Quinn's voice sounded like a child who'd sobbed himself to sleep.

Lucas made a sound behind his teeth, a look of dismissive irritation. "Always with you the obvious. You can't help but ask the wrong question."

"What's the right question?"

"What have you been given?"

"Fuck you," said Quinn.

This only deepened the irritation on Lucas's face. He stepped into the shower stall, the spray soaking his white shirt. "I've given you something Larisa never would. Your world has been expanded."

Quinn raised his fist and tried to swing. Lucas easily caught him, then grasped both of Quinn's wrists in his hands.

"You're nothing like her."

Lucas's gaze darkened. "Don't you think I know that? But you wanted me. This is me." There was something behind his eyes, the flicker of an open wound. "Most people will never know what you now know. You've been brought to the brink, stared back at your own powerlessness. What did you see?"

I'm nothing, thought Quinn. His gut reaction. But it rang false. He didn't know the answer. Turning his gaze inward terrified him. The idea that at some point he would be alone and have to sit with everything that had just happened was enough to make him go blank.

"If you're strong, you'll use this," said Lucas. "Learn to see its beauty."

Tears rushed up to fill Quinn's vision. After all of it, what his twisted mind took from that was, *You think I can be beautiful?*

"You're mine," said Lucas. "Tonight, you will not look at anyone or speak to anyone unless I give you permission." He turned Quinn so he faced the wall and clenched his hand against the side of Quinn's back above his right hip. The touch burned, but it would be bearable if he could just get one word of understanding or one gentle touch. Lucas dug his nails into Quinn's skin, holding him in place as he cleaned him. Silence. A brisk efficiency. But then Quinn thought, maybe this was all the caretaking Lucas was capable of giving. Who was Quinn to say it wasn't enough?

Chapter 9
Closing In

When they returned from London, Quinn went straight to his room. He didn't bother locking the door. Lucas had left him no illusions about his privacy. But he needed at least the feeling of being alone, away from Lucas's cold touch and penetrating eyes.

The next day, or perhaps it was the day after that, when Quinn ventured from his room, he found the villa a changed place. Guards in tactical gear had materialized both outside on the grounds and inside the living spaces. In the kitchen, Francie made him tea and asked if he'd seen the box.

At first, Quinn thought this was a confusion of translation. But then she mimed the shape of a box. "It came in today's morning," she said. "I heard there was blood leaking."

"Like in *The Godfather*?" Quinn asked, feeling more stupid than usual. But then, this was Italy, and he'd recently eaten dinner with three real-life mobsters. It seemed the kind of place where extravagantly impossible things ended up happening. For instance, Rifat and some guys Quinn didn't recognize were out beyond the back patio digging a casket-shaped hole in the gardens.

Quinn eased himself into his booth with his tea and adjusted the cushions so he could survive sitting for a little while. In his journal, Quinn made a list of all the other things a hole in the ground could be used for besides a coffin.

Treasure chest.
Giant time capsule.
Sewage line.
Bomb shelter.
Wine cellar.
What was in the bloody box?
Something is very wrong.

Quinn tried to apply this dread to the story he was developing. But his story of people colonizing the ocean, then, generations later, having factions fighting over resources, felt as real as his life.

Violence is coming, he wrote, then he tried to make a list of what it felt like so, when he could focus on his story, the details would be ready for him.

Everything feels charged and significant. A stillness, like the pressure change ahead of a stormfront, breaths being held, bodies tense even if its unconscious.
Pregnant anticipation.
What action does one take when there is no action to take?

By now Dansby would have delivered the messages to Larisa or else forgotten them entirely. The only other thing Quinn could think of to do was convince Lucas to tell him about the new buyer. But even with that information, Quinn didn't know what he could do with it. He had no phone, no phone numbers, no way to send an email without it raising suspicion.

A sharp rap on the mudroom door made Francie jump, even

more evidence to add to Quinn's feeling that life at the villa teetered on a precipice. He listened to the relief in Francie's voice when she opened the door and found only the butcher's daughter who'd brought the meat for that night's dinner party, an event Lucas was hosting for the Florence Film Society. Francie cooed over the girl, invited her in to sit and wait so she could give her a sweet.

The girl wandered over to Quinn's booth. She gazed at him shyly, then rattled off a few lines of Italian. Francie explained that Quinn was an American.

The girl beamed at him. "American? Write English?" She pulled a rumpled piece of paper from her pocket, then she pointed to his journal. "Trade?"

He tore a blank page from the journal. "What should I write?"

"Poesia."

Quinn wrote the poem every awkward middle schooler used to survive Valentine's Day and handed it to her.

"E cosa ci dice?"

"Roses are red, violets are blue, you're very sweet, promise you'll stay true."

She giggled.

Francie called her over to collect her sweet. She was out the door before Quinn flattened the paper she'd left him. He expected some gibberish of Italian. Instead, he found two lines of all caps block letters in English.

FINISH THE COUSIN'S WORK. THE USUAL PLACE. 3:00.

Quinn glanced across the kitchen. Francie had gone back to her work a little more relaxed than before, as though the interruption of the girl had shaken free some of her unspent nerves. He crumpled the note and dropped it into his teacup.

It was already past one. He wasn't even sure he remembered which church Hannah had been using to meet her handler.

Ignore it, Quinn.

There could be a message from Larisa.

She wouldn't be working for the CIA.

She is now if she got your message. They're the only ones who could have used the information you sent.

Fuck.

Fuck.

"You look more stormy than usual."

Quinn looked up as Lucas slid onto the bench across from him.

"Maybe I'm lonely," said Quinn.

"I detect a rebuke." Lucas sighed. "I suppose I deserve that. Such a nice time in London, and now I've left you all alone." He steepled his fingers. "One of my associates in Washington made several poor decisions that are just now coming to light at the worst time."

Quinn mustered a smile. "I heard you received a box."

"Everyone knows, do they?" Lucas cast Francie a dirty look. "It was nothing to worry about."

Francie released a stream of Italian that seemed to say otherwise.

"It will be fine. I'm not canceling my birthday because some money went missing."

"That sounds like a big deal?" Quinn stirred his pen around the table as though he didn't care.

"I'm not worried." Lucas twisted around to repeat himself to Francie. "I'm not worried."

"You think you'll be busy the rest of the day?" asked Quinn.

"I've only just escaped to make sure you'd stopped moping. How's the writing? Ready to show it to me yet?"

"Soon," said Quinn, praying his departure would come sooner. "Do you think I could go down to the city?"

"Alone?"

"If I must."

For a moment, Quinn was afraid Lucas would come with him, or worse, see through to Quinn's intentions. But whatever

Lucas was thinking, he shrugged it away. "As long as you're back for dinner. Everyone at the society has been asking if they'll see you again, you were such a hit last time."

"I'm looking forward to it."

"Did Hannah teach you to use the car service?"

"Can you do it for me?"

Lucas laughed. "This is the only truly submissive part of you. Absolutely unable to take care of yourself." It almost sounded like a compliment. He pulled out his phone, paused to look at it for a moment. "Ah, she speaks." To Quinn's questioning look, Lucas said, "I sent Larisa a video of our little experiment in restraint."

Quinn kept his face carefully immobile, but Lucas still said, "Don't look so shocked. It's a good faith gesture. So she doesn't worry. You two are still fighting, aren't you? This is what she said back. 'I'm better than he is.'"

"Probably true."

"Why do you think that is?"

"I like to think you were more invested in her safety and satisfaction than you are in mine."

Lucas's face lit up with delight. "Ah, you've thought about this."

"She trusted you." It almost came out as an accusation.

"And you do not."

"I'm slow."

"Well, I know a way to speed up the process." Lucas began typing on his phone. "We'll invite Larisa to join us. Then she'll teach you."

Quinn reached across the table, forcefully putting his hand over Lucas's to stop the typing. "I'm not ready to see her."

"It's been a month. Even Hannah went to LA to try to make amends."

"Is that where she disappeared to?"

"An impulsive departure. Guilt has been eating her alive since Christmas."

"And your guilt?" Quinn didn't have the stomach to make his

face into something that hinted at flirtation. He felt queasy, his legs jittery under the table. He didn't want Larisa anywhere near Lucas and his crumbling fiefdom.

She won't come.

"I can be as guilty as you need if it fits the scene." Lucas gave him a wolf's smile. "Il Direttore, if you write it, I will cast it. A ménage à trois."

"If only I believed you'd follow the script."

"If you are very good, I promise, when she comes, I'll be very good."

"I'll hold you to that," said Quinn as he watched Lucas pull up the number for his car service and pave the way for Quinn to be the opposite of good.

"Where do you want to go in the city?"

"I thought I'd wander."

"Don't walk beyond the tourist center where people don't speak English, or I'll never get you back."

Lucas dialed. While Quinn waited, he pretended to look over his journal and write down a few last notes as though he'd had a productive morning.

Write the scene so there is only one true outcome. How can he release his hold? Only the deepest betrayal. A regret that recasts all his dreams in shame.

Then he looked across the table at the man who didn't feel guilt. Who, as far as Quinn could tell, felt very little of anything.

What does he believe about himself that isn't true?

As soon as Quinn wrote the question, he knew the answer.

In this pageant play, Quinn was playing Larisa, or at least some fantasy stand-in of what Lucas believed it would be like to have Larisa back in his life. Despite all evidence to the contrary, he was determined to believe she could love him. And he believed Larisa was safe in his world. Despite his occupation, he could protect her.

Quinn hadn't been to Florence's city center since the day Hannah took him to her cooking class and they'd spied on Rifat's parents' bakery. In number of days, it hadn't been that long, but to Quinn everything felt different. Now he could recognize the significant historical buildings. He knew their names and had some association with the people who'd built them. He knew the difference between a loggia and an archway, a palazzo from a piazza. He knew the building materials for the roads, the buildings, and the statues.

Some of what he'd learned had come from Lucas and their rambling conversations in the study. Some had come from Hannah or from Lucas's guests talking about their lives, complaining about tourists. Most of it had come from reading, most of it aimless, some of it because Quinn thought he could use Florence and the rule of the Medici as inspiration for his own group of warring city-states under the sea.

The car dropped him off at the Piazza della Signoria. He marked the Medici Palazzo Vecchio to his left, paused to look at the statue that had taken him in before, the trio of figures trapped forever in a moment of violence. Now he knew the statue was marble, one of the most famous statues in Western history. He still didn't understand why the mass rape of a people group was something to be celebrated.

Once the car drove away, he glanced back over his shoulder.

Rifat's bakery was closed. Not just closed. The nameplate above the door was gone and the inside appeared completely empty.

Did I help make that happen?

What if his parents were innocents?

He didn't have enough time for regret. The clock on the Palazzo tower read two-thirty, and he had a lot of walking ahead of him to reach Hannah's church.

The Basilica of Santa Croce was more impressive in real life than in the pictures he'd seen. Similar in look and feel to the grander il Duomo, the church had a marble gothic-style front, or what Quinn now knew was called a façade. In the time of great churches, it had been the popular place to be buried if you were part of Florentine fandom. This preference had assured it a place in history. Tourists were lined up outside the door leading into the refectory to see the graves of Michelangelo, Galileo, Machiavelli, and others.

But like other churches in the city, the basilica also still functioned as a place for true worshippers. Quinn found the obscure side door marked CAPPELLA DI PREGHIERA and stepped out of the sun into a dim interior.

The church boasted over a dozen chapels, but this one, down by the nave and the entrance to the gardens, was the most removed from the noise of foreigners. Light came in through high, small windows, illuminating ornamental carvings on the walls and frescos by someone who'd eventually died in a plague.

Benches were set out parallel to a candle altar. He remembered a movie where a significant plot point was retrieving an envelope from underneath a candle alter cloth. Now, after seeing his first altar in real life, and how far away it was from the railing that guarded it, he found this scene implausible.

"This entire thing's implausible," muttered Quinn as he looked around for the guy who had almost blown his cover at the club.

"After last week, I didn't think you'd come."

Quinn turned and found the handler seated on a stone bench behind him. "Is Hannah safe?"

"Yes."

"Am I?"

"Is that your goal?"

"She said there'd be an attack. Or was that just you guys putting pressure on her to get results?"

"When a chemical weapon goes missing, and it can't be located, it's standard procedure to eliminate all knowing parties within a set time frame."

"And how close is that deadline? Do you know who the new buyers are?"

"There aren't any new buyers as far as we know."

"Why?"

"There's a rumor someone's been making calls to Lucas's network, telling them he doesn't pay his debts."

"Your people?"

"Someone else got to the accounts before we did. My stateside counterpart has been working with a source." The handler frowned. "I can't talk about that."

"I need a way home."

"Does he suspect you?"

"I don't want to end up dead. There's security all over the place, and all the staff is walking around like the place is going to explode."

"Not from us. Not yet anyway."

"Get me out."

"Get him to tell you where the gas is."

"I'm not supposed to know anything about the gas."

"You're clever. You can figure it out."

Quinn clenched his hands into fists. *This is exactly why Larisa didn't want to work with these people. They don't care about anything but their objectives.*

"What about the laptop?"

"What about it?"

"What was on it?"

"Haven't heard."

Quinn stared at him. All that work, losing his phone, surviving the Commissario, for nothing.

"Allora, maybe the gas isn't something you can find. But there are other things. Key figures, people who might be willing to turn on him. What about his man, the Arab?"

"I'm not doing that."

"So you don't want to go home?"

"Why don't you just drive up the hill and arrest him?"

"We want to keep the organization intact until we have the big picture. If he's arrested, they'll scatter, reorganize with someone new."

"That could take months."

"Give it a week. You're already more valuable than Hannah. He's sharing things with you, isn't he? Interests, weaknesses, fears?"

Quinn laughed bitterly. "At this point, his only weakness is me."

"You think he'd do something stupid if you were in trouble?"

Quinn thought of what Rifat had said the week before. He thought of the way Lucas had been in London, cold and distant, but invested. "What kind of trouble are we talking about?"

"I'll talk to my counterpart."

"Does this mean the villa's safe? I'm not going back there if your people are going to come in tonight guns blazing because you lost the gas."

"That isn't our style."

Quinn swallowed. "His old friends who are turning on him. Would they—"

"I would work quickly. This is the end one way or another."

I think I already knew that.

Instead of calling the car, Quinn returned to Umbras on foot. It was a long walk, but for the first time in his entire life, being outside and exerting himself felt good. *I'm his Larisa replacement. What did she do for him? What can I replicate?* Thinking about Larisa with Lucas inevitably led to thinking about his own experiences with him. *Is this how he was with her?*

At a half wall fencing an olive grove, Quinn stopped to catch his breath, looked out over the winter bare trees and the seamless blue sky above them. The call of a bird winging through the air. A perfect scene in a place he'd never imagined he'd visit. And all he could think were dark thoughts, a current of terror in him that had been there so long he almost didn't notice it except in these heightened moments when it became breathtakingly obvious how unlikely it was he'd succeed. Each day that passed, even the idea of success faded, became twisted up with ghosts of uncertainty. Death was too good for Lucas. But jail wasn't enough. And as long as he continued to live in the world, Quinn would never feel safe. He knew Larisa would never feel safe. The difference between them was she'd given up believing it was possible.

He doesn't want a submissive. He wants someone to try, and fail, to be a submissive. He wants to justify his disappointment in everyone.

When he arrived at the villa, instead of going to his room to shower and dress for dinner, Quinn took the stairs up to the second floor. He padded softly around the library balcony. And, not daring to pause, opened Lucas's office door and walked in. There was a meeting in progress. Lucas, Rifat, and three people who looked vaguely familiar, though Quinn couldn't place them. They all started up in surprise. One of the guys who'd been digging in the lawn that morning drew a gun.

Which was really, really scary, but Quinn pretended not to see it and kept on walking, right past them to the bedroom, stripping off his clothes as he went. "Plumbing in my room isn't working, sorry for the intrusion." And he said it like it was the worst imposition. He said it like they'd been fighting. Maybe, with enough tweaking of the narrative, they'd fought earlier in the kitchen, when Quinn hadn't convincingly pretended to be upset that Lucas had neglected him.

Yes, he thought, blood pounding in his ears as he turned on the shower in Lucas's bathroom, *that's what it will be. I baited him with a trip to town. He let me go by myself. Now I'm pissed about it.*

Lucas didn't come to find him in the bathroom, which Quinn found discouraging but also a relief. He didn't want to be naked with anyone, especially not Lucas. He dressed in clothes from Lucas's closet—layers upon layers, the opposite of those flimsy outfits that populated his own wardrobe—then stormed back through the meeting on his way out. On the ground floor of the palazzo, film society guests had already begun to arrive. Quinn hesitated only a moment to take a breath and summon some Dansby energy to work the room.

Here . . . we . . . go . . .

The perpetual early arrivals who acted like Umbras was their house included the film buffs Giovanni and Sven and the film society vice president, who approached Quinn and started a conversation about his critique of *The Red Shoes,* which they'd watched the month before.

"American taste is so particularly American."

An insult. But Quinn was past caring. "We're in the business of selling things," he said as though he believed the arts were a consumer product. And maybe part of him did believe that. The returns on his movie were solid, they felt like validation.

Winter and her companion from Quinn's first night in Italy had skipped the white wine aperitif in favor of liquor, which gave Quinn the perfect excuse to sidle up to her.

"He's going to be so angry," said Quinn, more teasing than anything.

Winter sounded much too serious when she said, "Let him. I've earned this drink and the next five. Where is he?"

"Still working."

Winter exchanged a look with her companion who shook her head.

"The birthday's still happening, I assume?"

"As far as I know."

"Fucking fool," muttered the companion.

"What did you expect? It's not like he'd weather this in a bunker. Last time—"

"This isn't like the last time."

Quinn looked from one to the other, his expression awash with worry as his mind strained to put the pieces together. "What should I know that I don't?"

"Nothing dear." Winter patted his arm.

"Did you hear about the bloody box?" he asked.

For a moment, Winter stared at him, then, like glass shattering, she let out a high-pitched gale of laughter. "Look at you, you're so sweet." But then there were tears in her eyes and a sadness crashing over her features. "Run along, now. Don't embarrass an old woman."

Winter wasn't old, and Quinn felt certain she didn't embarrass easily, but he moved on feeling he'd gained something of value. Winter was part of Lucas's business. They were here tonight to talk with him. Everyone else was here to watch a film and eat a good meal they hadn't paid for.

Quinn scanned the faces he passed as he circulated through the room. *There could be others.* If someone caught him staring at them or lingering too long eavesdropping on a conversation, he flashed them a flirtatious smile or left a light touch on their bare skin.

"The night's young and beautiful," he proclaimed like some young impresario. He blew kisses at the girlfriend of an art student who wore a striped shirt and beret and let a cigarette hang out the corner of his mouth like he knew some great secret about beauty.

When Lucas came downstairs to join the party and move them into dinner, Quinn turned up the volume of his enthusiasm and proceeded to flirt, chat up, and laugh at whatever inane joke anyone made except for Lucas. On the surface, the plan was so simple, so obvious, Quinn didn't think it would work. But when Quinn played like he was going to sit on Winter's lap for dinner, he caught the fire in Lucas's eyes.

During the first course, when Sven commented on Quinn's small portion, he loudly bemoaned his sensitive stomach and drew sympathetic acknowledgement from everyone on his side of the table. A conversation about the necessity of special diets followed, a topic on which everyone had something to say. In mere minutes, guests on Lucas's side of the table were leeching their focus away from some debate about the Dutch angle in cinematography and were chiming in to talk about IBS and the pills they were on, the herbalist they'd tried. Any gastronomic pleasure anyone might have taken from the meal vanished.

From the far end of the table, Lucas gave Quinn a long look. From the outside, it was just a look, but Quinn felt Lucas's bewilderment, his calculations, his interest in this new version of Quinn.

I'm winning, he thought. Winning what and to what end, he didn't consider.

Quinn's strategy faltered after dinner as they moved into the stone cellar viewing room and Quinn found himself cornered by the society vice president, a German named, Wolfgang, who said, "But isn't Tarkovsky the best director of the twentieth century?" right when Lucas was watching. For a moment, Quinn was so shocked by the proclamation that he couldn't think of a single thing to say in response.

No one wants to sit in a theater and watch obtuse philosophical musings ooze off the screen.

But such a sour response would have ruined his project. And Lucas was watching. Watching with a gaze that scorched and seared while Quinn flew about beneath it like a leaf in the wind. To stay still for a moment risked catching fire. He leaned in and whispered in Wolfgang's ear, "And we shall keep him to ourselves," then dashed away to a new hapless object of his attention.

The film of the night was Antonioni's, *La Notte*. Quinn didn't mind Antonioni, especially not his gorgeous actors, though, in a fair world, they'd be watching a film by Lucrecia Martel, who did what Antonioni did but with a much more natural style. In a different place with different people, Quinn might have said this aloud to start a fight, divide the room between the almost unknown semi-documentarian, Portuguese director and one of the unassailable fathers of Italian new wave.

Instead, Quinn's mind flitted and sparked, his eyes everywhere for opportunities to make a spectacle of himself. For weeks he'd been restrained, pensive, the emotional equivalent of Elinor Dashwood, with everything stuffed down so far inside it almost didn't exist. He'd been so focused on pleasing Lucas, being the good submissive. Now he'd released that control and channeled all the pain and uncertainty and fear and anxiety into this fission of trapped energy that was his body. No longer barrier, but invitation; almost as though, at long last, he'd put on the red shoes of a survival instinct he didn't know he had. He couldn't be still. He couldn't not spend every last minute making a bid for the future he wanted.

The film began.

First, he sat with two college students from Rome. He thought of Larisa sitting through a film that didn't interest her with the basket of fidget toys she kept at her parents' house. He played with a cocktail spoon, with the buttons on the coat he was wearing. One of the students giggled at his restlessness. But this wasn't enough. Lucas was four chairs over, glaring at the projection screen, but still composed, maybe not even thinking about Quinn, maybe thinking about the other things. Perhaps the thing that required a coffin-sized hole in the garden.

On screen, the 1960's goddess Monica Vitti was having a moment of uncertainty, beautifully pensive in black and white. Quinn tried to mimic her expression. Then he leaned over to one of the students and muttered something about hot girls, a nonsensical string of words meant to be jointed together by the unconscious. The guy grinned. The student on the other side of him shushed them. Quinn took this as a sign to continue.

He made smooching noises as Monica and her costar Marcello Mastroianni worked through their angst, not kissing, but wanting to, wanting so much. *This is a great film.* The thought came in and slid off the side of Quinn's tilting mind. He remembered there was a party scene coming. When he'd watched the film in college, he'd thought how romantic sixties parties always looked in films and wondered if they had lived up to their legacy. He despised modern club scenes in new films. They never captured the claustrophobia, the noise, the soullessness of the modern experience, the fact that human connection had been boiled down to intoxicated gyrating in strobe lights.

We're always reaching out. The nature of life is isolation, disconnection. That's what this film is about. He was strangely disappointed that he'd written an entire paper on Antonioni and never reached as profound a conclusion as he did in that moment, thinking of LA, of its lack of Romance. All the magic happened on soundstages and in the minds of the people who came there to dream.

As soon as the music for the party scene started, Quinn jumped to his feet and began to dance. At first, he imitated the actors on screen, then, when the camera cut away to not dancing, he made up his own dance, something a little like Fred Astaire and a little like Elvis. After months of Lucas's attentions, it felt so easy to throw his body around in front of this audience of film snobs. There was pain, but even in that, he felt powerful. He'd earned this moment. In the flicker of the screen, he saw Lucas watching, that fiery gaze darkening into something more dangerous than desire.

Finally, it happened. Lucas stood up, crossed the space between chairs and screen, took Quinn by the arm, and steered him out of the cellar.

"I was just dancing," said Quinn so that everyone could hear him.

Out in the hall, Lucas pinned him against the wall.

"What's your—?"

"Quiet." Lucas yanked off the coat Quinn was wearing, the sweater. He dug his hands into Quinn's waistband and released the shirt he'd tucked into it, digging down and down until fingers found skin, a bulge of soft meat to close his hand around. Lucas's hands were so cold, Quinn flinched.

"Is this what you want?"

"More." Quinn tilted his head to the side, an invitation. Lucas attached his mouth to the base of Quinn's neck, teeth, tongue, almost vampire. Quinn closed his eyes and told himself this was it. This was the next step, no holding back. Lucas grabbed his ass and squeezed.

"You have no idea what you do to me. Your resentment is so . . ." Lucas breathed into Quinn's neck. "I want to send everyone home so I can demolish you."

"Then do it."

Lucas stilled.

At first, Quinn thought he'd said the wrong thing. But no, the phone in Lucas's pocket had vibrated.

"Ignore it."

Quinn's heart sank as Lucas tore himself away and walked down the cavernous hallway toward the stairs, leaving Quinn breathless, coming down from the highest high to crash into the worst withdraw.

Follow him, thought Quinn. *This is the end. No more hiding. Follow him and what?*

Quinn picked up the discarded clothes. Down the hall, Lucas's voice echoed with a ripple of distortions that felt like opportunity dissolving into lost time.

Fuck it. Quinn followed Lucas at a distance, unnoticed, all the way up to his office.

Chapter 10

Witnessed Murder

Quinn couldn't help but think if Larisa had been in his place, she would have charged into the office and demanded answers. She wouldn't have stood outside the door listening when she already knew from attempting to eavesdrop on a dozen other meetings that only shouting could be heard from beyond Lucas's office doors. But Larisa's approach would have also lost the possibility of overhearing the truth. And the truth was what Quinn needed above all else.

There were no voices coming from the other side of the office door. Quinn had been standing there several minutes now and he'd convinced himself that, unless Lucas was whispering—which he never did—Lucas was in his bedroom not his office. Which meant Quinn was almost certain Lucas was in the dungeon he and Hannah had found. But believing this to be the case and acting on that information were two separate things. He lost several more minutes paralyzed with fear before he managed to grip the knob on the office door and turn it.

As he'd thought, the office was empty. And there, where the painting of Samson and Delilah had hung before Hannah had dropped it and broken the frame, the faintest glowing crack of blue-white light along the floor. Quinn crept forward. The door to the dungeon had been pulled closed but not latched. He paused to listen but couldn't hear anything. First with his fingernail, then with his finger, Quinn wheedled the door open by millimeters until he heard the soft hiss of a seal breaking and the ends of the door pulling apart enough for sound to leak through.

The first thing Quinn heard reminded him of lava, the gushing of molten metal, but less distinct. A human's wet, strained breath.

Lucas: This is very simple. Where's the money?

Man: I don't know.

Lucas: You're an accountant. The only thing you're required to know about is the money.

Man: I told you already, when the laptop was stolen, we did what you wanted. It's not simple. It takes time. Janne was sick. She sent things places and didn't keep track.

Lucas: That's not possible.

The sound of movement. The man groaned.

Quinn pushed his finger into the door and pulled it open another half an inch, just wide enough he could see inside. A man hung from the top bars of the cage at the far side of the dungeon. Blood bubbled up from holes on each side of his chest. They spat red into the air when he coughed. His breathing sounded more animal than human, like an animal in heat, except an animal didn't take things personally. And this was so, so personal.

For a moment Quinn stared, mesmerized by how very different this scene of torture looked from the movies. He drank in the details, tried to memorize the sounds. The blood soaking unevenly into the man's shirt, the spray of it on the floor. How clear the man's voice sounded even though he was breathing his own blood.

Then Quinn's gorge came up, so sudden and forceful he only managed to retreat a few feet back from the doorway before he pitched forward and vomited. They heard him of course. He turned to try to run, but the door rushed open and Rifat was on him before he even made it to the office door.

"Let me go," cried Quinn just like every other person in a movie that'd ever been caught doing something they shouldn't.

Rifat held him fast as Lucas emerged from the dungeon wiping his hands on a towel.

"Let me go," said Quinn again. This time, with Lucas's nod of permission, Rifat released Quinn. He fell forward onto his knees and vomited a second time. It wasn't the blood, or the sounds. It was the smell that made it all too real, the sticky, iron-scented humidity in the air, as though the blood that dying man was breathing had become the air in everyone's lungs. It mingled with the more subtle, drifting stench of the man's released bowels. The two of them together marking the most vivid premonition of death.

He's going to kill me, thought Quinn.

"This is unfortunate." Lucas turned his gaze down to the far side of the room, thinking. Tense moments passed as Quinn's head swam. He could barely hold himself upright to keep Lucas in sight. He expected to be hit, or at least reprimanded.

Finally Lucas said, "Go down and ask Winter to take over as host. The night was already lost to me anyway."

"And him?" asked Rifat.

"I'll take him with me to pray. We'll be back before Vegas goes live."

Lucas motioned for Quinn to stand. Somehow Quinn did. It seemed the only choice that kept his limited options open. *Get what you need. Don't back down.* But it was difficult to know exactly what this meant, or if Quinn was just feeding himself generalized inspirational phrases. He followed Lucas through the villa.

Outside, he sucked in gulping gasps of cool night air. He breathed in the scents of the potted lemon trees lining the driveway and the olive grove on the other side of the wall that bordered the street down into the village of Fiesole.

"A perfect night," said Lucas as he rapped his knuckles on the top of the wall, drew in a deep breath, then let it out with a dramatic sigh. "We'll never recover from what you saw, will we?"

Not waiting for an answer, he began to walk down the driveway. As Quinn followed, he thought about how much Lucas's question revealed. It startled him to think Lucas had begun to think of their arrangement as something lasting. He'd thought they were both operating from the same assumption that eventually the game would end, a winner in their unnamable duel would be proclaimed, and they would go about their lives.

Or one of us would go on and the other would not.

"When did she tell you about me?"

"What do you mean?" Quinn knew exactly what he meant.

"You just watched me interrogate someone. Two weeks ago, when I said I'd asked Larisa to kill someone, you barely blinked. So you've known I was bloody for a while."

"I thought you said that to test my reaction," said Quinn.

"But still, you knew what I was. You're not surprised."

Quinn had no idea if he should admit that Larisa had told him. He felt, perhaps at this point, it didn't matter, but a lie came easily to his mind, so he used it. "The Commissario told me. He thought I was working for you."

The words hung in the air, so flimsy Quinn knew they wouldn't hold. But then Lucas nodded. "That wanker. I never thought it'd be a fool who'd bring me down."

"It's easy to think only the smart people are dangerous," said Quinn, so flooded with relief he almost missed a cleft in the road and tripped. Lucas brought up an arm to catch him and pull him upright. In his touch, a rush of warmth, almost as though they were friends more than they were enemies. *Or lovers,* thought Quinn, thankful the dark of night hid the flush on his cheeks. *Will he want to fuck me before he kills me or after?*

They walked on. Lucas eerily thoughtful. The Tuscan countryside hushed with suspenseful quiet. In a few minutes they would enter the village. Quinn thought he could make a mad dash for a pensione's door and pound on it, or perhaps run into the olive grove and slip away into the darkness. Once he'd made his escape, he would walk down to Florence and hide until Santa Croce opened. He would pray Hannah's CIA handler would come to visit, then he'd tell him about the tortured accountant. Force him to make the arrest.

Il fine, thought Quinn.

The road split into two. Lucas turned down the right side. The walls of a monastery loomed up before them, the road ended at the wrought iron gates. *He's going to kill me here.*

"What did you think when you met me?" asked Lucas.

Quinn looked down the other side of the road, the darkness that sucked hungrily at its edges would hide him if only he managed to get there. How far was it? Thirty feet, maybe forty. Running on his wobbly legs. Lucas would chase him, catch him easily.

"I suppose we're past the point of conversation." Lucas waved a magnetic key fob at the gates. The lock clicked and the gate opened. "Did you know Cosimo de' Medici had his own monk's cell? It was down in San Marco. Frescos by all the great artists of his time. A lovely little room for his private thoughts. Meetings. Negotiations with God."

Quinn hung back from the gate. This looked a little too much like a horror movie for him to walk forward without pause. "I thought you were an actor who'd come to impress me," he said. "I had cast you in three movies I'll never get made while you were interrogating that bartender about his wines."

"Not interrogating." Lucas paused. "Perhaps interrogating a little. He knew nothing about wine."

"Not his fault."

Lucas shrugged, but Quinn thought perhaps he was flattered by Quinn's description. He hooked his arm through Quinn's. "Come on then. We're late for prayers."

If Quinn's life was a movie, this was the scene where the audience would start yelling at the screen for the hero to not follow the villain into the creepily quiet, possibly abandoned, building. Even as Quinn was aware that as a director he would never have his characters make such an irritating decision, he allowed Lucas to lead him across the courtyard, through a rounded doorway, and up a narrow column of stairs.

The hero follows because they want something, thought Quinn. *They know running doesn't get them that thing. They believe when the necessary situation presents itself, they'll find a way through.*

"I haven't thought of you as a religious man," said Quinn, if only to mask the pounding of his heart.

"Religion can be anything we make of it. In this case, I like the feeling of being a trespasser and committing unholy acts in a sacred place." Lucas raised his eyebrows suggestively. *Did he just say what I think he said?*

The hallway at the top of the stairs was too narrow for them to walk side by side. Quinn walked behind. He studied Lucas to see where he might have hidden weapons. He was wearing a long black coat, dark, narrow jeans, and boots that were stained, possibly with blood. There could be a knife in the boots, any number of things in the pockets of the coat.

If he's brought you here for sex, don't surrender, thought Quinn. *The disguise is gone. He knows.*

Make him fight you.

They passed several small doors before Lucas stopped and opened one. It led into a monk's cell with a spartan, metal-frame bed, a window with a wrought iron cross in its frame, and a shrine with a kneeling cushion in one corner. Quinn hesitated in the doorway, searching for a sign, for anything he could use that would keep this room from being a trap. There was a narrow chest of drawers beside the shrine just like the one in Lucas's dungeon. And there, half hidden along the frame of the bed, a spreader bar with cuffs.

"Welcome to my sanctuary." Lucas moved aside to let Quinn step in. He reached over and closed the door behind him, then turned the key in the lock.

"What kind of prayers do you offer here?" asked Quinn, trying to play along.

Lucas laughed. "I offer nothing." He pulled up the side of the bed frame so it was tilted onto its side and pressed into the wall. Iron brackets dropped down on either end to hold it in place. "I facilitate the offerings of other people's prayers. And now, finally, it's your turn. Your transgressions tonight—I think I've been more than patient."

"You have." Quinn stepped forward as though to kneel. It was such a small room Lucas stepped backward to make space, just as Quinn hoped he would. Instead of kneeling, he leaned in, set his hands on Lucas's hip, then moved them upward, feeling the line of his body up to his arms. As he leaned still farther, their faces inches apart, the warm air of their breaths mixing, Quinn gripped Lucas's wrists, drew them down to the cuffs, and snapped the cuffs into place.

Lucas's laugh ricocheted off the walls and pinged against Quinn's eardrums like deflated bullets. He tried to breathe, forced himself to smile like he was not fighting for his life.

"What do you think you're doing?"

Quinn studied the shrine. He opened the top drawer of the chest and examined the instruments inside. Unlike the dungeon at Umbras, almost everything in the drawer was a true instrument of torture, a rawhide whip, thumb screws, a corkscrew with dark pulpy residue stuck to it.

"You don't have much that's useful here," said Quinn.

"Depends on what you're wanting to do."

Quinn pulled out the only thing that felt remotely safe to handle, a stainless steel dildo, though it hardly seemed right to call it a dildo. It weighed at least a pound, was almost a foot long, and wider than a quarter. *A weaponized penis, how fitting.*

"You could kill me with that, just like everything else here," said Lucas.

Quinn sat down on the kneeling cushion and tapped the thing in his palm, trying to calm down, to think. He hated the feeling of Lucas's gaze on him, that knowing look in his eyes as though this was a scene he'd seen coming. For weeks, they'd been playing a fantasy, inching toward this moment of unveiling.

For Lucas, a submissive surrenders mind, body, and soul.

I can't.

No one should.

And yet, Quinn felt the draw to what he knew Lucas wanted. He could still submit, release Lucas's nearest wrist, kneel, trust that what came next was not death, if only because their work together wasn't finished.

"What do you want, Quinn?"

To kill you. Quinn pictured the long column of Lucas's throat being crushed between his hands. He wanted to feel the man struggle beneath him the way he'd struggled in London. He wanted Lucas to feel the low static hum of terror that had been in Quinn's ears since Christmas dinner.

"I want to make movies," he said.

I want to be recognized on the street and have strangers tell me they like my work. I want to buy a house with Larisa and host dinners that are more interesting than the ones her friends host. I want to forget you were ever part of our lives.

Lucas rolled his eyes. "You are so vexing. Really, I think you do it on purpose sometimes."

Before Quinn knew what he was doing, he'd reached up and slammed the dildo across Lucas's face. The blow drove his head back, bending him backward over the bedframe. When he straightened, there was a line of blood along his cheekbone.

"Did you know love and hate are sibling emotions?" asked Lucas. "They exist together, closer than anything else." His eyes glinted. "And I've made them as good as a collar around your pretty little neck. We both know I have you one way or the other." He might have stopped there and things would have gone differently. But Lucas couldn't help adding, "If you ever get back to her, she'll know I've marked you. Will she still want you then?"

Any restraint Quinn might have called on disappeared. He

stood, kicked Lucas's knees in so he fell forward, his arms raised behind him in the strappado position, his chest toward the floor to relieve the pressure on his joints. Quinn shoved the dildo into Lucas's mouth.

It collided with the hard palate before Quinn thought to grasp Lucas's hair and pull his head up, giving easier access to his throat. Then he pushed. The thing was so big, getting it in was harder than expected. To Quinn it felt like a crushing amount of force. But when he looked down, Lucas was gazing at him. It was a look that imitated love but acted like triumph. That gaze would be seared in his mind for the rest of his life, the marker of this eternal night when he stopped worrying about boundaries and acceptable risk and strategy and he became the thing Lucas wanted.

Quinn released Lucas's hair and pressed his hand against that throat, felt the spasms of muscle trying to swallow, choking, straining. The rest of Lucas's body remained still. Not once did his wrists pull to be free. Not once did he attempt to pull his head away from the dildo. His eyelids fluttered as though fighting against unconsciousness, as though he had resolved to live for every moment Quinn allowed him and die only when Quinn was certain this was what he wanted.

When at last Lucas's eyes closed and his body went limp, Quinn yanked the dildo free. He fell back, gasping as though he was the one who'd been choked. Then he staggered forward, released the wrist restraints before the weight pulling on Lucas's arms dislocated his shoulders. He pressed himself against the drawer, darkness drawing forward, then fading from the edges of his vision. He watched. He waited. *I'm not going to be responsible for your death, you fucking asshole.*

Just when he was sure he'd really done it, a hacking cough, the shudder of a body coming back to awareness. Quinn knelt beside Lucas in relief. He was so close he could taste his first ragged breath, could feel the aftershocks spasm along his bones.

"I'm sorry," whispered Quinn.

Lucas dragged a wobbly hand up and rested it on Quinn's shoulder. "Don't apologize," he said in a voice two octaves lower than normal and as raspy as a burn victim. "Don't ever apologize."

The film society guests had left Umbras by the time Quinn and Lucas returned. Lucas led the way out to the patio where two wine glasses and a bottle from Inverno sat waiting. Somewhere out in the sucking shadows of the night, the sound of men's murmuring voices and shovels clinking against rocky soil.

Quinn watched Lucas open the wine bottle and pour. He watched for pills secreted in with a slight of hand. He watched for fingers touching the rim of the glass where his mouth would go. But if he was about to be drugged, there was no evidence of it.

Lucas handed him a glass and motioned for him to sit.

"Now," said Lucas as he took his own seat, "we can be honest with each other. Drink."

Quinn lifted the glass to his nose and sniffed.

"I said, drink."

He took a sip. "I'm not feeling well."

"I don't care."

Quinn took a larger sip and felt the pungent liquid light up his taste buds.

"You'll continue to live because that's what I want," said Lucas. "When Larisa realizes the only way she can have you is through me, she'll join us. And then we'll see which one of us she loves better." Lucas sipped his wine. "You'll read and write. When things settle down with my business, maybe we'll make a film together. You'll dazzle my friends with your charming personality, you'll fuck whomever I tell you to fuck, and if you don't, I'll tear you apart and put you back together over and over until every part of you has been made by me."

He glanced over, saw Quinn staring at him. "You have a question? Am I unclear? My voice is a little strained tonight. Drink your wine."

Quinn took another sip. Already his stomach felt uncomfortably sloshy. He'd evacuated his dinner in Lucas's office. And now the wine was burning acidic holes in his empty stomach.

"Well? Anything to say? Do you wish you'd killed me when you had the chance?"

"I guess I'm surprised you waited this long," said Quinn. "We both knew you would keep me here until she came. But you wanted to pretend I was here for you." Quinn sipped his wine, filled his gaze with all the vitriol and disgust he'd kept hidden for the past month, and leveled it at Lucas. "As though there was the remotest chance I could actually love you."

For a moment, Quinn thought the blow had landed. Lucas blinked as though stung, then his face lit up with delight. "There you *are*. Wonderful. Now we'll truly begin. Drink." As though he could barely contain his excitement, Lucas bounded to his feet and came around to Quinn's side of the table. For a moment he stood over him, watching as Quinn forced himself to swallow the rest of the wine in three successive gulps, then he leaned down and cupped Quinn's chin in his palm. "Why would I want the love of a man who has wasted his life afraid of people seeing what he is?"

Quinn pulled away. "What do you know?"

"I know you're not a submissive. Everything you have with Larisa is false even if neither of you have figured it out yet."

"Then let me go. Let us ruin each other trying to make it work, then you can come gloat over the wreckage." Quinn's stomach cramped, not just from the wine. Speaking life into the possibility that all of this was for nothing; the idea that he could go back to LA and in six months or a year, one or both of them would realize it wasn't meant to be, filled him with dread.

"Tempting," said Lucas. "But you're here now of your own choice. And it's apparent my future is not so assured as it has been. I'll take what you've dangled in front of me and then we'll see what emerges from the carnage. Are you going to be sick again?"

Quinn nodded.

"Waste of wine." Lucas walked to the balcony door. "Rifat? When he's done, take him upstairs and put him up on the bed. I'm going to check in with Mario."

"Mario's gone dark."

"Dead?"

"Unknown. Boss, I think we should move out. There's chatter in Palermo. The family—"

"I'll look at the messages. You get him ready."

Rifat stood by, checking messages on his phone while Quinn bent over and regurgitated wine onto the balcony flagstones. When he was done, Rifat guided Quinn up through the villa to Lucas's bathroom where Quinn was almost sick again as Rifat supervised him undressing and washing himself. In his past life, Quinn would have been embarrassed, now he barely felt the exposure. It felt like he'd been walking around in only his skin for days.

"How bad is it?" asked Quinn.

"Bad," said Rifat without expression. Quinn thought he looked tired. He wanted to say something helpful. Maybe he only wanted to talk in order to stall what was coming next.

"Do you ever get to override his decisions for his own good?"

Rifat shook his head, and Quinn couldn't tell if Rifat thought the question was silly or because he wished such a thing were possible. "Come on."

The dungeon had been cleaned, but the orange-scented soap wasn't strong enough to block out the death that lingered in the air. Rifat brought leather restraints from one of the drawers and attached them to the posts at the end of the bed. There was a mirror over the headboard Quinn hadn't noticed on his previous visit.

I'll get to watch myself while he's inside me, thought Quinn. If he hadn't been so nervous, it might have given him a rush.

"Do you think he'll kill me?" asked Quinn.

Rifat was kneeling down, fastening restraints to Quinn's ankles. He looked up, surprised. "Just try and relax." Rifat stood and began on Quinn's wrists. The restraints weren't tight. He could shift his feet a few inches each direction. His elbows dangled below his shoulders when he let his hands rest on the chains.

I have enough freedom to trick myself into thinking this will be okay, he thought. *It's just sex.*

Maybe it won't even be that.

At this point, he thought it probably didn't matter what actually happened. It would be something more intimate than he wanted with a man who didn't care about how other people felt. A man who was angry, and in the middle of a fight with foes unseen for his business, if not his life. A man who loved Larisa and wanted to make sure Quinn knew his place.

Quinn tested the strength of the restraints. He looked at the solid posts of the bed that stretched from floor to ceiling. *Whatever he wants to do, I won't be able to stop him.*

Movement in the doorway. Quinn shifted his angle to the mirror so he could watch Lucas come in. At the door, he paused to take in the scene, eyes traveling over Quinn's body. He motioned for Rifat to leave. As Rifat walked out, he said softly, "It's not his fault."

Lucas laughed.

It was a strange sound, a thing that was both entirely natural and yet completely out of place. In three strides, Lucas had crossed the room. Before Quinn even fully realized they were together, Lucas had his hands on him—arms, chest, back— moving quickly so they felt more like searching than caressing.

"I know you don't want this," said Lucas. "I'm willing to negotiate. Something softer? On the bed perhaps, with the love of our mouths." He bowed his head over Quinn's shoulder and pressed a kiss into his collarbone. In the mirror, Quinn saw the thick, dark crown of his hair, slightly greasy from being left unattended, saw Lucas's hands on him like alien beings creeping in, looking for those soft places in which to sink their teeth.

"I want you even less in bed than I want you like this," said Quinn.

Lucas's head snapped up to him, his eyes bright with a kind of malicious delight. He stepped back, jogged around to the bed, and flopped down onto the mattress. "I'm really very excited about this. The real you. So dark and stormy." Lucas shivered. "It's much better than pretending you care. People like us, it's a waste of time to pretend when we're among peers. It's something we do for little people." He got up on his knees at the end of the bed, so his head was level with Quinn's chest, and gazed up at him. "My life is falling apart, but we're doing this now. It's perfect, isn't it? Everything heightened with the urgency." Lucas inhaled like he was taking in a field of wildflowers in a laundry detergent commercial. "You feel it, don't you?"

Quinn did feel it. And he didn't want to. The more he felt, the easier it would be to remember, the more vividly it would stay with him. In five years, he didn't want to have a wet dream fueled by the memory of Lucas's lips around his penis. That seemed to be what was about to happen. Lucas had his hand on him. Then, instead of lowering himself to Quinn's groin, Lucas pressed his face into Quinn's stomach, taking small nips of skin between his teeth, sucking them in, stroking them with his tongue, too hard, too aggressive. Quinn's wrists lurched against the restraints as he yanked back, shooting his hips backward so his skin was out of easy reach.

"You *are* sensitive, aren't you?" Lucas grinned, almost boyish in his joy. It was a strange thing to see. In these protracted moments of what Quinn considered agony, Lucas was the happiest he'd ever seen him. There was no way to tell if his delight came from Quinn no longer pretending to enjoy the attention, or from the joy of meting out such meditative torture. "Do you hate me?" he asked. "I think I'm like that kid in high school who knew how to flick all your switches. You were probably so serious, all buttoned up just like you are now. Do you want to be young again with me?"

"There is no you and me," Quinn growled.

"Once I'm inside you, that will change." Lucas slid off the bed like a jungle cat, crept around the end of the bed to stand behind Quinn. "Look at yourself." He set his hands on Quinn's hips. "This is the end of being only hers."

Quinn stared down at the bed. He didn't want to see what was in the mirror, the two of them together. Quinn naked, restrained, the clear possession of the man behind him who remained fully clothed and had given nothing of himself that Quinn could touch. He felt the impatient movements of Lucas's hands at his back as he unzipped his fly, used one hand to lift Quinn's cheek, the other to penetrate his entrance. Quinn gasped, his body instinctually pushing forward until his thighs dug into the bed's footboard. His breath sawed the air.

"Let's play a game," said Lucas. "You tell me about the last time you and Larisa were together and I'll be gentle." His fingers stroked the inside of Quinn's thigh, sending sparks of alarm bells, the nerves overfiring, muscles contracting as quickly as startled clams only to be held open by the restraints.

Don't think about her. Don't think about her.

But the alternative was the head of Lucas's cock greedily pushing into him, so much larger than Quinn thought it should be, so violent with its need, yet agonizingly slow. He didn't want to pay attention, or let the details of it sink in. Against his will, Quinn's mind leapt to that long ago Christmas morning in a Minneapolis hotel room. Cold winter light had come in between curtains they'd forgotten to draw closed. Larisa had fed him berries and put him on his stomach so she could kiss every verte-brae of his back. She'd been so very gentle, so interested in how she made him feel and what she could do better. He'd told her he wasn't that complicated; he didn't need to be studied. And she'd laughed.

Just as Quinn was remembering her laugh, Lucas pushed

himself all the way in. Quinn realized Lucas never expected Quinn to tell him anything about Larisa. He just wanted Quinn to be thinking about her as his insides were seared open and marked by the man who still believed he had the right to approve everything she did.

Chapter 11

Gloves Off

"What do you feel?" asked Lucas.

They were in bed, not the dungeon bed, but the bed in Lucas's bedroom in a position that had become so familiar it felt like it'd always been, Quinn naked, Lucas dressed, appearing as lovers if one didn't look too closely.

Quinn glared at him, which made Lucas grabby and impatient. He pushed Quinn onto his back and pinned his wrist against the pillow. "Tell me."

"No," said Quinn. The word had never felt so powerful, his defiance a new kind of armor even as it was also an invitation to violence.

Which was exactly what Lucas wanted.

Each day, each hour that passed, Quinn felt himself getting closer to that buried core of Lucas's heart. But it was costing him. It cost him now as his bruised body surged against Lucas in protest, a flighty moment of panic before he regained control and gazed cooly up at the man whose touch was now imprinted on his skin.

"Make me."

Lucas dug his fingers into Quinn's hair, then pulled back so Quinn's chin pushed into the air. Lucas bent down, his mouth inches from Quinn's mouth, teasing him, revving himself up.

"I'll beat it out of you." His grip tightened, making Quinn

arch his back to relieve the pressure. "Every thought, every secret. You'll beg to be free of them."

"You can try."

A knock on the office door, or perhaps the archway that led into the bedroom. Lucas sighed. "What is it?"

"Update from Vegas."

"Has anything gone wrong?"

"No, sir."

"Then don't bother me."

"There's something else." A hesitant pause. "Your parents have landed and are en route."

"Already?"

"Yes, sir."

With each exchange, the disembodied voice behind the curtain grew more and more uncertain. Quinn thought it was one of the men who'd helped bury the body of the accountant the week before, one of the hired guns who was now prowling Umbras's grounds watching for intruders. Actually, Quinn didn't know exactly what they were watching for. He just knew it made him nervous. As long as men with guns could be around any corner, he couldn't slip back into an illusion of the villa being a safe place. And he desperately needed that illusion. Because it was too much to try to survive Lucas and also live day-to-day with the possibility of being attacked by someone from the outside.

"I'll be right there." Lucas flopped back onto his half of the bed. "You have no idea what a gift you've been given, not having a family."

For a moment, Quinn thought about being insulted, but instead tried to be understanding. "They can't be that bad."

"Tedious, ignorant, condescending, more irritating than you."

"That's a compliment."

"Larisa was great with them. Since she left, they've been . . . well, there's no use complaining, is there?"

Larisa. Something sharp pinched across Quinn's chest. She was still there, somewhere in the recesses of his mind, but he couldn't feel her the way he used to. She'd become a ghost of an impression, so far removed from his life it sometimes felt she didn't matter.

"I can help."

Lucas laughed. "You're staying here. In fact—Barrett, you still there?"

"Yes, sir."

"Take Quinn into the dungeon and lock him up."

Quinn started in panic. "Why?"

"You know too much."

"What?" Quinn pulled up the sheets to hide himself as Barrett entered the bedroom, striding forward like one of those retired football players who still felt he could take on the world. "I can be good."

Lucas laughed. "You're never good, and we both like it that way."

Quinn scrambled across the bed, aching muscles straining from the rapid movement. He placed himself in front of Lucas as he moved to get off the bed. "Please, I want to be with you."

Don't you dare lock me up in that room with nothing to think about but being attacked by your enemies.

Lucas studied him. Quinn had no trouble holding his gaze now, there was no reason to hide. He was scared. He felt Lucas should be scared too. A day alone in the villa without a way to escape would be too much.

"So you do have a limit," said Lucas softly. His expression remained hard, and Quinn feared that in revealing himself he'd given Lucas ammunition to use against him. *You're not that cruel,* thought Quinn. Then, because he wasn't quite sure Lucas wasn't that cruel, he said, "Let me help you. I can be great with ignorant people." He mustered a half smile and saw immediately that he'd won.

"Heaven knows I don't have the energy to take them on myself."

Quinn thought he didn't have the energy either. But later,

when he saw Lucas's parents climbing out of the car in the drive-way, saw that they were extremely normal people by comparison, he rose to the occasion and became Lucas's American coworker from the lobbying firm visiting for an extended holiday.

For the next eight hours, he kept up a lively conversation drawn from small talk, attentive personal questions, and anec-dotes about their son who held a stony silence as he toured them around the city, scowled as they passed up authentic Italian coffee for Starbucks, ignored his menu recommendations because they were too exotic, and complained about all the naked statues. When Lucas's father insisted he knew the house where Dante had written the *Divine Comedy*, Quinn found a way to correct him before Lucas shouted at him. When Lucas's mother patted Quinn's hand and said, "Please don't take offense, but I wish he was lolling about with a nice, respectable woman instead of you," Quinn told her Lucas was happy. Didn't she want her son to be happy?

They finished the day on the Umbras patio watching the sunset and drinking brandy. Quinn quietly reveled in the fact that he could tell it was the aged barrel from the back of the cellar while the glasses for Lucas's parents had been poured with some-thing else. He could tell from the way the liquid coated the glasses. Even the smell spoke to him of a different quality.

As the parents sipped and pretended to know what they were drinking, Quinn glanced over and met Lucas's gaze. They didn't have to speak. Lucas saw that Quinn knew. He was rewarded with a nod before Lucas turned and gazed down at the garden. Quinn, unreasonably satisfied with this small victory, followed his gaze. Every so often the shadow of a person crossed the spotlights on the topiaries. Not invaders, Quinn told himself even as his nerves skittered to life, but the men paid to protect him.

Afterward, as they walked to Lucas's bedroom, he said, "You impressed me today. Where did all that come from?"

Quinn shrugged like it was nothing even though Lucas's praise melted over him like the most soothing balm. "It's just a character—the ideal son. You set up the rules, and if they're real-istic enough, the stories just flow out of it."

"I almost believed some of it myself. The story about almost crashing a boat over Christmas?"

"Apparently that happened with Rifat and that accou—the blond girl who visited once."

"One of my accountants," said Lucas. "How did you find that out?"

"She didn't seem like the submissive she was pretending to be, and it bothered me. Things that don't fit the scene bother me."

"She ended up stealing from me," said Lucas.

Quinn gave him a surprised look, which he hoped also masked the worry he felt, that the girl had been caught over her head and paid for it with her life.

"Not on purpose. Just through mismanagement."

"Not quite stealing, is it?"

"It's cost me."

They'd arrived in the bedroom. Lucas wearily began to undress. Quinn looked at the bed. The night waited for him like a mouth full of silent gnashing teeth, each sleepless hour ready to take bites out of him.

Quinn walked past Lucas into the bathroom and started the water for the bath. He added the salts, lit the trio of candles that rested on polished ebony blocks by the window, then held out his hand to Lucas. "Come."

To his surprise, Lucas did. He allowed Quinn to finish undressing him, to massage oil into his tense shoulders as he sat in the bath. It was the first time Quinn had initiated intimate touching and the first time either of them had been gentle with each other. Quinn found it easy to do, his own quiet revenge against the man who had no idea how to be a loving partner.

This is what Larisa would do for me if I were in your shoes, thought Quinn.

"Will you manage my parents tomorrow during the party?"

"If I must."

"They won't know anyone. And they don't go to parties at home. Without a minder, they act like they've landed on—" He broke off as his phone vibrated. From his view over Lucas's shoulder, Quinn could easily read it.

Rifat: Everything as planned. You still want to do this?

Lucas: Yes.

Rifat: You're being selfish.

Lucas set the phone face down on the ceramic shelf along the edge of the tub. "You should join me."

"There's not enough space," said Quinn.

"Excuses."

Quinn climbed off the shelf where he'd been sitting behind Lucas and undressed. He started to get in with his back to Lucas, thinking that from his example Lucas had picked up on the idea that Quinn might enjoy a softer touch, or at least a hint of the caring he'd given Lucas. Instead, Lucas gave him a push.

"Turn around. I want to see your face."

They sat facing each other with their backs against the ends of the tub. Lucas wasted no time in moving one foot between Quinn's legs, scraping his toes against Quinn's sensitive inner thighs until he flinched.

"Tell me something true."

"You think I'm lying to you?"

Lucas put on his condescending face. "A great truth about your life. Something no one else knows."

He almost said, *I'm afraid of death.* But he realized it wasn't that exactly. The fear keeping him up at night wasn't just about dying, it was about running out of time. "I'm afraid my life won't matter."

"You need it to matter because your mother lost so much for you."

"Maybe," said Quinn, if only to avoid an argument. It was his shrink's job to decide if his ambition came from childhood trauma. The way Quinn understood it, he wanted to be larger than himself, which he felt was a common enough thing regardless of parents. But he didn't want to be common. He wanted to be great. Sometimes, he knew it was possible. He was just waiting for other people to see it.

Larisa sees it.

As he gazed across the cooling water at the man who he wanted to blame for everything wrong with his life, he knew he wanted Lucas to see it. And until that happened, he would never completely believe when other people called him great. They would all be hacks, and moneymen and groupies complimenting him because they felt they'd get something out of it.

Larisa would always speak to him out of love, so her belief in him counted, but not the way Lucas's did.

"What are you thinking?" asked Lucas.

"I'm thinking, I don't want anyone to kill you."

Lucas laughed. "Things would be easier for you."

"But the story would be incomplete."

"What's our story?"

Quinn pressed his lips together in a wordless smile that felt like defeat. He couldn't imagine doing anything worthy of the approval he wanted Lucas to give him.

"Do you know what would really shock my parents? If you kissed me at the party."

"They're homophobic?"

"Yes and no. I'm not sure actually. But that's beside the point. They're not expecting it. We could tell them we're engaged."

"That would be something."

"I'll give you a signal. When the pavane comes on, that's when you'll do it."

"I'm not dancing."

"Tomorrow it'll just be atmosphere." Lucas's foot dug into

Quinn's thigh, pressed up into his groin until the pain became too much and Quinn reached down and pushed Lucas away.

"So you'll kiss me. You're doing it. And if you don't." Lucas's eyes lit up with malicious delight. "I know just how to punish you."

Chapter 12

A Birthday Waltz

Her room was exactly as she'd preserved it in her mind. From the gauzy curtains blowing in the wind of the open balcony doors to the particular smell of the villa that had to do with stone or lavender cleaning solutions or long years that had passed before its eyes, a smell that existed in Larisa's mind like an ancient willow but smoother.

The bed was round, custom made to fit into the curve of the wall and then extend outward around two similarly molded end tables set with vases of fresh cut white roses; they appeared golden under the spotlights of the wall sconces that framed the head-board. Larisa ran her hand over the satin comforter, hand-painted with vaguely Japanese looking cranes and cherry trees in an ochre sky. Across the room, a coffee table with a small village of candles just out of reach of the blowing curtains. The sectional couch, built around the corner of windows, sat exactly as she had left it, overcrowded with her pillows. Everywhere she'd gone with Lucas, she had purchased a decorative pillow. It seemed silly the reminder of how grown up it'd made her feel, shopping at bazaars and markets and high-end stores full of household goods, even though all she'd bought were pillows. They'd been a promise she was making to herself, an investment in their future.

"I thought you were in high alert," Larisa said to Rifat as she hurried to the windows to close them. There, she paused to look out on the grounds. The balcony faced north, the monastery tower of Fiesole dominant against a skyline just starting to turn gray with the approaching sunrise. To her left, the far distant orange dome of Santa Maria del Fiore in Florence. Not a hint of the ominous stories Rifat had told her as they flew across the ocean.

"You know Lucas," said Rifat. "Presentation comes before everything else. Besides, there's like twelve dudes outside on guard."

"And what will they do for the party?"

"Hmm?"

"Are they going to search all the guests?"

Rifat laughed, but when Larisa turned to him, he looked nervous. "It's a very specific guest list."

"So, no visible security. And they probably won't check the extra staff either?"

"Maybe I exaggerated what I said before. He's not expecting something that obvious."

"But you don't think I'm safe here."

Rifat opened his mouth to answer, then closed it. He turned and disappeared behind the dressing screen which hid the vanity, dressing room, and bathroom from the rest of the room. "He has everything set up for you, looks like. You have two options for the dress. And it looks like the queen's jewels here. Do you want breakfast or dinner before you turn in?"

"I'm not going to see him before tonight?"

"So, the thing I said about presentation? He'd really like it if you uh, make a grand entrance and all that. And he doesn't want to see you until then, kinda like a wedding."

Larisa shivered. "So I'm trapped in this room until then?"

"You love being trapped in this room."

Larisa couldn't argue with that. There were her books on the shelf by the door. Beside it, the antique curio where she'd spent hours making lists of the things she'd seen, the things she wanted to do, wine, music, films, flowers, fabrics, all the names the ancient Romans had for cement. There'd never been a time in her life when she'd been more purposeful about something that everyone else in her life would have called purposeless, as though she'd enrolled in a degree of learning for learning's sake. Wherever interest carried her, she went, and she never asked herself if it mattered or was adding up to something.

"Food?" asked Rifat.

"Does Francie still keep cold chicken for the stray cats?"

"Think so."

"That'd be fine. And whatever else you find that goes with it. I imagine Lucas has thought of this."

"He did, but I thought it'd be nice to ask."

Larisa remembered this also, the strange role of Rifat as middleman, pretending she had choices.

"I appreciate that."

"So, just make yourself comfortable and I'll be back up in a few minutes. And I'm going to leave the door unlocked, but don't leave, okay?"

"Why is it so important I don't leave? Isn't everyone asleep?"

"It's just a precaution thing. The parental units are here and I told them the same thing. For security, you understand."

"Why do I feel like you're not telling me something?"

"We can talk about it when I get back, okay? I bet you're starving."

"Rifat."

"Quinn doesn't want to see you." The words came out in a rush so that Larisa's brain took a moment to decode them, and when she did, they landed so hard she stumbled back, let herself drop onto the uneven terrain of her pillow-cluttered sectional.

"How do you know that?"

"Apparently Lucas told him I was over picking you up and he had a very strong reaction."

"What reaction?"

"I don't know, but it was bad. You know he's been through a lot."

Because of me, she thought.

"But he'll be at the party."

"I don't know how it's all going to work. But I'm sure he and Lucas have figured it out."

Larisa hated the thoughts that rushed to her head at those words. The too easily conjured picture of Lucas and Quinn conspiring to carve out their own corner of the world together, blocking everyone else out, especially the woman who hurt them. She barely noticed when Rifat left the room and didn't notice at all when he returned with a tray that'd clearly been arranged by Lucas, two covered plates and a little bowl. A primi pasta dish with capers and an oil dressing, a secondi dish of veal steak so rare it was bloody, three delicate spring carrots, and panna cotta in the bowl.

"Chef's compliments," said Rifat.

Even if he hadn't said that, instead of 'Francie's compliments,' Larisa would have known Lucas had made the meal himself. Francie didn't believe in eating baby animals, and even if she'd been convinced to cook one, she wouldn't have given up her beauty sleep the night before an event to make it fresh for Larisa whenever she managed to arrive.

"He's awake, isn't he?"

"Let's not make this complicated."

"It's already fucking complicated." Larisa grabbed the steak knife from the tray and began to saw into the meat. "What does he think he's doing?"

"He wanted you safe," said Rifat. "That's the thing to remember."

"We both know that's not it, though. He wanted me where he could control me. Was the whole Vegas thing meant to get me out of LA so I'd be easier to snatch?"

When Rifat didn't answer, Larisa decided this was the truth. She shoved a bite of meat into her mouth and chewed furiously. It didn't help that the food was delicious, an absolute perfect blend of texture and seasoning. *It doesn't matter that he can cook,* she thought. *He's still evil.*

She stared down at the steak knife and wondered if it was sharp enough to be her weapon. She'd planned to steal one of Francie's knives from the kitchen. But it looked like getting down there would be a challenge.

"Will you at least tell me how it's been going with Quinn here?"

"It's been interesting."

"That's not an answer."

"I don't know how to say what I'm thinking."

Larisa waved her fork through the air. "It doesn't have to be organized."

"I don't want you to be upset."

"I was just framed for a dead man's murder. Whatever you say I can take it."

"They're like fire and oil," said Rifat. "Whenever I'm in the same room with them I feel like something will explode."

A fist clenched around Larisa's heart. She didn't quite know how to interpret Rifat's analogy, but she felt it in her gut, a reaction that transcended language.

Rifat left her alone to finish eating, telling her he'd be back to escort her to the party at seven. The smart thing would have been to sleep, but when Larisa laid down on the bed, she felt transported back in time. In the dream state between waking and sleeping, she thought she was in college again, restless with sleep waiting for Lucas to fill the emptiness beside her. When she moved to the sectional, the effect was not as strong but still present, as though the lowered boundaries of her unconscious mind couldn't help but skitter back to that old life, a betrayal that would creep into her waking mind if she wasn't careful.

Because it was too easy to trick herself into forgetting everything that had happened.

It was easy because she wanted it to be true. That's what frightened her the most. How much she wanted to go back to those early days when she ceded her entire being to a man who seemed not only worthy, but also knew just how to please her.

Mostly.

Instead of sleeping, she made phone calls. First to Kahleah, then to Sid. Neither of them reacted well to the news that she was now in Italy. Sid filled the line with long, judgmental silences; Kahleah filled hers with ear-splitting yelling. They'd both been looking for her. Kahleah had thought she might be dead. Sid had thought something else, a vague thing that slipped between the meaning in what words he chose. He reminded her of Quinn and how he also got quieter as his feelings escalated.

We are in the same house, she thought. *I could go find him.*

But Rifat had said Quinn was still upset and didn't want to see her. Did she believe Rifat? Not completely, but she also felt this was a good situation to push back against her impulsive instincts and take things slowly, get a feel for the environment, consider her options.

Kill Lucas and run.

Grab Quinn and run.

Neither option was as simple as it sounded.

At five o'clock she took a shower and began to prepare for the party. It didn't matter that she hadn't been able to pack a suitcase, Lucas had provided everything she needed. Her old cosmetics had been replaced, her mirror, hair iron, brushes, everything in their usual places. Once upon a time, she'd reveled in his attention to detail because it felt like love. Now she wondered what it said about Lucas that he would take the time for such inconsequential things in the middle of a business disaster.

Perhaps Rifat was exaggerating, she thought.

A US senator hanging off the side of a hotel as he bled to death spoke to the opposite. Rifat had underplayed the degree of chaos Lucas was wrangling. But if that was true, it meant every moment she spent at Umbras was another moment closer to something going irrevocably wrong for everyone inside. Lucas should have canceled his birthday party. But she was probably the only person in his life who he would have listened to, and she hadn't been here to insist on caution.

She did her face once, found it inadequate and washed everything off to start over. Her hair also defied her. First, she left it down in curls, which felt too much like an invitation. When she put it up, she looked too old, almost frigid. She settled for keeping it up, but with loose curls swept across and down one side of her face, some pieces gentle against the crown of her head to soften the look.

Lucas had provided the same style of dress in wine-red or emerald-green. It was the kind of dress that hid its volume beneath the skirt. When Larisa walked, it hung straight down from her hips, but if she turned, it would flare out like the dresses of old Hollywood movies, a dancing dress complete with a ribbon to loop around her wrist to hold it away from her feet.

When she'd finished, she stood before the three-sided mirror in the vanity. It was impossible not to see the woman reflected back to her as Lucas's ideal woman. Yes, she'd made herself up more than usual, but it also showed in the way she walked, the severity of her posture, the almost self-conscious elegance that had descended like a shroud when she'd put on the dress. Her best self, Lucas would say. Because he demanded no less than her best.

A knock on the door sounded before she'd decided which jewelry. She'd lost track of time. Scrambling across the room, Larisa rushed to grab the steak knife and tuck it into her cleavage before Rifat came in.

"You went with green," said Rifat.

"He expected red, didn't he?"

Rifat shrugged. "He's allowed to be wrong."

This felt like a comment overburdened with meaning, so Larisa let it go without a response. The jewelry Lucas had provided was all too large and showy for a birthday party. She chose to wear only earrings and leave behind the necklaces. There was something about fastening a collar around her neck that felt like it would be going too far. She needed to keep some part of her free.

"Ready," she said.

How many times had Larisa watched this scene in a film? A woman in formal wear standing nervously at the top of a staircase, the staple of so many Hollywood romances, Jane Austen and her copycats, etc., etc. to infinity. Except those scenes involved a blushing debutant. As Larisa stood, looking down at the guests milling around the palazzo floor, she couldn't think of a single example where a woman as old and experienced as Larisa made a grand entrance. Barbra Streisand in *Hello Dolly!* perhaps, but without the feathers and peppy song. Like Dolly, she hadn't come to meet her old love, she'd come home.

It *did* feel eerily like a homecoming. The music, the smells, the way the orange trees had been pruned, the soft lighting that crept up the walls instead of shone down from below, a choice she'd once made for a birthday years before and that Lucas had adopted for all his Umbras events since.

You can do this. Larisa took a breath. *Find a target and walk to it.*

Just beyond the base of the staircase, she spotted Winter and her partner chatting with a couple who looked vaguely familiar. *By the time I reach them, I'll remember their names,* thought Larisa. She picked up her skirt with one hand, set her other on the railing, and began a slow descent.

There was no fanfare announcement. Rifat was somewhere behind her either watching or waiting to make sure she didn't trip. She wouldn't—never had—but he always worried. People nearest the staircase began to turn and look. None of the faces belonged to Quinn. She scanned the crowd and didn't see anyone who looked like him even though she knew he had to be there. If he'd really installed himself in Lucas's life the way Rifat had implied, he wouldn't have had a choice.

Unless he's hurt. Larisa's grip on the railing tightened. She misjudged the step and would have tumbled forward if a hand hadn't reached out to steady her. Immaculate white gloves, antique, gold leaf cufflinks with the Medici crest.

"There you are," he said.

Slowly, Larisa raised her gaze to Lucas's face, forced herself to smile as they walked down the last few steps together.

"Thank you," she said.

"It would be a terrible start to the night if my guest of honor fell down the stairs."

It felt like a criticism, as though she'd already disappointed him, but his smile remained. And she saw in his eyes that old pleasure, like the banked embers of a fire stirring to life, a look more predatory triumph than joy, the foreplay of a devouring.

"Guests of honor aren't usually required to plan the dinner menu."

"You made excellent choices." His hand came around her waist, drawing her against him so they walked hip to hip. People approached them to say hello. Some she remembered, some she didn't. One man, whose name escaped her, gave Larisa a funny look.

"We should have a dance before dinner. Like we used to." Lucas's fingers tapped a melody into her waist, playful but insistent. She couldn't have detached herself from him if she'd wanted to.

She didn't want to.

"You've been visiting my dreams." He spoke with his mouth against the side of her head, heat rushing into her ear and down her neck. People were watching, which made his touch even more intense. She felt herself falling into him, surrendering to those possessive hands as they guided her across the palazzo into the villa's ballroom.

"Teasing me with promises you won't keep. Running away

just when I've reached you." He breathed in her scent. "I've been thinking of you in a cage. My daring girl, trapped with no one to appreciate you."

The ballroom was empty, a pool of golden light, multiple Larisas as a column of vibrant green copying her movements in the walls of mirrors. People began to file in behind them and spread out around the dance floor to watch.

"I was appreciated," said Larisa.

"Did they make you beg?"

She shivered. All around them now, people watching. Faces and faces and faces. No Quinn.

As Lucas released her to walk to a starting pose, she sent him a knowing look over her shoulder. "What do you think?" She placed one foot, then the other, accentuated the arch in her back as she struck her pose. She did it without thinking, as though every moment had come pre-packaged, and she was merely following the steps to an arranged conclusion.

She couldn't remember the last time she'd felt more powerful, more beautiful, more confident. In her head, she heard Lucas say, as he'd said so many times, *Assume the position,* and her body obeyed without guidance from her mind. Even as her limbs snapped to attention and her muscles pulled taut, she felt a sinking softness that was like a dream, like being high. When the music began, she closed her eyes and felt him come to her, a shadow in her mind, heels hard on the floor until they fell silent and a hand reached out, the current that sparked her to life.

They only ever danced to one song on Lucas's birthday. The first year they'd been together, he'd commissioned a musician friend of his to write them a waltz. Together, they'd choreographed a dance to the music. It did waltz things, but it was also more than that. In the first measures, they stayed still, their bodies finding each other with all the slow sensuality of a tango. Then they'd begin to move into the formation. They'd built flourishing turns into the pattern. Lucas sent her out from him and drew her back in as she spun. The dress of her skirt flaring in a dazzle of rippling color. At the midpoint, a slowing, a return to the stroking, long-armed movements that carved the air and outlined her body in heat. They became an accelerating climax of fast steps that ended with Lucas lifting her above his head and holding her there as she gazed down at him, the man who somehow still continued to hold her dreams in the palm of his hand.

All dreams except the one where he no longer existed.

When he lowered her back to the floor, they'd always ended the dance with a kiss, his hands pushing into her hair, drawing her head to his. But this time, Lucas lowered her and stepped back, left her panting like a dog in heat as he took his bow, then turned to applaud Larisa as she also bowed. The applause of their audience echoed off the ceiling. Larisa blushed as though she'd been caught doing something, but she couldn't say what. It was hidden beneath that ribbon of dissatisfaction she felt winding its way between her legs and up her chest. To not kiss her was as good as rejecting her. Her mind scrambled to push away the feeling she wasn't enough.

"I've worked up an appetite," said Lucas. A few people laughed at the inuendo, a few others—male voices—gave him a cheer. The party moved into the dining room. As people flowed past, they said how nice it was that Larisa had come. Some complimented her dancing. Then, coming in behind her too quickly, someone took her arm and steered her against the flow of traffic.

"What do you mean by this?" It was the man from before who'd given her that strange look. She recognized his voice.

"By what?" she yanked her arm away before Lucas saw.

"You said you wanted him to pay," he hissed. "But now you're here just as before." His sweaty hand again reached out and seized her arm. "Did you betray me?"

"I don't know what—"

Larisa stopped as the pieces clicked into place. It was Goku, one of the men in Lucas's black book. She'd called him less than a week ago to tell him Lucas was losing money to the wrong people, that he had spies in his organization, and that he needed to get his balance from Lucas or risk never seeing it.

"What are you doing here?" she asked.

"He invited me." Goku blinked. "We're to meet after the party to discuss my concerns."

Larisa ran a hand down her chest to try to settle her over-heated nerves. She felt the knife there prick her skin. Lucas never discussed business on his birthday. Something about what Goku said didn't make sense.

A gentle melody began to waft down from the villa's speakers. Larisa was momentarily distracted placing it, *Pavane for a Dead Princess*, by Maurice Ravel. Not the kind of music one played at a party, not even one of Lucas's favorites unless his taste had dramatically changed.

"He didn't kiss me."

"You're back with him now? Is this a trick?"

Larisa shook her head as though to clear it. "Did you tell him I called you?"

"Of course not."

He didn't kiss me. It's a punishment for something.

From the dining room, a rising tide of applause and laughter. Larisa pushed Goku away and hurried to the doorway. At the far side of the dining room, framed perfectly by the wall of windows that opened onto the balcony, Quinn stood in Lucas's arms receiving the kiss that should have been hers.

"Thank you everyone, thank you." Lucas waved his hand to quiet the cheers. "I'm so pleased to start this next chapter in my life with Quinn at my side. We all know I've been floundering these last few years." He raised a champagne glass toward the corner of the room where his parents stood, their faces washed white with shock. "I know you've been after me to settle down and it's wonderful Quinn has your stamp of approval. Cheers."

Lucas put his arm around Quinn's waist as a roomful of champagne glasses lifted. She watched Quinn bashfully rest his head on Lucas's shoulder, lean into him as though their bodies had been made for each other, two halves of a whole. They looked like the perfect couple, but Larisa saw the way Quinn's hips put up resistance to the pose. She saw how hard Lucas's hand pressed in to hold Quinn against him.

She pulled the steak knife from the bodice of her dress.

"Get your hands off him, you fucking bastard."

Chapter 13

A Labyrinth Courtyard

Quinn had decided the best way to survive Lucas's birthday party was to hide in the kitchen until he was summoned for his big moment. Since he was also supposed to keep Lucas's parents company, they sat in the kitchen with him, first in his booth nursing cocktails, then wandering aimlessly about watching Francie oversee the hired staff as they plated the dinners. It turned out, even though Lucas's parents had money, they were not the kind who threw dinner parties; the three of them found the behind-the-scenes process a novelty.

Four courses, ten waiters, a warming oven. Three special diet plates that were supervised exclusively by a woman named Kirka who guarded those three special plates as though they contained codes for nuclear missiles under their servings of orange glazed duck. After Quinn had that thought, he couldn't unthink it. His eyes kept drifting to those plates, wondering about special diets and if one of them was for him.

"Quinn," Lucas's mother pulled him back from the food action. "I know my son isn't the easiest person. I just wanted to say that I appreciate you being with him. I hope you feel able to come to us if there are any problems. Not that he needs his parents anymore, but his father and I have both felt if we'd been more involved with Larisa" —she stopped, probably because she saw whatever was happening on Quinn's face— "I'm sorry, you probably don't want to think about her. I just think you're very sweet and he needs that in his life."

Not once had Quinn ever been called sweet. He wondered if Lucas's mother needed glasses or if she'd picked up some of those rose-colored ones they sold in Paris. He was saved from finding a reply by Rifat bustling in to announce the party was moving into the dining room. He went over to Kirka. "Are you ready?"

She nodded.

"You know your people?"

"I'm a professional."

Rifat gave a nervous laugh. "The effect will be delayed, right? We don't want anyone keeling over at the table."

"You worry too much."

Rifat grinned. "That's my job."

Killing over at the table, thought Quinn, an innocuous enough expression. Except when you're serving dinner at the house of an arms dealer whose business is on the ropes. Only half aware, Quinn walked into the dining room. Lucas was coming to his parents, trying to put on a good son show. Lucas's mother was repeating a different version of what she'd just said to Quinn about how lovely he was, and Lucas was saying, "Of course I plan to keep him around." And then Lucas took Quinn by the hand and was pulling him forward.

"Poison," said Quinn.

"Hmm?"

"You're going to poison three people at dinner."

Lucas laughed. "You know, I do actually love some things about you. Never subtle, are you?"

"Stop." Quinn pulled against Lucas's grip, but it only tightened, continuing to drag him forward. Then they were at the table, the focus of fifty pairs of eyes.

Who does he want to kill? Quinn felt his throat constrict, the first warning sign of the oncoming panic attack.

"My dear friends!" Lucas called the room to silence. "Thank you so much for being here tonight."

Quinn frantically scanned the crowd. Only a few familiar faces, members from the film society, Winter and her partner, someone else—there, Quinn's gaze screeched to a halt and zeroed in on a familiar face poking uncomfortably out of a tux collar. Hannah's CIA handler. They made eye contact. Or rather, the handler had been watching Quinn since he'd entered the room, and now Quinn was looking back at him as Lucas said, "I'm pleased to introduce you to my fiancé, Quinn VanderVeer."

The guests erupted in cheering, not one person showing any hint of surprise except Lucas's parents who'd sequestered themselves in the corner by the door. Either everyone else had been told ahead of time to expect an announcement, or they were all so afraid of Lucas's disapproval that they'd become actors in the scene. The engagement was fake so it seemed reasonable enough that the reaction to it might also be fake.

Lucas really does care what people think, thought Quinn. It was just a side thought, something his brain was doing to distract him from the oncoming panic. Then there was no more thinking. Lucas pulled him close, gripped Quinn's hair on the non-audience side of his head, while he cupped the visible side more gently, both hands drawing Quinn forward for the kiss.

A kiss with tongue.

A mouth that tasted like sulfur and mint.

It lasted so long the strangeness of the taste faded and Quinn began to think it was something he liked. When Lucas drew back, Quinn felt his absence, felt his mouth humming, lips so swollen that for a moment, he thought the strange taste might have been its own poison.

"Did you just—?"

"What do you feel?" asked Lucas, eyes glimmering.

Quinn reached out and touched Lucas's lips, which were also swollen, a pair of ripe, pink lines Quinn wanted to suck into his mouth and explore on his own terms.

Lucas's smile widened. "Good boy." They turned to face the crowd, and Lucas was talking, holding Quinn against him as though he thought Quinn might collapse, which only made the poisoning seem more likely.

I'm going to die, thought Quinn. *He's found me out and I'm going to die. That CIA guy won't even try to help me.*

The liquid matter in his brain crashed from one side of his skull to the other, the room swimming before him. The sounds of laughter and more cheering fading in and out. He knew he was still playing his part. Everyone believed how much he was in love with Lucas and this made Quinn proud. At least he would die performing well.

An absurd thought. One that made Quinn want to laugh.

Then a familiar voice shouted, "Get your hands off him, you fucking bastard."

Quinn's head whipped around to the far archway to see a flash of green, a head of almost-red hair, slashing through the crowd. Larisa brandished a knife at the level of her shoulder as she broke through the guests and came around the edge of the table to charge them. Not them, just Lucas.

They had only a moment. Quinn stepped into Larisa's path and raised his arms to block the blow. "You have to get out of here," he said. "The dinner's been poisoned." He couldn't tell if she heard him. She barreled past Quinn and drove the knife into Lucas's shoulder. Someone screamed. Someone else laughed, which seemed the more appropriate response. There was no blood obviously visible through the jacket. With all the layers Lucas was wearing, she might barely have nicked him. But Lucas stumbled back as though mortally wounded. As people rushed forward to help, Quinn dragged Larisa back, and finally, finally, she allowed him to pull her away.

They pushed into the crowd, through the archway, and out into the palazzo atrium. Two men waited there. The handler and someone Quinn didn't recognize. Across the palazzo a woman in a black dress was making a guilty looking exit through the front door; he would remember her later when things got much, much worse.

"We need to leave," said the man, reaching toward Larisa. "I've called for my car."

"Who are you?" asked Quinn, suddenly worried Lucas had foreseen this and provided Larisa an escape route that would turn into an illusion as soon as she was beyond the sight of witnesses.

The man glared at him.

Larisa was trembling in his arms. Her rage spent. Quinn didn't have a suit jacket to give her. Lucas had dressed him in the backless jumpsuit he'd worn for the London red carpet. Instead, he rubbed his hands up and down her arms.

"Larisa."

She hiccupped a sob.

"Larisa, you need to leave."

"Not without you."

Quinn glared at the CIA handler. "Are you here to finish it?"

"I'm here for you. My superiors have a plan. Is it happening tonight?" the handler asked the man.

The man shook his head.

Quinn struggled to fit the pieces together and realized there was too much that didn't make sense. All that mattered was getting Larisa to safety. The rest would come, and he'd deal with it in the moment.

He looked to the handler. "Then you're leaving and taking her with you. I'll meet you at the usual place when I can." Quinn's voice sounded remarkably steady, almost like it belonged to someone else. "Larisa." He couldn't bear to look at her. He wanted to kiss her but who knew what Lucas had put on his lips. It was too much of a risk. Instead, he held her, tried to press his heat into her so she'd stop shaking.

"You should have let me kill him," she whispered.

"You don't deserve that curse."

Another sob, this one harder, deeper.

"We're in the third act," he said. "It's almost over."

"I can't—"

"You will."

"Come with me," she said.

"I love you." He pushed her away, made eye contact with the handler that he hoped looked threatening enough to motivate the guy to do his job, then he turned and fled back to the dining room where Lucas was laughing hysterically.

"Tosca's kiss," he said, eyes running with tears that didn't all seem attributable to his laughter. "Daring girl, you always play the role so well. Don't you see it?" He looked around at the faces of his guests. "If only she'd had better aim." His eyes landed on Quinn's and his face fell like a curtain dropping as his voice broke. "She tried to kill me."

"No, she didn't," said Quinn, pulling at Lucas's jacket. "If she'd meant to kill you, you'd be dead."

Lucas began to laugh again, the grief wiped away. "You're right. I've been spared the knife so I can enjoy this fine meal. Everyone, let us feast!"

The guests took their seats. Quinn watched in his peripheral vision as Lucas noted the two empty chairs at the table. Only two, which meant the CIA handler had been present without an invitation and hadn't planned to stay for dinner. Quinn looked down at his plate. It looked just like all the others down the line of the table, but he couldn't bring himself to eat.

I should have left with her, he thought. *This is madness.*

But staying made sense in the slanted way that many impossible things now made sense to Quinn. He'd spared Lucas's life, and with that action, bought himself the last step across the boundary of Lucas's rotten heart. The gesture would mean something. Quinn finally had Lucas where he wanted him. That, combined with whatever action the CIA had finally decided to take, would be enough. Soon, it would be over.

Out of our lives forever, thought Quinn as Lucas's hand reached over into his lap and his fingers became a steady warmth on Quinn's thigh. Not unwelcome, more than a little comforting, so familiar, unlike the feel of Larisa against him trembling. Quinn leaned his head back into his chair and closed his eyes, focusing hard enough he tricked himself into believing it was gentle instead of possessive, caring instead of power hungry. He let that comfort soak into him until it was real.

"I'm glad you're alright," he whispered.

"Are you really?" asked Lucas.

"You know I am."

The party continued late into the night. Sometime around eleven a man named Caruso abashedly approached Riffat to admit that he'd become horrendously ill and asked to have a room for the night. Later, as Quinn slipped out onto the balcony to take a break, he heard the steady crunch of shovels in the darkness. A new grave was being dug, but it seemed only one.

Lucas came out to join him still somehow full of energy, bouncing on the balls of his feet. "I think I've rolled back a year instead of gained one," he said.

"Near death experiences have that effect."

"Hadn't thought of that." Lucas followed Quinn's gaze out into the darkness hiding the gravediggers. "Of course the evening isn't a complete triumph. I brought three traitors to my table and two of them escaped."

"So we're still not safe?"

"Safe enough here. The cowards," Lucas spat.

"Larisa was working for those people?"

"Hard to imagine, isn't it?" Lucas sighed. "Honestly, I can't say. Our relationship has become so clouded. It's always that way with true passion."

Quinn looked at him in surprise. "You like that she tried to kill you."

"Well, it surprised me. Very little surprises me. I rather enjoyed—"

Quinn slapped him.

"What was that for?"

"Mocking me."

"Come now."

"I saved you."

"Yes," said Lucas softly. "You also surprised me."

"I was scared for you."

Lucas made a tsking sound behind his teeth. "Were you now? And what else?"

"What do you mean?"

"What else did you feel?"

Quinn stared into the darkness. *A man died tonight and I'm standing beside his killer like it's nothing.*

"What did you feel when you saw her?"

"I felt lonely," said Quinn.

"Why?"

"She didn't feel like mine anymore." Quinn closed his eyes so Lucas wouldn't see the tears pooling there. They came anyway, so insistent they overflowed and began to roll down his cheeks.

"You were never going to be enough for her."

Quinn forced himself to nod. "I know."

"You belong with me," said Lucas.

"I want to."

"Then I have a question for you." Lucas dropped down on one knee and pulled a velvet box from his jacket pocket.

Oh no.

"Quinn, I've never met anyone like you. Your stubborn ignorance used to be so annoying I had fantasies about drowning you, but now your resentful glare is the reason I get out of bed every day. Every hour we've spent together has been a challenge and I love it. You make me want to live just so I can convert you to my side. Marry me."

Inside the box was a ring that looked old with a polished stone held in place by metal teeth forged to look like leaves. There was writing engraved on each side of the band and a craftsman's seal on the inside. A ring so full of history Quinn would never understand it, let alone live up to its value.

"Stop thinking about it," said Lucas. "Just say yes."

"Yes," said Quinn.

"Brilliant."

"Are you sure?"

"Of course I'm sure."

"It seems fast."

"Maybe, but life is like that sometimes. Besides, you know where the bodies are buried now. I can't just let you walk away." Lucas grinned as he slipped the ring onto Quinn's finger.

"How long have you been planning this?" asked Quinn.

"About forty-five minutes." His hand reached around Quinn's shoulder and danced soft brushes of his fingertips down Quinn's bare back. "But it feels right, doesn't it?" The hand reached up and pulled at the ribbon of fabric that held the top of the jumpsuit around Quinn's neck. When it came free, the whole outfit would drop straight down and pool around Quinn's feet. As Lucas had instructed, he wore nothing underneath.

"Your guests," said Quinn.

"I don't care if they see."

"I don't want to be shared," said Quinn trying not to sound desperate. Lucas's worst tendencies fed on the smallest hints of desperation, like parasites sinking their teeth in and engorging themselves.

"Come then." Lucas took Quinn's hand and led him down the balcony stairs into the garden. They walked all the way down the hill and around to the labyrinth. Here, the rise of the garden blocked most of the view of the house. The gravediggers could no longer be heard. The moon was a dim gray shadow behind thin clouds that left them with just enough light to see the labyrinth's entrance. Lucas led the way inside.

Endless twists and turns later they arrived in a small courtyard with a statue standing in each corner and a trickling fountain in the middle. The dark hedge rose around them like a protective shield, blocking them from the rest of the world. In this space nothing mattered except beauty. It seemed a place born of beauty, woven from the satin of dreams, and animated with the stillness of life that did not age.

As Quinn was distracted taking it in, Lucas pulled the ribbon at the top of the jumpsuit. Quinn's skin fritzed and sparked as the fabric slid down and exposed him to the cool night air.

"Do you know what the fiancé of Lucas Onslow wants most in the world?"

"Tell me," said Quinn.

"To always have his master inside him. Empty, he's worthless, a puppet without strings."

Quinn bowed his head. "I want to be filled."

"Get down on your knees."

Without hesitation, Quinn knelt on the frigid flagstones of the courtyard. He was already getting hard. It took so little to get him going when Lucas spoke like that, in the voice he both hated and craved.

"Beg for it."

"Please."

"Not like that." The disgust in Lucas's voice brought bile surging to Quinn's mouth.

"Beg for exactly what you want."

Quinn stared down at the stones, at the delicate green grass growing between them. The only fantasies in his head were the things he wanted to do to Lucas, which seemed an entirely different thing. And now that he'd let his mind go there, he couldn't think of anything else. Lucas as the one naked, Lucas on his knees for hours, unable to speak or move. Lucas bent over the edge of the fountain unable to breathe as Quinn showed him which one of them was the bigger man.

"Beg! Or you'll spend the rest of the week sleeping in a cage."

The threat struck home. If Quinn was locked in a cage, he wouldn't be able to sneak away to meet the CIA handler the next day. Whatever else he did, Quinn needed to keep his freedom. He swallowed down the bile. Once he made up his mind, the words came easily.

"I want you to fuck me," said Quinn.

"More," said Lucas.

"I'm nothing alone. The only time I'm alive is with you inside me. Please, take me. I'm already your slave. My body, my blood, my seed is yours. Please fill me, stretch me until I bleed, break me, choke me. If only my last breath is yours, I'll be happy."

"I don't need your permission," growled Lucas. "Head down."

Quinn lowered his head to the flagstones.

"Arch your back." Lucas came around behind him, slapped his bare right cheek. "More."

Quinn arched harder. He heard a splash of disturbed water as Lucas reached into the fountain, poured a handful of shockingly cold water down Quinn's crack. Water was a poor substitute for lube. Quinn would have braced if he'd had time, but the entrance came so quickly he cried out and pulled away.

"I thought you wanted it," said Lucas.

"I do."

"You're going to take it this time?"

"Yes."

"All of me and all the pain?"

"I want all of it," said Quinn.

Chapter 14

The Guise of Escape

It felt like hours before Lucas was satisfied. When he gasped out his last orgasm, he zipped up his pants and walked away. If Quinn had been thinking more clearly, he would have realized following Lucas was his easiest way out of the labyrinth, but he wasn't thinking about much by then. Even his usual 'grit his teeth and wait for the end' had failed him. It didn't feel like an ending when Lucas pulled out and left him there without a word, a used-up husk easily discarded. Even with Lucas gone, Quinn still felt him inside.

Which of course was the point. For Lucas, sex would never be about love or caring for the needs of another person. It was a powerplay, a driving force of ego that couldn't be satisfied until he knew his partner had been pulverized on every level.

Quinn dragged himself over to the edge of the fountain and dropped down into its shallow pool. Using hands that had been clenched into fists so long he couldn't get them to release, he washed himself, then washed himself again. The cold soothed him at first, then it became a problem. He was in the middle of a maze with no light, no phone, no warm clothes, and no strength left to save himself.

Walking was out of the question. He managed to crawl over and pull on the bottom half of the jumpsuit, a flimsy covering that did nothing to mask the lingering fire of Lucas's hands on him. Quinn lay on his back with the cold seeping into him. Soon he'd be shivering, and he'd have to pick himself up and try to find his way out. But not yet.

The clouds across the moon faded, bathing the courtyard in clear silver light. Quinn looked up at the statues towering over him, two female figures, two male, all unabashedly naked, which made him think Lucas had commissioned them.

"What's your story, nymph of the moonlight?" Quinn asked the nearest one. His voice came out as an agonized whisper over raw skin, but somehow the statue heard him. Then it answered.

"You've taken a wrong turn."

Quinn laughed. "That's obvious."

Another voice, male. "Well, you lead then. It can't be far."

"This better not be a trap."

"Pete saw him walk up the hill alone. This is our chance."

Quinn tried to push himself up to a sitting position and quickly gave up. Whoever was coming, he wouldn't be able to fight them off.

Americans, he thought.

A moment later, they came through the opening in the hedge facing his feet, a man and a woman dressed in commando black with visored hats on their heads.

"See? I told you," she said.

The man shrugged as though still unconvinced. "You're the fiancé?"

Quinn opened his mouth for an answer he couldn't form. The truth was yes, he thought, but he wasn't really sure. It wasn't true for him in a way that he felt other people should be involved in the lie.

The woman came up, grabbed his wrist, and held it up. "There's the ring. Can we go now?"

"Fine."

"Go?" Quinn asked.

"We're taking you out of here."

"You're with the CIA?"

The woman cackled.

"Don't be difficult," said the man as he reached for Quinn's arm to pull him up. Pain shot through him, not just his arm, but everywhere. His cry cut through the still night much louder than any of them wanted it to be.

"I said don't be difficult!"

"I can't—" Quinn didn't know what else to say. Here, finally, was the rescue the CIA handler had promised, and he wasn't able to get his feet under him.

"I've got it." The woman unzipped a pouch on her shirt and pulled out what looked like a bandage.

Quinn wondered if he was bleeding somewhere and didn't know it. This thought was overwhelmed by a rush of thoughts about all the things that had just happened and how it all felt both too real and also like a dream that he'd watched happen to someone else.

Larisa had come for him.

Tried to kill Lucas.

The poison, both real and imagined.

Engaged to Lucas.

Fucked within an inch of his life in the most peaceful place he'd ever seen.

And now these people wanted him to move.

A tearing sound, then a tingling sensation on his bicep as the woman pressed the bandage against his arm.

"Codeine patch," she said. "Give it five minutes."

"Do we have five minutes?" The man stalked to the edge of the fountain and back, scanning the edge of the courtyard. "Why would he have been left here if he didn't know we were watching?"

They were watching? thought Quinn. No, not watching if they'd gotten lost in the maze, but they'd probably heard everything. The memory of a nightmare's soundtrack echoed between his ears. It only got worse when the man nudged him with his shoe. "I recorded it. Pam will love it."

"Don't," whispered Quinn. The rest of his protest was lost as he wondered, *Who's Pam?* Then a wave of chemicals washed across his system taking away the pain and carrying him away on a tide of oblivion.

Quinn jolted from sleep at the slamming of a car door. There was a cloth bag over his head and his wrists had been restrained in front of him. *Not the CIA,* he thought. But what did he know? Maybe they were deep undercover and needed to make it look like he'd been arrested as Lucas's accomplice. As a narrative device, the narrative felt thin, a placeholder for what he didn't want to think about.

I've been kidnapped.

His door was opened and hands hauled him out, brought him forward a few paces, then let him drop to his knees on what felt like a gravel road. This time, as the pain coursed through him, he managed not to cry out. There was something about the quiet that made making noise frightening. There seemed to be people around, but no voices. Behind him, the engine of the car remained running. To his left, a bird's call and another's response, then a different pair of hands took hold of him, pulled him to his feet.

"That's him?" asked a woman, not the one from the labyrinth, also American. "Put him in the processing room. There's more light there."

'Processing room' sounded ominous. But Quinn clung to his patience. Yes, everything hurt. Yes, this was scary. But he was alright. He was away from Lucas, and he was alright. He had to think that an enemy of Lucas was his friend.

Not remotely that simple.

The scrape of chair legs along a stone floor. A new room, a strong wine fume, something a little chemical, and the smell of machinery. The person pulling on Quinn's arm sat him in the chair. He thought how civilized it felt to be seated in a chair after all his time kneeling, though kneeling hardly seemed the right word to describe what he'd been doing as Lucas plundered him.

No one released his wrists or pulled off the hood.

"What angle do you think?" asked a man, another American accent, but not the man from the labyrinth.

"Do half the machine, half the wall there," said a second man, a thick accent not American or Italian.

Shuffling. One of them grunted. The other sucked his teeth in judgement. "I think more to the left."

"You do it then."

"It doesn't really matter as long as you get the sound."

"She wants it to be effecting."

"Well, she better not be expecting art. I'm security not a press secretary."

Footsteps sounded of a third person joining them. The men fell silent.

"Is it ready?" asked the new person, a woman. "Good enough. Go back to work."

Retreating footsteps. A soft breath of women's perfume drifted in to greet Quinn as she lifted away the hood. Quinn blinked. The light in the room was low but the freedom of nothing in front of his face felt more significant than he'd expected. He'd probably only been hooded a handful of hours and yet free of it, his skin tingled as though he'd worn it for days.

The woman standing before him appeared surprisingly ordinary, short, straight hair dyed to keep the gray out, a plain face but well balanced. She wore a Padres sweatshirt and leggings, as though she'd just been out for a jog and stopped by to say hello. *A woman who central casting sends when you ask for Midwest, suburban housewife,* thought Quinn. Except for one thing. In her left hand, a baton with electrodes on one end.

You've got to be fucking kidding me.

Quinn scanned the room for an exit. His legs were free. He could run. The room—he was sitting in the processing room of a winery—was empty, the adjacent room also appeared empty.

It's just for show, he thought. *She won't use it.*

If she does, you'll survive.

But show for who? And why? He didn't have any idea who this woman was or why she'd taken him. He wanted to say, *Please don't hurt me,* but the look in the woman's eyes, their quiet, cold purpose, told him begging wouldn't help him. Besides, he'd had enough of that for a while.

"I don't want to die," he said.

"Do your job and I will evacuate you before the detonations."

"My job?" echoed Quinn.

The woman moved over to a tripod with a camera set on top. "Today is the last day of Lucas Onslow's life. But only if he comes here to rescue you."

Oh.

Well fuck.

"You want me to act?" asked Quinn.

"You do whatever you think's necessary." The woman pushed a button on the camera, then she stepped forward and drove the electrode end of the baton into the right side of his chest. Fire surged through him, setting his tender body aflame. When she pulled back, Quinn looked down at his chest expecting to see scorch marks or smoke. Instead, there were just two pink marks like bug bites.

"Why you?" she asked.

Quinn was still breathless, his body sizzling on the inside even if there was no outward evidence. The baton came again, the soft flesh of his belly this time, harder, longer than the first.

"Please," he said, thinking she might give him a moment to catch his breath.

"What are his favorite places?" The baton traced a circle on his middle without activating. It dropped down to his waist.

Please God, no, thought Quinn. In his panic he raised his knee to knock the baton to the side. "Why are you doing this?"

"Lucas killed my husband." The woman looked matter of fact, colder than ever, as though this, the most intimate reason for anyone to do violence to another person, was a plain fact and nothing more.

She's going to kill me. The thought rushed over him in a brief buzz of terror that died back into something quieter, something that felt like disappointment. Maybe it was true what Lucas had said, Quinn had wasted so much time trying to be acceptable, following the rules of other people. And now, none of that would matter.

"Your death will be slower than his," said the woman. "More painful. More humiliating. Do you think he'll care?" She raised the baton and stroked it down one side of Quinn's arm.

There was only one thing that mattered now. Quinn looked into the camera. "Lucas, tell Larisa—"

The baton filled his mouth. "This is a place he likes, isn't it?" said the woman. "Close your lips around it the way you do his cock."

Quinn kept looking at the camera; he put all the pleading he would have given the woman into his face and prayed Lucas would be moved, maybe not by him. But by the thought of Larisa. Somehow. Someway.

The woman pushed the baton back into his throat so he started to cough, then choke. It knocked against his teeth, a fore-shadowing of the pain to come. Still, Quinn kept his eyes on the camera. Tears welled up and leaked down his cheeks. It felt like an ending. *If I die here, Larisa will see this someday,* he thought. *And the recording they made of what we did in the labyrinth courtyard.*

He wished he could tell her he loved her. Even in their short grasp at happiness he hadn't said it enough. He hadn't known himself enough to promise her what was now so obvious; the weight of it burst his heart.

I love you.

The baton vibrated as the woman pressed the button and sent electricity coursing down the barrel into the velvet tissue of his throat.

Chapter 15

Rage of Heart

The CIA watched the news. This surprised Larisa for some reason, probably because she'd felt for a long time that the news was just another form of entertainment, facts dressed up and embellished, or at least that's how it had always felt when she'd been the object of a news story. Now, in a warehouse building in the industrial suburbs of Florence, she sat on a folding chair watching the coverage of John Hagan's murder on a big screen that was probably using up more electricity than an Italian household used for all their appliances.

She chose to focus on this, the very American-ness of the CIA office, the insta coffee machine, the McDonald's wrappers that hadn't quite made it to the trash, the sprawling tables of surveillance technology she was pretty sure was illegal, but then, they weren't spying on Italians, so maybe Italy didn't care. Her focus didn't quite wipe out the horror of hearing that Hagan had hung on the side of the Regis Grand Hotel for five hours before emergency workers figured out how to rig a harness to support themselves as they cut him loose from the iron hooks that'd been soldered into the side of the building, then stabbed under the ends of his shoulder blades. He had died just before they got him free. A terrible ending made even worse by the fact that the media couldn't stop talking about it, the spectacle, the humiliation, the strange surprise of a man who'd already been given a funeral dying again.

I'm sorry, she told the giant television over and over.

Sudden movement at her side made Larisa jump. She'd been twitchy since they'd left Umbras, as though every nerve stood at high alert. Of course they did. She'd tried to kill Lucas. If any feeling of safety had been an illusion before, it was all gone now. He would come for her. All she could hope was that Quinn had found a way to keep himself safe. She prayed he had a plan and that it was better than the CIA's because everything about the body language of the agents rushing around and whispering to each other told her they were scrambling.

The movement at her side was Goku pulling up a chair. He leaned in to whisper, "I found us a ride out of here."

Larisa glanced over at Agent Jensen, the man responsible for Hannah being a spy and who knew what else. He was on the phone, talking rapidly in Italian, his free hand a fist pressed against the table. Two other agents, both Americans, were on computers manipulating video feeds. They were too far away for her to see what they were watching.

Get Quinn out, she wanted to shout. But she felt she'd done that already. In the car leaving Umbras, or perhaps when they'd first arrived at this office. Like her rage at failing to kill Lucas, her urgency had also faded to a quiet thrum in the back of her mind, visible only in the tapping of her heel against the floor.

These heels, her old, favorite Louboutins Lucas had bought her during their first trip to Milan. This dress, custom made, a ballroom gown that emphasized all his favorite parts of her. Sooner or later the CIA was going to sit down and ask her questions and it wouldn't matter what the truth was or how well she told her story, she'd dressed for the part Lucas had cast her in, and appearance always mattered more than words.

I killed Hagan.

I let Lucas take me from prison.

I failed to end him.

End this.

"We should leave now while they're distracted," said Goku.

Larisa turned and squinted at him. They barely knew each

other, but he was acting like they were allies in this situation. What situation? Being caught by the CIA. Not quite prisoners because they'd come along nicely, but how long would that last? Goku was sweating through his suit shirt, agitated in a guilty kind of way. Maybe he felt trapped. After all, he was a criminal. Larisa couldn't remember exactly what kind. They'd met years back at a party. Lucas had asked her to keep Goku entertained. She remembered being excited by it, honored Lucas had trusted her with his important friend.

Now she just saw a small, nervous man who was anxious to escape. And she couldn't tell if it was her job to keep him here with the CIA so he could be questioned, if she should just send him on his way, or if she should take his offer to escape together.

"What's he saying?" She nodded to Jensen on the phone.

"Something about an operation in Orvieto. They had a plan, but it's gone wrong."

"What plan?"

Goku sighed. "We don't have time for this."

"Do you know what's in Orvieto?" she asked.

"Why should I?"

"Lucas kept a cache there in a winery."

"Not anymore apparently. It's been rigged to explode." Goku listened. "They're all down there. Lucas, the fiancé, Agent Smith, the CIA people."

Larisa lurched to her feet and walked over to the operations table. Not that anyone was paying attention, but she walked on her toes so her heels wouldn't click on the floor. Doing this, she was able to walk right up and look down over the shoulder of the agent with the video feeds, three camera angles of empty rooms that could have been anywhere in Italy. The screen beside the video feeds was a satellite feed. She recognized the winery's alfresco patio and the wind break of cypress trees.

Across the table, Jensen hung up his phone, leaned over to stare at a screen, pointed to something and hissed out a command.

The agent at that station swirled a mouse around, clicking, clicking, then Jensen was back on the phone.

It wasn't how covert operations looked in the movies. For one, Larisa didn't understand the need for a phone instead of a radio feed. The difference between the urgency in Jensen's voice and the low murmur of the Americans also pacing around on phones at the other side of the room seemed strangely at odds with the stillness on the feeds she could see. On the screen it felt like nothing was happening, but the voices said the world was ending.

Then, in a corner of one of the video feeds, two people ran through the camera's field of view. They moved too fast and were too small to easily be recognized, but Larisa thought one looked like Pam, a brightly colored sweatshirt with a blooming red stain, the right color hair. But in the next moment, Larisa's confidence in that recognition faded.

The agent at the station played back that portion of the feed, paused it, switched to a different feed. "They went through the north tunnel," he said.

A momentary silence. The two American agents both rushed up to the table and watched the playback. On the other side of the table, Jensen jabbed a finger at another screen. "But they haven't come through to the loading dock," he said. Back on the phone, in English this time. "She's on the move. Spotted in the north tunnel."

More figures on the video feed. This time Larisa had no trouble recognizing them. Lucas and his impeachable posture even as he carried Quinn in his arms. Quinn still wearing his golden jumpsuit from the party, his pale skin stark against the earth tones of the tunnel, the low light. Larisa's hand flailed out and gripped the back of the nearest office chair.

Gunfire sounded on the phone, so loud Jensen pulled it away from his ear, then began shouting. He ran around to the end of the table to another agent, and said, "Tell the car to move in. Move in now!"

And then a bright bloom of light scorched across the camera feeds. Everything went black. A moment later, the same bright bloom appeared on the exterior feeds as it obliterated the walls of the winery, then billowed out until it consumed one side of the roof, the patio, the cypress trees. An SUV that had been rushing up the drive, stopped short of the blast. Figures disembarked, spread out to watch as flames began to articulate in small clumps around the building. Light danced behind the windows as their panes shattered.

No one emerged from the building.

"Confirm no one came out," said one of the Americans into his phone.

"Perimeter search," said the other American to his phone.

Jensen's eyes were jumping from screen to screen on his side of the table, his phone pressed to his ear. Italian again, repeating a name over and over. Finally, he said, "Agent down."

Larisa grabbed the sleeve of the nearest American agent. "Send your people in. There could be survivors."

The agent jerked away, glared at her, then turned his back.

She went to the other one. "There are innocents in there. You have to help them."

"What innocents?" His look said everything. He knew who she was, who Quinn and Lucas were to her, and he'd already passed judgement. She wanted to argue with him, but there was nothing to say.

"He was helping you!" she shouted. "He did everything for you!"

An agent snapped his fingers and some enforcement officer entered from the adjacent room, took Larisa's arm, and began to pull her away.

"No! No, I have to see! He'll come out."

"What about the weapon?" asked an agent. "Is it secure?" A pause, an exchange of eye contact between the two Americans. "Good, move out. Make sure no one sees you."

"You can't leave," said Larisa. "You have to help them. You have to—"

In his effort to pull her from the room, and Larisa's deranged efforts to pull away from him, she slammed into the side of the doorway, which left the room spinning. Maybe the officer had pushed her. It felt like too much force for a fall. But then, she hardly felt her body. It had become a creature unto itself, spasming, dissolving and coming back together, clawing at the air. But in her head, the calm eye of the storm, an unnatural stillness with one thought gently seeping through the ether.

They can't be dead.

The officer locked her in a bedroom that had been turned into an interrogation room with two uncomfortable chairs and boards nailed over the windows. Larisa yanked off her shoes and flung them against the door as the officer retreated. She screamed insults at him that only made half sense, then, when she was alone, she let herself collapse. The skirt of her dress billowed up around her like a deflating air balloon, still somehow beautiful, even though it clothed a ruined woman. Larisa beat down the air pockets as she cried. This dress, the last gift Lucas would ever give her. This dress, the last thing Quinn saw her wearing and they hadn't even had time for him to say if he liked it or not.

They were together at the end.

It's over.

And yet she felt no relief.

It would never be over. She'd been a fool to hope there was any future for her where she would be free. Now, instead of being haunted by one man, she'd be haunted by two.

He can't be gone. Lucas wouldn't have allowed it. As though he could thwart death and defy not one, but two conspiracies working against him. Impossible, and yet the hope refused to die.

Lucas had taken Quinn from her, but he wouldn't have allowed someone else to do the same. He was like that with his possessions. No one else was allowed to touch them unless he gave his permission.

The tears gradually drained themselves dry. She lay down on the floor and stared at the plaster ceiling, her mind floating, pulling together fragments of information. Pam had come to Italy for revenge. That part seemed clear enough. She'd lured Lucas to the winery by threatening the gas deal, or maybe she'd posed as a seller. For some reason, Quinn had been with him.

He'd been hurt. A fresh round of tears, a blur of thoughts only half intelligible, more feelings than ideas. Time became meaningless until Larisa heard the lock on the door turn. She didn't bother sitting up to greet her visitor, so she had a severe angle looking up at Agent Osna as he oozed into the room, paused, then looked down at her. He held a bottle of vodka in his fist, two paper cups in the other.

"You," she said.

"Afraid so." He stepped over her, walked to the wall, then slid down it until he was at her level. "Thought we'd share a drink." His hand shook as he poured the vodka but was steady when he pushed the cup across the floor to her. Larisa considered refusing. But there was something about Osna that piqued her interest. He'd changed, as though something had fractured inside him.

"What are you doing here?" she asked.

"I followed Pam from the States."

"And once again failed to control her."

Osna swallowed down his drink and poured another. "You were right. We were working together. I *thought* we were working together." The way his voice broke seemed oddly compelling even though he wasn't saying anything Larisa didn't already know and had hated him for. She wanted to relish in the crushing of his ego, instead she only felt empty. Maybe the vodka would help.

"People are dead because of you." She glared at him a moment or two before she pushed herself into a sitting position and took up her cup. "The man I love is dead because of you."

Osna passed her the bottle as though it was an apology.

"Did you get your fucking nerve gas?"

"Yes." He took a drink. "If it helps any, we're pretty sure your boyfriend was on the other side. He might even have been planted in Hollywood to spy on you."

"What makes you think that?" Larisa gave him her best impression of the doe-eyed ingenue, as though grief had suddenly transformed her into a woman who believed anything.

"He had an alias, Volpe Rossa, an infamous middleman no one's ever identified. He moves weapons through Europe into Russia."

Larisa held up her cup so she could peer at Osna over the edge of it. If he kept talking, she might fling it at him even though what he deserved was a crack against the head with the vodka bottle.

"I'm sorry, Larisa." He even looked like he meant it. This threw Larisa off, made what he was saying almost possible. But then she began to laugh. She laughed and laughed until her belly ached and the vodka in it began to churn. When she could speak, she said, "Let me see if I understand what you're saying. A key player in illegal arms trafficking put his life on hold to come to LA and make movies for the past five years just so he could eventually meet and seduce me."

"I know it sounds elaborate—"

"It's preposterous, Osna. Who gave you that information?"

"We had multiple agents witness VanderVeer at key meetings. Lucas identified him as Rossa."

"My God," she whispered. "Are you even listening to yourself?"

"During the cold war, Russian agents infiltrated—"

"Just stop."

"It might help you feel better knowing—"

"Who do you think I am that someone that important would

come to LA for me? I am just a girl who fell for the wrong man and got on with her life."

"There's no way to know that for sure."

"There is actually. It was on that laptop you didn't want because you're afraid of porn."

He stared at her.

"Volpe Rossa isn't a man. It's an organization of terrorists working together to control natural resources in developing countries so they can leverage influence to decide who sits in power."

It was a little frightening seeing his face break open, the realization dawning so slowly she wished there was a fast-forward button. It was almost painful.

"That man I was with in the operations room? Goku? I called him last weekend and asked a few questions. He told me all about it. Lucas was their chief supplier. But sometimes he also asked them for things, gambled favors with the expectation that a destabilized country would be good for business, but it didn't work out that way. He owed lots of money to them and others."

This was the first time she'd said it all aloud. Her last and greatest secret. It hadn't all come from Goku. Dozens of phone calls had given her only a hint of the scope of Lucas's treachery. He'd become not just someone who did business, the person he'd always presented to her, but someone desperate for more, uninterested in who was hurt, how many lives destroyed in parts of the world the bigger countries didn't care about, as long as he got what he wanted. It had been surprising, and it hadn't surprised her.

Because somehow, she'd known what was inside him.

She had known and chosen to ignore it because he'd given her what she couldn't find anywhere else: a life beyond her parents. What he'd asked for in return hadn't felt like enough to complain about.

Maybe it's good Quinn is gone, she thought. *He would have wanted to know everything. It would've changed us once he knew what I'd done.*

Larisa closed her eyes and sipped her vodka. It was cheap and too sharp and tasted like chemicals.

He died in pain because of me.

"Well, it doesn't matter now." Osna coughed like he was suddenly feeling sick. "He's gone. We got most of his contacts through the accountant. The Rossa people are probably part of that."

"What will you do with all those names?" Larisa couldn't help but smile. It was a bitter, little smile, one she hoped made Osna's balls shrink to the size of raisins as he realized what a waste of life he was.

"That will depend on you since you're obviously an expert."

"I want a retainer. A hundred grand every month when you call me with a question. Double that if I have to travel somewhere to help you sort out a mess you've made."

"You've planned this."

Larisa sighed. "No, Osna. You're just so predictable, I only need five seconds to think ten steps ahead of you. In LA, I was a kinky therapist, now I'm most likely a suspect in the most visible murder of the century. My career as a therapist is over. I have access to information, I need money. You're going to give it to me."

"Thinking of money the same day your boyfriend dies. I knew you had a black heart."

Here was the vodka bottle in her hand, ready to slam into the side of Osna's head. Larisa watched it happen, saw the face he'd make as his head slid sideways beneath a shower of glass. She thought if she swung it hard enough, and he fell and hit his head on the floor, the combination of the two blows might kill him.

So she resisted the temptation and left the bottle where it was on the floor. Killing him for being an asshole didn't seem worth it. The fact was, she did need money. She wouldn't be able to pick up the shards of her life, nor did she want to. The only thing that made sense was making sure Lucas's people were brought to justice. If the CIA wouldn't do it, she'd find a way to do it herself.

"I suppose you're sending people to search Umbras?"

"It's already started."

"I'd like to go see it."

Osna leaned forward, took the bottle from her, and poured himself another drink. "I suppose we can do that. Looking for anything in particular?"

"My phone, passport, wallet. Some mementos."

"We'll have to be careful no one sees you or the game will be up. You working for us and all."

It's already up, she thought. *The wolves were circling. There were probably a dozen people watching Lucas's movements. By now, they'll know Lucas was assassinated. They'll know government agents have taken possession of his house.*

The thought made her incredibly tired. Every turn her life took, it seemed to lead to another moment like this, her thinking she had a way forward, then discovering someone had gone ahead and ruined it. Working for the CIA, she'd be fighting their incompetence more than finding justice.

Maybe that was what she was meant to do. A perverted kind of penance.

When Osna gave her a scarf and farmer's hat to wear as a disguise, but no new clothes, she didn't argue the obvious problems. It was enough to be away from the CIA operations center where agents continued to rush around, speak urgently into phones, and replay footage. Part of her wanted to force herself into the conversations until someone gave her an update. But she didn't believe there was an update she wanted to hear. And she didn't think she could bear it if someone said one more insulting thing about Quinn and his loyalties.

She gave them the finger as Osna guided her past the doorway. Then she had to catch him as he almost stumbled on the stairs, just drunk enough to not realize his equilibrium was impaired. For her part, the vodka just added a layer of surreality to Larisa's already drifting headspace. When she touched the car door it felt spongy. The seat against her back, somehow less solid than a real seat. The feel of the tires on the road, not quite gritty enough. She briefly fixated on the impression that the car could fly.

The drive to Umbras felt like hours. Maybe it was, they were coming from the far opposite side of Florence and traffic was horrible. Outside the window, the sun was shining across a bright, cloudless sky. Vespas zoomed past and startled pedestrians shook their hands at the drivers' retreating backs in anger. The alfresco patios along the roads were full of diners. Larisa thought it must be five or six o'clock in the evening. But that didn't make sense with the sun being high in a winter month. She realized it was February, which meant she'd known Quinn for a year.

One year, she thought, *that's all it took to ruin his life.*

She lost herself wondering if this timescale felt like too long or not long enough. Both and neither felt true. She thought back to that night at Club D. The couple she'd helped even though she'd known they were going down two different roads and would break up soon. The way Quinn and Parish had watched her through the viewing window. The way he'd looked at her when she'd come out, his mouth open with a hunger that had struck him sideways and was still bowling him over with the shock of it.

Hadn't she enjoyed shocking him like that?

Hadn't she enjoyed how obviously he desired what she could offer before he'd known anything else about her?

And what if she'd loved him for exactly the same reasons she'd loved Lucas? As though they'd been interchangeable, just bodies slotted in to fill the hole of her need?

No.

"Beautiful house," said Osna. "Typical that villains always get the nice houses."

Larisa climbed out of the car and resisted the instinct to glance around to see who might be spying as she walked up to the front door. It stood open, probably from someone's carelessness, as though the house deserved to be punished for its owner's misdeeds. As she walked through, she closed it behind her.

"We've already found a couple fresh graves," said Osna. "Any secret passages or tunnels we should know about?"

The cocktail tables that had populated the palazzo for the party had been picked up and taken away by the rental company. Larisa walked over and poked her head in the dining room to confirm what she already knew, everything had been cleaned and returned to its usual order.

She went to the kitchen half thinking to find Francie there, but the kitchen was a cold, empty cave.

"What have you done with the staff?" she asked Osna as she came back to the palazzo.

"Lucas had all his people with him when he went down to Orvieto."

Larisa nodded as though this made sense. "So, you saw Lucas and Quinn and how many other people get into a car and drive away?"

"Not Quinn. He was already gone. Lucas, his assistant, the goons he keeps with him."

Larisa pressed her hand against the cold terra-cotta wall and tried to breathe. "Tell me what happened," she whispered to the house. Francie was a big person and obviously not a security guard. Also, she wouldn't have gone with Lucas to Orvieto. She never left the villa.

Except that one time.

She gripped the staircase banister as she walked up the same steps she had slowly descended not long before. Up on the second floor there was a bare spot on the wall where a painting used to hang. Here and there in the bookshelves, books were leaning into each other marking the gaps where books were missing.

They evacuated.

Which meant Lucas had known he was walking into a trap.

Osna had followed her up the stairs. "What are you looking for?"

"Nothing particular."

"You think he left you a note? Signed a confession?" Osna sounded as hopeful as he sounded mean.

Larisa wondered which 'he' Osna meant. At the office door, she paused. *If it's locked, it means he's alive,* she thought. Because if the door was locked, it meant Lucas had left Umbras with a plan.

"We have a video of Quinn with Pam. I can show you."

"Not right now," said Larisa. Instinct told her she would never want to watch that video, even if they were Quinn's last moments. Especially if they were his last moments.

"She took him from the house, didn't she? And Lucas went to rescue him."

"I think that's a bit romanticized. VanderVeer was wearing a tracking device. The ring Lucas gave him for their *engagement.*" Osna smirked. "It was broadcasting so loudly, it blocked our comms for hours."

Larisa gave him a look she hoped told him, *That was probably the point, you idiot.* Then she rested her hand on the doorknob, gave it a gentle turn. The office door opened without resistance. Something barbed and poisonous dropped through her gut. She swayed, suddenly lightheaded, then pushed inside.

The office was almost as she remembered it, except Samson and Delilah was missing thanks to Hannah. And there were pictures framed and sitting on Lucas's desk. She almost didn't recognize her younger self; the girl in the pictures looked so happy.

"Is that you?" Osna brushed past her and snatched up the pictures. Larisa moved on before he could say anything else. Bedroom, bathroom, everything neat and clean and well-ordered. Lucas's favorite suitcase was gone, as was the larger, secondary suitcase he used for long trips.

The closet appeared full. Larisa brushed her hands through the clothes as she tried to think of what might be missing that would signal to her Lucas had planned for everything that had happened.

He knew things were falling apart. He knew what he did to Hagan would make it all worse.

Even if he planned to escape, it doesn't mean he didn't get caught.

Osna's voice came to her from the bedroom. "Where'd you go?"

Larisa pressed into the clothes feeling along the closet wall until she felt the button, pressed it, felt a gasp of cool air as the panel slid open. She ducked down and showed herself out into the broom closet that opened into the hallway of the north wing. Walking again on her toes just in case there were still CIA agents around to hear her. Just a few feet, then the door to her room. A breath to open the door, another to close it behind her.

She rushed behind the vanity screen and changed clothes. A T-shirt and long skirt, neither of which fit her like they had when she'd been twenty-one, but they would work. Ankle socks and the sneakers she'd worn the day she and Lucas had toured the Ville d'Este in Rome and planned out a new section of the Umbras garden based on what they'd seen.

From the back of the vanity closet, a suitcase with her name on the Italian leather tag. She packed all her favorite clothes. If the CIA was going to control the villa, she wasn't going to let them have her things. The gowns didn't all fit, so she had to leave a few behind. She wheeled the bag into the bedroom, found a tote in a drawer where she'd kept all her travel supplies, and began to stuff it. Her favorite pillows, dustables, the lists from her desk.

Each time she moved to a new part of the room she expected to pick up an object and find a note, however unlikely. After what she'd done to him at the party, Lucas wouldn't have expected her to return to Umbras. She'd shown him her cards. Perhaps he'd even died thinking she hated him.

This thought brought fresh tears. A new permutation of rage she hadn't known existed. That he could die without giving her the chance at a true revenge. Even in death, he'd won. Larisa seized the letter opener from the desk and began to stab her pillows. Feathers filled the air, stuck to her wet face, obscured her vision.

"Whoa there," said Osna, somewhere behind her. Only then did Larisa realize she'd been screaming as she murdered her beloved pillows, telling them that they wouldn't get away with it. When Osna came up behind her, apparently to try and stop the violence, she turned and attempted to stab him.

Not attempted.

The opener plunged into his chest. Not easily, but Larisa was beyond being able to judge her own strength and use of force. She watched it disappear into the fold of his shirt. Like a magic trick. He looked down and they both watched for what felt like eternal minutes before two lines of red appeared on either side of the blade.

"Well, you're the doctor. Any vital organs there?"

Larisa opened her mouth, then closed it. What she did next would be very important. But why it was important felt murky. Everything was already ruined. The concept of consequences felt like something she wouldn't be able to explain to Martians.

On the one hand, if she let Osna die, she could leave and probably get away with it.

On the other hand, being an asshole didn't quite make him worthy of death.

On the other, other hand, she really didn't feel like saving him.

"I've been drinking too much, haven't I?" he said.

"It's a small cut." But the opener was almost eight inches long. And the only part on the outside of him was the handle.

"How about this? You help me not die, I forget we know each other. You can walk out the door, take yourself to the spa, do whatever—"

"I accept." She dashed across the room to the bedside table where she'd left her phone plugged in and called the emergency service in Fiesole that existed solely to take care of the wealthy foreigners who liked to live hard and party harder in the hills around Florence.

The number was in her new phone because Lucas had known she would come back to Italy. He'd planned for her to come, for the three of them to be together.

A sob ached through her chest as she ran down the hallway back to Lucas's bedroom and the dungeon where he kept a mini fridge with ice cubes (for play) and cold packs (for after). Her Basic Medicine rotation was ancient history, but she remembered something her ER attending had told her about field dressing. Localized cold would slow down blood flow around a wound.

The dungeon smelled terrible. She didn't want to know why. It was strange to be in a place that looked exactly how she remembered and yet felt entirely different. Tarnished. Maybe it had something to do with the truth of Lucas finally crashing home in her mind. The realization that even during her happiest, hottest moments with him, he'd always been keeping some part of himself back from her. When she thought they were coming together in shared ecstasy, he'd been thinking about his work. And if he'd been able to write off so many lives for the sake of his profit, what had he really valued of her?

She grabbed a Velcro restraint from the top drawer of the dresser and hurried back to Osna. He'd lowered himself onto the couch and was bleeding onto her massacred pillows.

"I thought you'd left," he said.

"You'd like that, wouldn't you? It would prove what you think about me."

"You can't be that close to evil and not like it," he said.

She slapped the cold pack against his chest, then pulled his hand over to hold it in place as she threaded the restraint under his back.

"Aren't you going to pull it out?"

"I can't remember if that's what you're supposed to do."

"You're a doctor."

"I'm a psychiatrist. My medical rotation was three months

internal medicine, three months in the ER. Almost everything I was taught, I never used. And I can't remember if what I think I was taught actually came from a movie. So just sit still. The doctor will make the big decisions."

"Why didn't you kill him?" Osna's eyelids were fluttering as he fought to stay conscious. "You had so many chances."

"I could ask you the same question," said Larisa bitterly.

"It's not the same."

"No," she said. "It wasn't my job to protect people. It was yours. I'm a therapist. I clean up after people like you fail."

Osna's eyes closed before she finished. Did he hear the end? She couldn't tell. He appeared unconscious but his pulse was still present and she didn't think the blood loss was catastrophic. With the Velcro cinched as tight as she could make it across his chest, she went downstairs to wait for the doctor.

She wondered if it would be the same one she'd called before and if he'd remember her. It didn't matter, it was just something to think about. She sat down on the stairs and looked at her phone. Over a hundred notifications. At first, she wondered what catastrophe she'd missed, then she realized news of the winery explosion must have reached the US and everyone had seen.

But no, half of the messages were from the sisters' group chat about last minute plans for Italy. Departure was less than forty-eight hours and Larisa was MIA. It seemed her friends were divided on whether or not she was really missing, or she'd just abandoned them to ruin their trip.

There were angry messages from her mother. Apparently, Larisa had missed a mother-daughter-cousin 'send Hannah home in style' manicure appointment.

Two messages from Sid wanting to know how the party had gone.

Two more messages from Sid saying that FilmStreams Studios had reached out to him with a contract for Quinn giving him everything he'd demanded to make a new *Poseidon* film.

Three messages from Kahleah.

> Kahleah: I've decided it's over.

> Kahleah: I've packed more than I need and I'm staying in Italy after our trip. Let him have a month alone with the kids and see how he feels.

Larisa opened her social feeds app, which had saved her location as LA so it would give her US news. She searched her name. The latest thing that came up was that guy from the radio show in November. Even her BDSM discussion streams didn't have enough hits to make it to the first page of results.

No one knew she'd been arrested for murder.

No one knew Lucas and Quinn were gone.

She went back to Sid's last message and typed as she began to cry.

> Larisa: That's great. He'll be so excited.

> Sid: Did you talk to him?

> Larisa: A little.

> Sid: So what's next?

Larisa stared down at her screen. She couldn't tell him. Not yet.

As tears blurred her vision, her phone began to vibrate with an incoming call. Thinking it was Sid, she held it still, watching. The ringer began to play music she immediately recognized as her waltz, which was confusing until she managed to clear her eyes and see the name on the screen wasn't Sid's.

"Yes," she said, certain it was a trick, possibly even a hallucination.

For a moment, a breathless silence, then his voice, *that* voice. "Say something else so I can listen to you."

"Everything I have to say, you won't like."

"I suppose I can understand that."

"Then you understand there's only one thing I want to hear you say right now."

More silence. Larisa held her breath.

"It's been a challenge, Larisa. I can't help but feel you've had something to do with it."

"Tell me, you fucking bastard."

"He's here with me. Rifat gave him something to sleep. Want me to take a picture for you?"

Larisa pressed her hand to her mouth to suppress a sob so painful it felt like her throat was splitting in half. When she could speak, she said. "Promise me he's safe."

"Of course he's safe."

"Lucas—"

"I'm sure those CIA goons have been feeding you juicy little tidbits about my demise, but none of it's true. I wouldn't let anything happen to him, just like I'd never let anything happen to you."

But look how close you came to failing.

"My mother's making me come to Milan."

"The full week?"

"We arrive on Friday." Larisa pulled up the words she knew she needed to say, arranged them in her head so they were easier to say naturally. "I'd like to see you."

Lucas laughed softly. "So you can finish Pam's work? I think not."

"I was angry about Quinn. How did you expect me to react?"

"I suppose I understand. But I'm not up for socializing."

"How do I find you?"

"You don't."

"Lucas."

"This is goodbye, Larisa. Quinn chose me. We're riding off into the sunset. You're getting a courtesy call. It's more than you deserve."

Panic zipped through Larisa's mind, momentarily wiping her

thoughts into a blank. It sounded like he was going to hang up, maybe never speak to her again.

"How do you know he chose you?"

"Don't play games."

"You said he chose you. But, given recent events, isn't it possible he had ulterior motives?"

Silence. Larisa prayed she was making the right choice. If Lucas was feeling trapped and suspicious, he might discard Quinn out of hand without bothering to test the accusation. She was betting everything on the fleeting image she'd seen on the CIA surveillance video of Lucas carrying Quinn out of danger like he was the most precious cargo.

"You're jealous," said Lucas, and Larisa couldn't tell if he was making a statement or posing a question.

"When you invited me home, I thought" —she made a strategic pause as though she was struggling to speak, not that she had to pretend very much— "I thought you wanted us to be together. All of us."

"That's what made you angry?"

"I didn't want to share. But now, today, thinking I'd lost both of you." She let the tears well up and the hiccups of several painful sobs echo into the phone. Outside a crunch of tires on the gravel. The doctor had arrived. She was out of time.

"I could bring you a gift," she said. "The CIA has a laptop they say they stole from you. Some kind of database with names and accounts."

"Do they know what it is?"

"Do you want it back?"

One beat, two. The doctor was knocking on the door. Finally, Lucas sighed. "*Norma* is playing at La Scala next Tuesday. First intermission, the mezzanine bar."

Before she could ask if he'd bring Quinn the line went dead.

Chapter 16

Life of the Dead

Quinn woke unable to breathe. The pain was everywhere but what he felt most was the fire in his throat closing in, shutting off his air. Lurching upright, he didn't even manage to open his eyes as he floundered like a drowning man. His reaching hands landed on something solid, an arm, which he pulled forward, clutched it to his chest like an anchor.

Another arm came around the back of his head, drew it down so the side of Quinn's face rested on the anchor arm. A soft voice that sounded far away and underwater, "Shhhh." The hand at the back of his head gently stroked his hair. "You're safe now."

Slowly, Quinn found he could breathe, just not in the usual way. His throat was swollen but not closing over. If he could just calm down, it would be better. One breath, a focus on the process, a reprogramming of his expectations. The second breath was easier. Quinn dragged open his eyes and squinted against pristine morning sun made all the more brilliant by the white stucco walls, the shards of wood embedded in the rounded windows that framed the double doors. They stood open to a balcony. Beyond it, the red tile rooftops and scattered greenery of a medieval Italian town.

Naked. Understanding this brought the burn of tired tears to his eyes. To have endured so much and still wake up exposed felt like failure. All he wanted in that moment were three layers of hoodies and a soft pair of joggers. He wanted the respect of the person who bought them for him, a person who cared more about his comfort than their own desires. Even worse, he found he still wanted that person to be the one who was now stroking his hair, bestowing this rare moment of tenderness.

This is what it takes for Lucas to be gentle, thought Quinn.

He struggled to draw himself from Lucas's arms. His captor/lover/enemy/friend sat in a carved wooden chair at Quinn's bedside wearing an expensive looking shirt and vest. His pocket watch. The beginnings of a goatee, which meant Quinn had been out for a while.

"What happened?"

"What do you remember?"

"You left me in the labyrinth. And these people took me."

The accusation only made Lucas shrug. "You were never in any real danger. That ring I gave you tells me where you are."

Quinn found it difficult to move his head to look down and find his hand. Not that hand, the other one. They seemed alien parts of him, connected and yet aloof. He wanted to pull the ring off and fling it across the room, but his arms weren't working yet.

"I was tortured." The words were too forceful. Pain shot down his throat making the muscles spasm. Panic rushed at him as once again it felt impossible to breathe.

"I didn't expect she'd move so quickly." Lucas almost sounded regretful, then he added, "But a baton's nothing that would've killed you."

"It wasn't nothing," rasped Quinn. "She put that thing inside me. *Inside me.* I thought I was dying."

"And yet here you are." Lucas gazed at him without an ounce of visible remorse, that old condescension, the iron will. And yet, he had to have felt something. He was sitting there. He'd been waiting for Quinn to wake up.

"She's gone now." Lucas had the nerve to smile as he reached forward and stroked the side of Quinn's arm. A touch that set off small electrical fires in Quinn's skin. Lucas's hand moved down to Quinn's belly. His thumb stroked over the swollen bruise of skin where the baton had been held in place so long the smallest blood vessels had ruptured.

"If she's gone, why don't I feel safe?" asked Quinn.

Lucas's expression still revealed no story of compassion as his eyes did their work of devouring Quinn's body. "Rifat wants to give you something for pain. Are you in pain?" He pushed away the bedding covering Quinn's waist. "I told him you were tougher than that." Lucas pulled Quinn's knees apart and touched the insides of his thighs. The baton had been there and closer, had brought its unquenchable fire to all the places Lucas wanted, the soft places.

Quinn whimpered. Instead of retreating, he leaned into Lucas's arm, took hold of him, and wrapped it around his waist in a hug, a brief grasp for comfort stolen when it should have been offered. "I'm glad it was me and not Larisa."

The words had their desired effect. Lucas flinched backward so forcefully his chair legs scraped the floor. "Larisa would never have been in that situation."

"Because you wouldn't have used her as bait?" Quinn leveled his gaze on Lucas with what he hoped was a look that showed every modicum of justified rage. "Tell me you never put her in a situation like that."

Lucas opened his mouth for a ready response, then closed it.

"Admit you weren't good for her," said Quinn.

"You're being dramatic."

"If she'd stayed with you, sooner or later one of your enemies would've come for her. They still could."

By all appearances, Lucas was the same as he'd been before, the perfect posture, the immaculate clothes, that smooth veneer of a curated self. But Quinn's kidnapping had cracked something beneath the armor and now his words struck there, that invisible, epicenter of shaken faith.

"She loves me," said Lucas.

"It isn't a fair love, and you know it."

Lucas threw up his hands. "You think I should be a monk,

swear off all passion for the sake of my work?" He shook his head. "It doesn't matter now. I'm presumed dead." To Quinn's surprise he said, "The CIA had set explosives. I went in early, got you, left behind some bodies. That woman is dead and all her people. The explosives went off. Buried about half a million euro in wine. An underground restaurant collapsed in the process. So many bodies. They'll be half decomposed by the time they're uncovered."

"Larisa thinks I'm dead?"

Lucas sighed. "I really wonder what you think I am." He pulled out his phone and showed Quinn his screen of messages with Larisa. Lucas had sent a picture of Quinn sleeping and the message, *All fine.*

Quinn thought there was nothing remotely true about a status update of 'all fine,' but at least she knew. And he was relieved to notice that his hands had been hidden beneath the bedding so Larisa hadn't seen the angry red ligature marks the ropes had left on his wrists.

"Now what?" asked Quinn.

"Now we plan our future."

"Our future," repeated Quinn. His brain couldn't process the words. He was about to blurt out, *My future's with Larisa,* when the door opened and Rifat came in, impatient in a way that made Quinn think he'd been listening in. "Lay off him." Rifat carried a glass of water, a bottle of pills, and a tray of the Italian version of saltine crackers.

Rifat laughed at Quinn's expression. "These are the crackers you like, right? When you were doing those interviews in London, the actor said—" Rifat stopped like he was embarrassed. Of course he was. He worked for a man who saw the consideration of other people's needs and desires as a weakness.

"They're perfect." Quinn tried to get the package open, but his fingers couldn't grip, so Rifat did it for him.

"You're interrupting," said Lucas.

"What's the hurry? You're dead. There's nowhere to go."

"Not true. We're still going to Milan."

"What? Why?"

"Quinn needs to hear music in the greatest opera house in the world."

Rifat stared at him. "The Sforza think you stole their two million deposit. The CIA just tried to kill you."

"And we'll let them think they did. Call Letto, have him start the process for a declaration of death."

"But—"

"It's fine. Actually, it's better than fine. We'll start over in Milan."

"At an opera house with hundreds of people?"

"Buy the tickets with cash. My usual box."

Rifat nodded slowly, a motion that appeared against his better judgement. "But not Winter's ball, right?"

Lucas laughed. "If we can go to the opera, we can go to a masked ball. In fact, we'll leave tonight."

"Quinn isn't ready to move."

"Sure he is."

They both looked at Quinn. He had taken the smallest nibble of the corner of a cracker and was trying to chew it. Everything felt wrong. The motion of his jaw, the feel of the cracker crumbs on his tongue. He kept chewing because swallowing would certainly be worse. If Larisa were with him, she'd hold his hand and walk him through it. He'd feel safe knowing whatever happened, she'd fix it. They'd get through it together. *Larisa.* Tears filled Quinn's eyes as he washed the cracker down with water that burned his throat like liquid glass.

The painkillers Rifat gave him put Quinn to sleep. The first time he woke up it was dark. The next time, he was in a car, laid out in a makeshift bed in the backseat with one of the guys from Umbras driving and Rifat in the passenger seat. More pills, more sleep. He woke in a modern bedroom with cement walls, a lamp in a frosted glass dome, and buffed industrial flooring.

Still naked, as though Lucas wanted to punish him by withholding clothing.

The pain was still terrible in the places he'd been shocked with the baton, but the full body agony had begun to diminish. As he lay in bed, Quinn tested his limits with small movements, fingers reaching to touch each other, hand to chest, to neck, to face. It was a strange thing to touch himself, as though his brain had lost its footing and was surprised to exist in relation to the rest of him. Ears, nose, mouth, teeth. His jaw, the most painful of all the movements he'd attempted. He abandoned his project of awakening his awareness and lay still. It was enough to know he was still intact, startling to realize that, aside from some rough scraped feeling of his skin, he hadn't been seriously injured. The damage was all on the inside.

The sky out the window of his new room was an indeterminate overcast. Sounds of conversation drifted in from under the door, which sat in its hinges several inches up from the floor, a strange urban chic design. He heard high-pitched laughter with a nervous undertone and answering lower-pitched voices, as though Quinn was missing a dinner party.

Eventually, the door opened and Rifat arrived with a plate of cheeses and cured meats in one hand and a bowl of risotto in the other. The prospect of eating anything made Quinn's stomach knot with anxiety.

"I'm not hungry."

"You haven't had anything but crackers for four days."

"Where are my crackers?"

"You finished them yesterday."

The concept of yesterday had no meaning. He thought he could ask about the date, but then he would have to attach himself to some fixture of a reality involving other people and events. He wasn't ready.

"Pills?"

Rifat looked uncertain, and Quinn's anxiety compounded as he understood what that meant. "One more day full dose."

"Lucas doesn't think—"

"Fuck Lucas." Quinn took the risotto and held it waiting. "Two bites and I get one."

"Four bites," said Rifat as he pulled the pill bottle out of his pocket.

Quinn had been living without his stomach. To draw it back to life would be a fresh agony. But he knew Rifat was right. It'd been too long. He'd gained some weight living with Lucas, but not enough he could afford to starve himself. Quinn filled the spoon with creamy rice and smelled it. Gears that had been still began to churn, saliva filled his mouth, the empty place below his ribs began to cramp and gurgle.

"I'm going to regret this."

"Let's think long-term," said Rifat. "Not dying, yeah?"

"Did Lucas tell you to keep me alive?"

"Are you trying to kill yourself?"

Quinn shoved the spoon in his mouth and swallowed what it left there as quickly as he could. The pain made him cough, which sent shards of fire along his jaw and up the sides of his head. One bite down, three to go, then the pill, its thirty minutes of heavenly floating, then sleep.

"How long until the opera?"

"Two days."

"Does that mean its fashion week here?"

"It does."

Quinn wondered if Suzette had managed to steal Larisa's friends for the trip she'd planned. It felt like ancient history now to think of that fall, the drama of Larisa and her friends trapped by her mother.

What if she decided to come? Then Quinn remembered. *She's already here.*

"Where's Larisa now?" he asked.

Rifat gave him a funny look. It took Quinn a moment to

realize it was because Rifat had been caught unprepared and he didn't know if he should tell the truth or lie. Finally, he said, "You don't need to worry about her. Just focus on getting better."

"I'm going to be sick."

"If you're sick, those bites don't count."

"I can't help it."

"Try."

Quinn sucked in a breath and held it. He tried to think about something that wasn't food or Larisa. The nice smooth floor, the exposed beams and ductwork in the ceiling, the abstract art on the walls. But his mind was a dead weight, as stubborn as Sabrina when he tried to move her from her favorite sleeping place. All he could think was, *I'm not ready to see her.*

The thought didn't go away. If anything, it intensified. Eating brought Quinn's dormant physiology online so that he needed to use the bathroom, which brought more pain. He felt like he was pissing seeds and his shit was full of teeth. The agony made him want the pills. But with food in his stomach, they weren't so powerful. He was awake too much, thinking too much, slotting characters into scenes he'd never film, scripting beginnings, middles, and ends of stories he'd never tell, all in a flimsy effort to keep the ants of dreadful anxiety from crawling in and colonizing his brain.

Time passed in a sludge of impressions, sometimes pierced with shards of sunlight, sometimes by the din of distant conversations that came too loud across his ears. Lucas came to visit him in the stillness of the afternoons and stayed into the evenings, restless with his new entrapment.

"Winter's out again," he said. "Gone to an influencer banquet. She wore the worst dress." Lucas kicked at the globe light on the floor. "I've decided it's not so easy to be dead."

Quinn looked up from his journal. "Did you change your cologne?"

"No, why?"

"It's stale."

Lucas turned from the window to peer at him. "Yesterday, you said I reminded you of green oranges."

"Did I?" Quinn wrote that down. He didn't remember yesterday as a defined space. There was just the struggle of eating, of getting out of bed and moving around, of relieving himself.

"What are you writing?"

"Just notes."

Lucas crossed to the bed and snatched the journal out of Quinn's lap. "A list of smells? Why?"

Before Quinn made up his mind to answer, Lucas was flipping through the pages. He sat down at the end of the bed and began to read. The pages stilled as Lucas settled on a section where script filled the space. Quinn leaned forward to see what it was.

"That's not finished."

"What is it?"

Quinn leaned back against his pillows, awash in a wave of fatigue that made his bones ache. "It's something I wrote about our night in the labyrinth."

"And these notes? 'There's no going back now. We're both lost.' So dramatic." Lucas's eyes flicked up to examine Quinn's, missing nothing of his discomfort, how he was working to hold himself back from reaching for the journal and stealing back its secret thoughts.

The eyes lowered again. Lucas continued reading, "'Three cannot live as one, so the game is played, the one most knowing finds their object of desire. The other must honor the loss.'"

Quinn watched Lucas's tongue move in his mouth as though siphoning the words through his teeth.

"It's true, this hasn't turned out as I'd hoped."

This, thought Quinn bitterly, as though they'd embarked on some ordinary affair, as though there'd been choices, with each of them able to define what they wanted with the expectation the others involved would respect them.

"But I still believe your accusation unfair. What happened to you wouldn't have happened to Larisa. She's always been obedient. Your inclinations invited catastrophe from the beginning."

Quinn compressed his face into the hardest, soulless glare he could muster so Lucas could have no doubt exactly how much bullshit Quinn saw hidden in that belief. He said nothing. Now Lucas's armor had been cracked, the silences worked as well as they did with ordinary people. He shifted uncomfortably in his seat.

"Anyway, it's an interesting idea." Lucas stood. "I'm keeping this."

Then he walked out, leaving Quinn alone in bed with his pen and nothing to occupy his mind but the clawing dread of falling through darkness with no floor in sight.

Forgiveness

"I don't want to go tonight," he told Lucas on Tuesday afternoon when they were deciding what to wear to the opera. Or at least, Lucas was deciding. Quinn was sitting up in bed holding his stomach.

"You're going."

"It's safer to stay in."

"You're worried about my safety?" Lucas laughed. He held up a new, open-backed jumpsuit almost identical to the one Quinn had worn to *The Key*'s London premiere in one hand and a black off-shoulder blouse in the other. "I think the jumpsuit."

"The black's formal," said Quinn. He didn't want to wear the blouse any more than the jumpsuit but at least it covered more. If he was allowed a coat, he might be able to keep it draped over his shoulders and burrow inside it where Lucas couldn't touch him.

"Black it is."

"Isn't there a hat with it?"

Lucas looked across the contents of the suitcase that erupted around the room. "I don't see a hat. Did you ask for a hat?"

"It doesn't matter."

"So grouchy," muttered Lucas. "Why don't you want to go?"

"I feel terrible, and I don't want to sit in a public place for hours on end."

"It's a short opera. Two acts, then we'll eat dinner somewhere quiet. My last outing as myself."

"The transgressor dares death," muttered Quinn.

"What?"

"I think you don't want to be dead. Or are you testing it out? Seeing if you'll be recognized?"

"The CIA has no reason to look for us here." Lucas narrowed his eyes. "Unless there's something you'd like to tell me."

"What could I possibly be hiding from you at this point?" Quinn pushed himself out of bed and snatched the blouse out of Lucas's hand, took up the matching pants, and marched to the bathroom.

After he'd dressed, Quinn sat at the vanity and let Lucas do elaborate things with his hair while quizzing him on Milan's famous opera hall. At first Quinn resented both the hair styling and the quizzing. He didn't want to be touched. He didn't want to parrot back information from reading he'd done when he'd been a different person; it just reminded him of how much had changed. Some of that resentment certainly had to do with his fear that he wouldn't be able to provide satisfying answers and Lucas would become angry. His mind was a swamp with only a limited number of very sharp thoughts stabbing through the muck.

La Scala was . . .

"Commissioned by Archduke Ferdinand."

"Named after the church that used to stand at the same site. The church was named after a royal family from Verona."

They walked through Winter's house out to a waiting car. Quinn remembered sitting in Umbras in those fresh, early days when he was still reeling from the revelation about Parish's pregnancy and the opportunity to sink himself into reading had been a balm that paired perfectly with gray Tuscan winter days.

"There used to be a casino in the foyer. Mary Shelley complained about it."

Out the car window, Milan was a city full of cold white stone and modern lights, a world away from Renaissance Florence. "The chandelier was so bright the people of Milan resented it, assuming it was a tool the Austrian empire was using to spy on them."

They arrived. With his arm around Quinn's waist, Lucas steered him through the foyer he'd just mentioned, up the first level of stairs, and up to the second mezzanine. Someone who actually loved him would have found the elevator. Walking was a special kind of torture. Quinn's insides felt like they'd been shrunken and were pulling everything around them too tight.

"And is this the original chandelier?" asked Lucas as they walked into their box on the third level.

"That chandelier is a copy to replace the original which was lost in World War II when bombing collapsed the roof."

"Very good. Pam must not have shocked you too much. Your memory is intact."

Pam, thought Quinn. *The name of that woman was Pam.* It seemed a fact exceptionally large and also irrelevant. Large because it filled in a gap in the narrative; every villain needed a name, a status of belonging. Irrelevant because she was dead now, and all Quinn wanted to do was forget he'd ever met her.

The box was long and narrow, decorated with red silk damask and gold, furnished with two chairs and a banquette. The door of the box led to a private coatroom with another door to the hallway that the usher had locked behind them. Anytime they left, the usher would need to escort them back and unlock the door. An antiquated system from the days when opera viewing was a more opulent affair with champagne or a full meal and boxes became the staging rooms of small pockets of entertainment with conversation and flirtations and perhaps even sex, while the action on stage played in the background.

Their box was on the third level stage right, low enough to the floor Quinn could see the faces of the people sitting in the rows of chairs directly before the stage, but not anyone sitting in the boxes stage left or at the top of the horseshoe at the back of the theater. He hadn't imagined it would be so big.

"What do you feel?" asked Lucas as he opened his bag and pulled out a velvet purse.

"It's nice," said Quinn, intentionally pedantic because he knew it would irritate Lucas. But tonight, for whatever reason, Lucas seemed immune to the ribbing. He smiled. "So you like it. Finally, something that reaches you."

You have no idea what reaches me, thought Quinn even though he thought that probably wasn't true. If he'd been a better actor maybe it would have been true, and Lucas would have one less piece of him claimed. Maybe his old way of thinking, as though his body was a map of barricades, was still true. As long as only some of them remained intact, he could remain untouched.

No, that was certainly no longer true. Lucas had laid claim to every part of him. If ever there was a day when they were separated, Quinn would still feel as he did now. Every memory he reached for, everything he understood about the world and his place in it, contained Lucas.

At his side, humming to himself, the man who'd marked him lifted a pair of opera glasses from the velvet purse, gold plated, etched with what looked like a family crest on the sides of the viewing cones. The lights dimmed. Lucas held the glasses to his eyes and turned his head to look down on the stage. As the orchestra began the overture to *Norma,* Lucas's free hand reached out and planted itself along the inside curve of Quinn's thigh, as though, in the act of looking away, Lucas wanted another way to keep Quinn in his presence.

That hand ruined any chance Quinn had of enjoying the opera.

The music blurred across Quinn's ears, sometimes too loud, sometimes grating. When the curtain rose to reveal the titular character, Quinn was looking down at that hand, which rested with so much confidence in the rightness of its position. If Quinn moved it, or shifted his seat back, the hand would find him again. It would insist on its presence in his life until Quinn challenged it, then they would fight, and Quinn would lose because Lucas was always going to have the stronger play.

It smells like dead roses, thought Quinn. And then, *I can't do this.*

His stomach cramped, he retched, but not strongly enough to throw up. Not yet. He stood, rushed to the coat room. *No trash can.* The walls and floor were covered in red velvet. There wasn't an inch of expendable space ready to receive the contents of his stomach. Quinn bolted out the door into the hall.

"Bathroom?" he asked the first usher he saw.

She pointed him around the corner. There. The door with the friendly blue wc sign.

He vomited in the urinal, a first purge that banished Lucas's hand. A second purge followed as soon as he got a full breath of the smell of his insides mingling with the soap cake at the bottom of the urinal, except the soap cake smelled like peaches, and his vomit smelled like sewage. When it was over, he locked himself in a stall.

If he's angry I didn't come back, I'll tell him I couldn't find an usher to unlock the box, thought Quinn even as he hated himself for this kind of peremptory thinking, the fact that he was already bracing for Lucas's displeasure.

What if I run?

Where? No passport. No money. No phone.

The bathroom door opened. Quinn held his breath. But the shoes walked past his stall to the urinal in the far corner.

If this was a movie, everyone would hate it. The main character is passive, trapped, waiting for someone to save him.

There was no one to save him because Quinn had come here to do the saving. He was supposed to find a way for Larisa to live without Lucas. That had always been the plan.

Fool's errand, he thought. *Larisa was right. I should've just accepted he was going to be involved.*

It has to end, he thought. But the question remained. *How?*

He rested his elbows on his knees. As he tried to slow his

breathing, he began to compose the scene, a fitting climax to the drama of the past several months. He'd be the hero forced into violence by the violence that had been forced upon him. Afterward, he wouldn't be the same, and maybe Larisa wouldn't want a murderer as a partner, but at least she would have choices for herself.

The door swished open. Several men entered at once. Voices echoed out in the hallway. Intermission.

Quinn gathered himself and made his exit. Out in the hall, Lucas stood just to the side of the bathroom doors. When Quinn came to his side, Lucas gave only a bare nod of greeting. His eyes were fixed at some point down the way where the hallway opened into an atrium with cocktail tables. Waiters were walking around serving champagne.

And there, at one of the far tables, wearing a tiered ball gown with bustle and corset, her hair up in tight curls as though she'd just stepped out of a Victorian painting, was Larisa. She was laughing at something her date had said. The red-clad fingers of her long gloves came up and brushed a curl out of her eyes as she gave the man a look. Quinn was too far away to see exactly what kind of look, but it was enough. He shivered.

"Who is that?"

"Roman Acharya." A dark smile pinched Lucas's mouth. "Clever girl."

"What?"

"If I approach them, he'll know I'm not dead."

"And?"

"I owe him money." To Quinn's surprised look, Lucas laughed. "You think I allowed Rifat to declare me dead just because the CIA got too close? The business isn't what it used to be. I've had some . . . difficulties."

"She knew we'd be here."

"Apparently. But the question is, why the staging? What's she hoping? To steal you out from under my hands? To force me into —" Lucas laughed softly. "Ah, yes."

"What?"

"After the incident with that Minnesota man, she told me she was only going to fall in love with men who deserved to die. It was a joke we had."

Quinn wondered how much of it was a joke on Larisa's side. "You killed Hannah's boyfriend?"

"Don't judge me like a simpleton. The man was a waste of air taking advantage of vulnerable women."

You have no idea what you've done to her, thought Quinn.

"So, she's signaling that she's moving on from us. What do you think about that?"

Quinn watched Larisa down the end of her champagne and reach for Roman's, toying with him when he refused to give it up. It was a scene Quinn might have enjoyed in LA, the mystery of an unfamiliar man, the thrill of watching Larisa ply her charm from afar. He wasn't the least bit jealous. Rather, he felt a gentle warmth rising through his chest as he saw how many other people had noticed her, how people walking by turned their heads to look. One man crashed into another's back. All the looking just made her more radiant, as though the spotlight cast by so many eyes made her glow with a secret.

"I think I'd like to watch the second act of the opera," said Quinn. And he meant it. He'd seen her. He knew she was okay. That was enough.

"Let's go test her." Lucas hooked his arm through Quinn's and drew him forward.

Quinn dug in his feet. "Go by yourself."

Lucas yanked on his arm. "Don't be silly."

"I'm not ready."

As soon as she sees me, she'll know.

"Just look like you love me."

"Lucas, stop—"

She'd seen them coming. For a moment, her expression froze. Her eyes skidded over Quinn, an inventory, then a breath of relief.

He hoped whatever she saw was convincing. He didn't want her to know the ruin he was hiding.

They were approaching too fast. Quinn's eyes swam across the balcony, searching for an escape. He thought that balcony was actually called a mezzanine. The columns were Corinthian ivory, the floor travertine. He thought he was beginning to understand the power, the intoxication, of knowing. Or was that lightheadedness caused by something else? He was so far out of his body it seemed the only sense he could rely on was his sight. What a thing to walk into a room and apply names to what he saw, to draw on a store of knowledge and add the weight of meaning to it. In that moment, he could have given a speech to strangers on theater architecture and post-war reconstruction, but he couldn't meet Larisa's gaze.

"There he is, back from the dead already," said Roman. "This is your new friend who got you into so much trouble?" He glanced at Quinn without interest. "Surprised you didn't put him in a trunk and send him down the Arno."

The circumference of the cocktail table meant Larisa was on the other side, so close and yet so far. An onslaught of smells, all of them half rotten. Quinn managed to pick out what he thought was Larisa, a scent just familiar enough to be hers, but slanted, putrefying. For a moment, he thought he would be sick again.

Lucas laughed. "I considered it. But finding love isn't as easy as it used to be. Isn't that right, Larisa?"

She rolled her eyes. "I'm not having any trouble. Are you, Roman?" She didn't wait for an answer before moving on. "We've both agreed the tenor's not wonderful. What do you think?"

"The alto was the low point," said Lucas, like opinions on the quality of the singers were fighting words.

"We thought she was rather good."

Quinn saw Lucas's mouth press into an irritated line as he held back from arguing further. Larisa had won round one in whatever strange game they were playing. It didn't feel real that she was there within arm's reach. He wanted to tell her to run. He wanted to pull her into his arms, but he was terrified she wouldn't feel the way he expected. What was Lucas doing? It didn't seem like he remembered she'd tried to kill him at his birthday party.

Smells: Roses and champagne, not quite as Quinn remembered them. Larisa's freshly done nails, a bruised pink color. He was invisible, a small thing among these three towers of confidence, going through their lines. He tried to hold his breath. He didn't know where to look.

"Well, it's a tragedy anyway," said Roman. "There's no greater love than fated love."

"Otherwise known as human folly," said Lucas.

"Otherwise known as, you just lost everything you had for this boy." Roman clicked his tongue against the top of his mouth. "When Larisa told me you were still breathing, I couldn't believe it. The great Lucas Onslow touched by the fated folly? Impossible. I thought the shame of it alone would have stopped your heart."

"You should be glad it hasn't. Otherwise, you'd never see any of your money."

"On that subject—"

"Let's not talk about business," said Larisa. She hadn't looked directly at Quinn since they'd approached the table. But he could feel her taking him in, noticing, reaching out with her mind, while her body played this game of words with the other men. He didn't know what she saw. His face was no longer a finely tuned extension of his thoughts to meld to his will. It showed what it wished, and he didn't have the strength to stop it.

Lucas set his hand on Quinn's shoulder, again that possessive, overlarge hand, and the smell that came with it. He flinched. Larisa saw it. A hard knob in her throat bobbed as she swallowed down her reaction, kept that winning smile on her face. Her gloved hand came forward and rested in the middle of the table. A moment later, Lucas moved his hand from Quinn's shoulder and rested it over Larisa's. Their fingers moved under the caves of their hands. Quinn blinked, hardly trusting his eyes. If this was a movie, he would have believed she'd just passed Lucas a small, silver object.

"I agree," said Lucas. "No business. Now we all know we're in town at the same time, I'm sure we'll see more of each other. If that's what you want." Lucas focused on Larisa. "To move forward I think the first question is, have you forgiven him?"

Quinn looked up in surprise. Roman also looked surprised, his smile stiffening as though he felt he'd missed a vital step in the conversation. The him in question was Quinn, but he felt he'd missed the introduction of this new topic. Not a new topic, an old one. What did Larisa have to forgive him for?

Leaving her for Lucas.

He was so disoriented by the stirring up of the memories of those early days, Christmas, the rush of desperation that had fueled his equally desperate decision, he barely heard her answer. Then, as soon as he processed it, he hungered to hear it again.

"A thousand times and more," said Larisa, but she still didn't look at Quinn. "Where does that get us?"

"An impasse," said Lucas.

"What exactly are we—"

"Quiet please, Roman," said Larisa. "What are you offering?"

What is happening?

"A final performance to seal our fates," said Lucas.

"I'm listening."

"Quinn has written us a scene."

Now Quinn was staring. Lucas was pulling an envelope from his pocket. "Your script, madam, for the conclusion of our passion play. Whoever finds the person they most desire will possess them without contest until they are no longer wanted."

Did Larisa's hand tremble as she took the envelope, or did Quinn imagine it? He could barely breathe. He didn't quite understand what was happening. But he felt he knew enough to feel it was impossible Lucas would make such an offer. Surely Larisa saw it just as clearly. But since nothing felt clear, he felt the need to warn her. "What's the catch?" asked Quinn.

Lucas ignored him. He extended a hand toward Roman. "Do I ever go back on my word?"

"Never, but you're stretching your limits."

"I have your money. We can discuss it whenever you like. After Friday?"

Roman shrugged as he looked uncertainly between Larisa and Lucas. "After Friday." He reached into the pocket of his tuxedo jacket and pulled out a business card.

"Well, this has been productive. More than worth an evening of horrible singing." Lucas ducked his head toward Larisa. "Until Friday." And again to Roman. "After Friday." Then he cupped his hand around Quinn's neck to turn him around and steer him back toward their box.

"What just happened?" asked Quinn.

"Exactly what we've planned."

We had a plan?

"I will have her back. She'll never find you before I find her." Lucas stared at nothing, his gaze focused inward as they waited for the usher to unlock their box. "I know her too well. It's impossible to fail this time."

In the coatroom, Quinn held back as Lucas went forward. He wasn't ready to take his seat. Larisa's voice lingered in his mind, a song, a whisper. *Have you forgiven him?* Lucas had asked. And she had answered, *A thousand times over.*

Heat warmed Quinn's face. He wished Lucas had given him a chance to answer the same question. *Have you forgiven her?* Then he could have looked at her, could have held her gaze and transmitted everything he wanted her to know when he said, "A thousand times and more."

Chapter 18

Tollbooth of the Heart

"How was it?" asked Jaden.

"Did you take Quinn in your arms and—"

"Don't be ridiculous, Rosa," said Kahleah. "They weren't alone."

Larisa flopped down on the sofa in the suite the designer Fast69 had rented for her mother for fashion week. Only four hours had passed since she'd left to meet Roman at the opera, but she was exhausted with a deep-boned fatigue, as though she'd spent her time swimming against a river current instead of sitting in a theater. Her friends, the old clan of sorority sisters, leaned in, eager to hear her news. It felt like too much to tell them.

She knew the opera had nothing to do with how she felt. It'd been those ten minutes during intermission, standing across from Lucas knowing she couldn't yell or scream or cry. By not allowing any of her true feelings to show, she'd presented herself as someone open to him. He was the current she'd held herself against, the magnet drawing her forward. And the whole time, Quinn in her peripheral vision, like a rock in the waves; she hadn't been allowed to reach for him.

Even more disturbing, it almost felt like he hadn't existed. Those ten minutes had been all Lucas. As soon as she'd seen him coming, it had felt impossible to look away. She'd been like a trapped lamb, smelling the blood, but unable to save itself.

Which didn't bode well.

"It was fine," she said, an answer that revealed nothing.

Because she didn't want to say that giving Lucas his spreadsheets had felt so, so validating.

Because she didn't want to describe how beautiful she'd felt when his eyes had undressed her and his mouth crinkled at the side with that pleased smirk. As though their interaction at his birthday had ended at their dance and their meeting at the opera was a continuation of that moment, the attempted murder erased so completely, Larisa no longer had access to the rage that had driven her to that point.

She was so glad to see him. Alive. Unhurt.

Jaden sighed. Kahleah rolled her eyes. From the corner, where Suzette was ensconced in an overstuffed chair with her computer, her assistant at one elbow, a sound that was like a puff of frustration. "No, use this one." Suzette pointed at her screen. "It'll be better."

"Did you talk about Friday?" asked Rosa.

"He suggested it actually. Quinn had already created a proposal." Larisa pulled the envelope Lucas had given her from her clutch. She'd read it during the second act, hunched over in her seat using the light from her phone to trace every line of Quinn's boxy, all caps handwriting. It looked like the pages had been copied from a journal. *He's been keeping a journal,* she thought. She could hardly imagine Quinn sitting down and writing even though she knew he'd been a serious writer when he'd been younger.

What else has he been doing? She tried not to let the question overwhelm her. They were so far away from worrying about how they'd changed while they'd been apart, and yet her mind kept jumping ahead.

"I don't think I understand," said Krissy, who'd taken the pages from Larisa.

"Here, let me." Kahleah took them and began to read aloud. "'The darkness does not lie, it reveals. In the labyrinth of a baroque garden, three statues come to life under a full moon. In the north, a woman who still dreams of the stars. To the east, a king who once ruled the world. To the west, an artist who once painted scenes. The three of them, trapped forever in the maze, until one of them finds another who will be their fated mate and thus reveal the maze's exit. The third, left alone, loveless returns to statue's form and waits for the next month's illumination.' Alright, that doesn't make sense to me either."

"The ball on Friday is the maze," said Larisa. "Lucas, Quinn, and I will dance until one finds the other and those two will be joined without challenge. If I find Quinn first, Lucas will leave us alone."

"Obviously, he wouldn't do this if he didn't think he'd find you first, right?" asked Jaden.

Rosa drew her eyebrows together to create a wrinkle. "I don't like this."

"But it's very romantic," said Krissy, swooning onto the couch beside Larisa. "If it's meant to be, you'll find him."

"Unless the game's rigged," said Rosa.

"It will be." Larisa's eyes met Kahleah's, her new ally in all things unvoiced and over complicated.

"Yes, but I'm still confused," said Jaden. "If he finds you first, you'll have to go with him? To be like his girlfriend again? That's not what you want, right?"

"Right," said Larisa, but she said it a beat late, and too softly to sound confident.

For a moment, no one said anything. In one of the bedrooms, Rosa's new daughter Maria Josephina Raphealla started crying. Rosa tilted her head, counting under her breath to see how long it took the nanny to quiet the baby. At ten, when Maria was still crying, Rosa got up and went to intervene.

Krissy yawned. "I think I might go to bed, unless we're doing any strategy? The line to get into Gucci is going to come really early tomorrow."

"I should call Adrian," said Jaden.

As the two of them left, Kahleah moved over and sat beside Larisa on the couch. "You look like a wreck."

"That could be more than accurate."

"You going to tell me what happened last week?"

"I don't think I'm ready for that."

Kahleah reached over and laced her fingers through Larisa's, squeezed tight. "I could talk about how excited I am to be here and not at home."

Larisa nodded her permission, then looked up when Kahleah didn't start talking.

"Maybe that's for later also. You're not going to hear a word I say."

"I'm sorry."

"What would shrink Larisa tell you right now?"

"She'd say, 'Hold onto your dreams.'" *And she wouldn't realize Lucas said that to me once.*

We'll make it if we hold onto our dreams. What he meant was they should hold onto each other. It'd been a perfect moment, now tarnished along with so many other perfect moments.

"Why do I feel like you're worried if he makes you an offer you might say yes?"

Have you always been able to read my mind? wondered Larisa, a little irritated with herself that the friend she'd fallen for in college had been Jaden and not Kahleah.

"The way I've managed to keep him away is by saying maybe over and over and over. It was never possible to close the door on him and turn the key. And now I'm here, I'm supposed to say no and trust him to honor that even though it's never been possible before. I'm so tired of being afraid. Even worse, when I think about it, you know the last time I wasn't afraid?"

"You were with him."

"I was with him. Logically I know I'm not going back. Everything from last week should've convinced me that he's a monster. But brain chemistry still lights up and fires off all these chemicals that tell me, 'That was a good life, you were happy then.'"

"But Quinn—"

"Quinn's an unknown. We've barely begun, and look at the beginning. Shrink me would tell real me this is a transition relationship, a bridge to something I don't know how to find, that we're a boom-and-bust combination." To Kahleah's questioning look, Larisa said, "I love him too much for it to ever live up to expectations."

"Your brain's a scary place."

"Thanks."

"Not that you'd ever ask me for advice, but I'd tell you to just go for it. You know he's not a criminal. That's a step up."

Larisa laughed. "You make it sound easy."

"It can be that easy."

The days between Tuesday and Friday's masquerade ball stretched into a shrink-wrapped eternity. When Larisa wasn't attending a show, she was behind the scenes, narrating socials videos for Fast69. She survived an after-party where someone recognized her and asked very loudly if she thought she was kinky because she'd had bad parents. She tried on clothes and staged fashion moments around Milan, sometimes with her mother, sometimes with other models. It often felt like everyone, including her mother, had forgotten Larisa wasn't a model. Even when the sample size didn't fit her, no one complained, or said how she had the wrong body. They just found something else.

In her spare moments, Larisa sent messages to every person in Lucas's black book who'd answered her phone calls weeks earlier. To trap Lucas, she needed one plan and three redundancies. She couldn't trust any of his former partners to do what they said. Most importantly, she couldn't trust herself. In the mirrors of a dozen dressing rooms, she practiced saying no.

"This is the end for us." *Not strong enough.*

"Lucas, I want you to know I can't do this anymore." *Don't use his name. He'll see it as an invitation to parse words.*

Do what? he'll ask.

Have you in my life. Then he'd answer, *I'm not in your life.*

"Why do you want me if I'm in love with someone else?" *Again, don't invite a conversation. Don't act like you want him to talk you out of it.*

"No more."

"Leave me alone."

"Leave *us* alone."

Thursday night was the dinner honoring her mother. They sat side by side at an elevated table under hot lights listening to commemorative speeches from three decades of fashion icons. Suzette received a plaque. The pictures were endless. In a few of them, Larisa lost her smile because she thought she saw Lucas lurking along the wall of the restaurant.

That night, she dreamed of him stealing into the suite through her bedroom window, pinning her to the bed, and stroking her ear with his tongue until she agreed to kiss him. She woke on the edge of an orgasm, Krissy sound asleep in the far bed, the only other person in the room.

Friday afternoon, which was very early LA time, Larisa called Dr. Bade for a phone consultation.

"I'm making a choice tonight," said Larisa. "I'm afraid it'll be the wrong one."

"Why?"

"I need to tell someone no and I'm not sure what he'll do."

"You're afraid he'll reject you?"

I'm afraid of what he'll do if he believes the rejection's real. But then she thought, maybe yes, there was an element of fear of his rejection. She hated to think it. "Maybe part of me has been putting this off because I wanted to keep him as a backup. Everything until now, maybe I felt it was okay if it failed because I could fall back on him."

"Are we talking about college man?"

She and Dr. Bade hadn't talked about Lucas since she'd first come to LA. Even in therapy, Larisa had hidden how present Lucas remained in her mind. It made it easier to forget. What kind of convoluted mind trick was that, to hold on to someone while also erasing them?

"I don't want to hurt him."

He's hurt me.

"But having boundaries isn't malicious," said Dr. Bade. "If he cares about you, he'll respect what you want."

Those aren't things he understands.

"Maybe," said Larisa.

"And if he doesn't respect you—"

"I know."

"Larisa. Let me finish. If he doesn't respect you, what you're giving him is more than he's earned. That's something we talk about, right? You're a giver. You're always giving. You have very low expectations for what people give back to you."

"He has given me . . . some things."

"Not respect. Not trust."

Silence filled the phone line. Larisa thought, *I already know all this. It's not going to matter when I'm in the moment.* She'd had her chance to turn him in. She'd had so many chances. *Why didn't Quinn let me kill him when it felt possible?*

"It feels like I'm punishing him. And he's not able to understand why I would do that."

Dr. Bade's breath wisped across the phone speaker. "You've been hiding this from me."

You have no idea.

"We don't have enough time to unpack what you just said. So I want you to focus on this. None of what you just told me matters. Put it away. Only allow yourself to think about one thing. You're doing this for you. How he'll feel, or what he'll think, or do, or anything that happens after your decision, doesn't matter. You do it for you. Not the you who cares about him or the you who rationalizes every decision to within an inch of its life, just you, your emotional core. I know you have one of those."

A knock sounded on the bedroom door.

"I need to go," said Larisa. "Thank you. I'm sorry."

"We'll talk about it when you're back, or we won't. That's your choice as well."

Suzette bustled in with Larisa's masquerade costume in her arms. "You haven't done your hair yet?"

"I'm wearing a wig." Larisa pointed to her bed where her corset, mask, and a blond wig lay waiting for her attention.

Suzette made a face. "The girls seem nervous. Is there something going on tonight I should know about?"

"I think they're thinking about maybe cheating on their husbands if a situation presents itself."

"I suppose that would be exciting if I was your age."

"It could happen to you. The mask evens the playing field." Larisa took the corset to the bathroom and began to undress.

"But I always hope to find your father and if it isn't him, I lose interest."

Larisa poked her head out of the doorway to see if her mother was being sarcastic.

"You're surprised?"

She thought of what Quinn had said on the jet to Minnesota at Christmas about how her parents' love had worn into each other's grooves. "If you wanted him to be here, why didn't he come?" she asked.

"Meetings. Gio Corito was caught with a fifteen-year-old actress in her trailer. The studio has called in your father to arbitrate so the production doesn't get shut down."

"Someone else could've handled it."

Suzette shrugged as though this was an old story and she was past letting it bother her. "Your father's a savior. Something needs to be done, he does it better than anyone else."

That's where I get it from, thought Larisa, although it had been a while since she'd felt that old buzz of confidence in a job well done.

"I'm glad I came," said Larisa. "I'm glad you asked for what you wanted."

"One of us has to be selfish." Suzette fluffed her hair like a drama queen. "Can't say I hate that it's me. But I hope you've had fun."

"I have."

"And you're going to try to be better when we get home?"

Larisa came out of the bathroom holding the corset up over her breasts. She turned so her mother could tighten the laces. "Why does it matter so much to you that I'm good?"

"It's a hard world. All a woman has is her looks and her reputation. If you were in my business—"

"I'm not."

"That's right. You're currently in no business, following the plan of a junior PR manager who thinks you can make a career freelancing as a mental health consultant."

"What's wrong with that?" Larisa took a breath as she felt her torso contract into the line of the corset.

"What if the studio had hired you for this Corito production? You're called in, Corito or one of the producers says, talk to this girl. Tell her she's not upset. What do you do?"

"I ask for her side of things. I tell her she has options."

"If she wants to work in this town again, she doesn't. And you're paid by the studio. You're biased. But that won't matter. They won't hire you because everyone thinks you're a nymphomaniac who likes to beat men. Literally and figuratively."

"I see your point."

"Do you?"

Larisa was surprised to see moisture shimmering in her mother's eyes.

"You're not going anywhere you want to be, Larisa. And the clock's ticking. I don't understand why you can't see that."

"I'm working on it."

Suzette gave her a long look, then brushed at her eyes. "This is beyond. I've already done my face."

"It's a masquerade, Mom."

"Krissy said Lucas would be there."

Larisa was thankful she was bent over, gathering up the skirt of her dress so she could easily step into it. "He comes every year."

"You knew that, and you didn't mention it? I could accidently dance with the man who burned down our Christmas tree? Abused Hannah? Stole your boyfriend? Will he be there as well?"

"Probably."

"Larisa. This life you have."

Larisa slipped her arms into the sleeves of the dress and turned so Suzette could close the zipper. Unlike her usual style, Larisa had brought a dress that covered her from neck to toe. The sleeves even had diamond shaped extenders with finger loops to cover the tops of her hands. Lucas believed he could find her in a room full of people. Maybe that was true, but she wasn't going to make it easy for him.

"It's okay."

"Is it?"

It will be.

Chapter 19

Masquerade

Winter Duryea's end of fashion week masquerade was meant to mark the beginning of the Carnivale festival in Venice. The year Larisa had been with Lucas, they'd come to Milan, seen the fashion shows, gone to the ball, then taken the overnight sleeper to the city of canals where the true party began. She didn't remember much about the ball except how happy she'd been. Deliriously, gloriously happy.

Now with a clearer head, she thought the mix of fashion with Carnivale ambiance produced a unique atmosphere where almost anything was possible as long as the masks stayed in place. From the moment she stepped into the venue, it was as though her foot touched down on enchanted ground, a current went up through her foot and shivered across her body. It felt as though she'd crossed a threshold into a different realm with different rules, a mingling of desire, and energy with only the boundaries of one's imagination to limit their dreams.

Dreams can also be nightmares, thought Larisa. Despite the enchantment, she knew too well how easily the underbelly of her mind could rise up and thwart her. She stood in the middle of her posse like a queen ensconced in her retinue and told herself she was stronger than that. She wasn't going to let Lucas trick her again.

Suzette, Rosa, and Jaden had all decided on sleek modern gowns that showed off their bodies with matching masks that covered the bare minimum facial real estate. Krissy was wearing a hand-beaded, couture pantsuit she'd bought off the runway for a price tag that would have covered the rent on Larisa's apartment for three months. And Larisa and Kahleah had opted for full Carnivale vintage in matching silver and navy blue. Kahleah wore breaches, a vest, and a knee-length blue coat with feathers along the collar and cuffs. Larisa wore a voluminous gown that increased her wingspan by three feet, hiding her body. More importantly, her mask hid the circumference of her face and the giant, tricornered hat with a peacock's worth of plumes engulfed the back of her head.

They left Suzette at the door and migrated up to the organ balcony to look down on the festivities. The ball was being staged at an old church that had been turned into a trendy rental venue. Modern glow globes rested on a net suspended from the ceiling. Bunting had been draped between the columns of the vestry, illuminated with electric candelabra. Green velvet benches lined the walls and a security guard at the stairs up to what had once been a belfry, but was now a hostel, kept track of who was going in and out of the private rooms. A sixteen-piece string orchestra played everything from Renaissance two-steps to polkas.

"I like your mom's fall gala better," said Krissy. "This looks complicated."

"I'm the only one who has to dance."

"How are you going to dance in that get up?" asked Rosa.

"Carefully," said Larisa.

"But don't we all have to be dancing if we're going to find Quinn?"

"Quinn doesn't dance," said Larisa. "Once you find him, don't leave him."

"And we can't leave until the end of the night," said Kahleah.

"But what if one of us meets someone who—" began Krissy.

Rosa giggled. "I think we'll manage."

"Well, I don't want to mess it up. I've never been in the same room as a criminal before," said Krissy.

"He came to graduation."

"That's right." Krissy sighed. "If I find him on accident and the evening evolves . . ."

"Oh my God, Krissy," said Kahleah.

"I'm just saying, the whole idea is that we won't recognize him, right? So an accidental encounter could happen."

They looked down at the party. Rows of dancers filled the central floor of the church with everyone else standing on the sidelines watching or drifting in and out from the nave, where the food had been set up, or from the gardens where strings of white lights illuminated a meditation pool and pairs of lounge chairs.

It was the perfect setting for bodies to come together, parachute off the cliff of passion, and walk away unscathed, or not, as Larisa had years before.

"I don't think this is going to work," said Rosa. "There are hundreds of people down there. Half of them are dressed like you two, can't even see their eyes. Anyone could be anyone."

"That's what makes it the labyrinth," said Larisa.

"How do you truly know someone?" muttered Kahleah philosophically.

"Can we take a picture?" asked Jaden as she ducked around a support column, flagged down a person dressed as a court jester, and shoved her phone into their hands.

Larisa and Kahleah stood together with the other sisters around them posing. Buried beneath her costume, Larisa found she didn't need to do anything besides stand. Her mask was her face, frozen, wiped clean of any recognizable features, facial tics, or inflections. She was even more anonymous than when she'd been playing the Queen at Club D. Only her voice would reveal her. Down in the din of the party, even that would be difficult.

The mask allowed her to hide her own doubts as she descended the staircase, her hand on Kahleah's shoulder so she wouldn't fall down the narrow, stone steps. Once on the floor, surrounded by the movement of the party, she took hold of Kahleah's hand. The two of them turned outward from each other to compensate for their lack of peripheral vision in the masks.

"We should've practiced at the hotel," said Kahleah.

Masked people rolled past in an unending stream, all of them seeming strangers. Tall, short, fat, skinny, most in the middle ground of average, too many wearing costumes similar to theirs that masked body shape and gender performance.

Quinn might not even be here. Larisa pushed the thought away. Lucas had committed to this scenario. To win it without following the rules he'd designed would be a hollow victory.

A woman wearing Valentino came up and asked to take a picture with them. As soon as she left, an Italian couple asked if they would dance the quadrille. Kahleah laughed, but the woman took her arm and began to lead her into an empty space on the floor. The man took Larisa's arm.

"It's easy to learn. No worries," he said.

Larisa strained to hear his voice beyond the words. A higher pitch than Lucas. He was too short to be either Lucas or Quinn. The four of them danced a haphazard quadrille that became repetitive after the first pattern. Larisa watched the other quads of couples on the floor. She counted eight in total, thirty-two people. Many were learning the dance, were laughing, or already halfway to a blissful intoxication that turned historical pattern dancing into something sensual. She marked two people in tuxedos who could be Lucas. When the dance ended, she made her way toward the first one while she argued with herself over the chances that Lucas would deign to wear something as ordinary as a black tuxedo to Winter's ball.

He'd do it just to throw me off.
Who does he believe I'll look for?
Quinn.
So he'll have made sure it's hard to find him, but Lucas himself might not be hiding.

The first tuxedo was clearly not Lucas. Larisa danced a minuet with the second tuxedo. Halfway through, a man in colonial costume and extravagant gold and black mask that wrapped around the back of his head cut in. Lucas's height and general body type. Her heart leapt with possibility. Her hands began to sweat in her gloves as her fingers brushed his, as their eyes, hidden deep behind the holes in their masks, searched each other for recognition. A graceful dancer, poised, practiced. But then he spoke and the spell broke. Not Lucas, a man with a Russian accent saying he was jealous of her hat.

After that, Larisa retreated to the nave for a drink. Straws had been provided so those wearing the traditional masks with no mouth holes wouldn't have to lift them too high to drink. She stood back against the wall and slowly sipped as her eyes combed over every person who approached the refreshment tables. Here was Winter on the arm of a designer who Larisa had met the night before. There was Suzette, surrounded by admirers, most of them easily recognizable beneath their small masks.

None of them were Quinn.

He would stay near the walls or find a place to stand and observe, she thought. *He won't be comfortable out in the crowd.*

"Are you excited?" Lucas asked Quinn as they stood at the edge of the dance floor and watched the rows of dancers move toward the apse of the church in a rush of hurried steps that matched the quickening rhythm of the music. "Your bid for freedom."

Quinn glared at him from behind his carnival mask, which had been painted with gilded playing cards, its edges tucked up under a frilled puff of a baby-blue hat that hid all of his hair and his ears. There were holes for his nose but not the mouth. Not that it mattered. Lucas had taped his mouth shut beneath it, making his already reduced capacity to breathe even smaller.

His dress was the same pastel blue as the hat, a halter style with an open back that dipped all the way down to the top of his ass where Lucas's hand rested. The skirt was a gathered puff of tulle hiding the bulge of flesh between his legs. Because the back was so low, he was going commando. Every time someone looked at him, heat rushed up his neck and bloomed sweat along the edges of the mask. He was sure everyone knew, that they were all imaging what they'd find if they lifted his skirt or dipped their fingers past the flimsy barrier of that plunging back.

Nothing about this scene felt like a bid for freedom. Even as the word caught in his mind and turned itself around in a tornado, Quinn knew what Lucas meant was, *This is where we bid for the chance at Love. May the best man win.* If Quinn's life were a movie, the only way he'd be the one coming out the winner was if this was a comedy of the 1990s cross-dressing variety as seen through the eyes of straight white, slightly homophobic men.

This wasn't a comedy. And Lucas, in his elegant evergreen coat with silver trim and a mask that only covered his eyes, looked the part of the hero. He wasn't trying to hide, which Quinn thought was an error on his part. He had only thought of this scene as a game of chase. He hadn't thought that if Larisa spotted him first, it could also be a game of avoidance.

Lucas moved his hand from Quinn's ass to his wrist and checked the ring with the tracker in it. "You have until midnight, Cinderella. Find her and she's yours. You cannot remove your mask, you cannot speak to her. She must see through your disguise without help. You cannot leave early. Buona fortuna."

Quinn watched Lucas plunge into the crowd with the predatory air of a jungle cat on the hunt. He touched his hand to his face and felt the plastic, painted lips of the mask, his imprisoned mouth underneath. It would be easy enough to remove the ring, set it somewhere, gift it to a stranger, then turn and walk out, refuse to play Lucas's game.

What if he finds her?

Rigged game though it was, Quinn couldn't leave until he knew Larisa was safe. If there was a best man in this scenario of spotting Larisa incognito, it had to be Quinn, who'd loved her first when she wore a mask. And he knew Larisa wouldn't be standing back and observing. She would be out in the crowd, hunting for him the same way Lucas was hunting for her.

The dance floor was clearing. The PA announced that the next dance would be a quadrille. Some people were moaning that they didn't know what that was. Some drunk person shouted, "Stick to the nineteenth century!" Not that it did any good. The church was long, the musicians sequestered all the way up on the ambulatory. The high ceiling sucked up sound and sent it back in distorted reverberations so that everything was muddled.

Find Larisa.

Quinn saw a man eyeing him in that way that made him feel like he needed more clothes. Without giving himself time to think about it, Quinn reached for his hand and led him out onto the floor.

"I don't know how," said the man. Quinn quieted him by pressing a single finger to his lips. They got into line. There were enough people who knew what they were doing that his partner had others to mimic. The hardest part for Quinn was remembering he was dancing the woman's role. He'd done both at New Year's. And neither since then.

An eternity.

But as soon as the music pushed into its full melody, Quinn remembered his steps, remembered Lucas's hard instructional gaze, and the softer moments when Quinn had felt the thrill of his first triumphant seduction mingling with the fission of first true fear. He allowed the memories to wash over him and fade into the hypnotic pattern of the dance. He listened to the feel of strangers' fingertips in his hands. He looked into the eyes of the women dancers when they all danced the circle around their kneeling men. His mind pieced together camera angles, shots, cuts. It would focus on the couple two down on his left, the most authentic dancers. It would focus on the woman four couples down on his right who wore one of the most extravagant of the carnival costumes, a blue and silver gown with a skirt that wouldn't fit through most doorways and a tricornered hat stuffed with feathers.

The camera would linger on her if only for the play of color, it would allow the audience to marvel at how something so large and puffed could convey elegance with so little movement.

As the song ended, Quinn retreated to the sidelines to catch his breath and push back the tears suddenly threatening as despair clutched at his throat. *I have no idea how to find her,* he thought. *What kind of hell have I written for us with no assured escape? There'll be no point to any of it if Lucas finds her first.*

He'll claim her and she'll have to go with him.

Al fine.

Down the line, the woman in the blue and silver costume was also coming off the floor. Maybe he'd caught her eye. Now he'd have to find a way to refuse the next dance without speaking. His throat ached from the swallowed back tears, from the dry cavern of his mouth, and the thick tongue trapped within.

If this were a movie, it'd be—

If this were a movie, I'd just—

So many people. Every time he tried to look closely at someone, their movement rushed them out of focus. Someone put their hand on the exposed skin of his back and he flinched away, stumbled into someone else. He couldn't breathe. The tape—

As he reached up to pull at it, if only to get some air flow against his skin, that woman in the blue and silver came up to him, pressed something into his hand and said, "Find the man dressed like me." And then she was gone, diving through the crowd without even a paused step.

Quinn looked down at his hand. There, nestled in the wrinkled palm of his glove, was his prayer bead bracelet, the one that'd been his nervous talisman for years until that past spring when he'd given it to Larisa as a toy to entertain baby Sabrina.

Dizzy with surprise, he turned to try to find the woman in blue and silver. She was already halfway down the length of the church, visible only by the fluff of feathers bobbing above the crowd. *Larisa.* He wanted to follow her, to grab her, and hold on, and never let go.

This isn't over.

But what is she doing?

The rules, as Lucas had explained them, a convoluted interpretation of Quinn's labyrinth scene, said whoever found the person they wanted first won the night. Larisa had found him and passed on, had in fact gone out of her way to make sure no one had cause to notice their interaction.

She's going after Lucas, thought Quinn. A tremor rippled through his chest. It felt like failure. *I should help her.*

He started to follow Larisa, then stopped. His fingers massaged the beads in his hand. She'd given him instructions. She had a plan. He needed to follow it. *Find the blue and silver man first, then both of us help Larisa.*

The other blue and silver costumed figure wasn't hard to find. Quinn had taken only a few steps toward the front of the church when he saw him coming down the belfry stairs. *Sid?* he wondered. But as he closed the distance between them, he thought not. The posture didn't seem familiar, the gait decidedly different than his friend's.

As soon as the figure cleared the security guard at the base of the stairs, Quinn stepped up to them.

The figure took a step back, surprised. "Oh, hello."

A familiar voice. One of the sisters.

"Do you speak English?" she asked.

He recognized the voice. *Kahleah.*

Quinn held up the beads.

"Oh. Oh fuck, Quinn?"

He glanced around to see if anyone had heard her. Being named felt like it was against the rules, and it suddenly felt absolutely important that they not get caught. He took her hand and led her through the archway into the room with the food, picked up a plate, and began to fill it even though he wasn't free to eat.

"I'm confused," said Kahleah.

He could only shake his head.

With their plates full, they found a place in the shadows along the walls. He spread his fingers in a hang ten, then held his hand to his ear like an old-fashioned telephone. The expressionless oval of Kahleah's mask stared at him for a moment before comprehension dawned and she dug her phone out from the pocket of her jacket.

Quinn typed a message, then, watching for anyone who was looking their direction, he passed the phone back. Kahleah read it and then said,

"The plan was to find you and stay with you until midnight. The Kahn's jet is waiting."

He took the phone back. It was ten-thirty. Far too much time for something to still go wrong. He typed another message.

"Larisa's doing her thing," said Kahleah, reading over his shoulder. Quinn sensed she was holding out on him, so he slapped at her heavily padded shoulder. "She said we don't need to wait. If she's not there by twelve-thirty, we leave without her."

Not happening, thought Quinn.

He typed another message asking if Larisa had been pulled in with the CIA. If yes, had they set up a meeting point?

"She didn't tell us," said Kahleah. "There's a lot that's happened. I'm not sure about all of it. Here, let me just tell the girls I've got you. We'll set up a rotation so it still looks like you're playing the game. Do you think he's watching?"

Quinn thought the answer was yes, but he had no idea how. He scanned the room for Lucas's green coat. As he searched, he realized the question wasn't if Lucas was watching, it was why Larisa hadn't told her sisters the whole plan. *What's she planning to do that she doesn't want them to see?*

The gardens were cooler than inside the church, but with all the layers of her costume, Larisa felt more of a suggestion of cool than an actual breeze on her skin. She'd run from Quinn as far as she could and now she was breathless, and her neck ached from her headpiece bouncing around.

He's safe, she thought.

As quickly as the thought came, doubts squirreled it away. *Safe for the moment.* What they were doing here was the work of the rest of their lives.

Dramatic, Larisa.

And yet, it felt true. Tonight she made up for years of failing to be selfish as Dr. Bade had put it. The term rested uncomfortably in Larisa's mind. She thought if Dr. Bade had been a better therapist, she'd have recognized that positive words always had a stronger motivating factor than negative ones. Selfish was a negative word to its core. Who wanted to be selfish? Even when Disney villains got their own movies, they worried about the strength of their own desires overpowering the greater good. Plus, selfish didn't play well with others.

That was probably her point, thought Larisa as she pressed her hand against her stomach to try to ease her breathing. *I'm supposed to make a decision that's just about me and what I want.*

What I want.

What I want.

She should go back inside and get a water before she passed out. As Larisa turned to go back down the path, a figure emerged from one of the awnings of the swinging benches that lined the garden path.

"Larisa."

She stepped back as though to run the other way. Lucas grabbed her arm and held her still.

"I knew you'd come out here."

"Did you?" she asked.

"The quiet outside, away from people. It's where you'd expect Quinn to go."

True, thought Larisa. *But Quinn had gone out onto the floor because that's what he knew she'd do.* That's how she'd found him. It'd been too easy.

"But he stayed inside because he thought that's where you'd be. And now I have you."

Larisa looked longingly toward the door into the church as though she was still wanting to look for Quinn. Then she reached up and released her mask. *Time to make my move.*

"I suppose you think this illustrates the wrong kind of love," she said.

"It illustrates that I'm more capable of taking care of you. He's just a boy following a passing passion. In five years, eight, ten, will he still think of you in the same way?"

"I hope not." She let the words hang in the air without explanation even though it felt that Lucas was waiting for one. She began to work her gloves off her fingers.

"You're allowed to see him before we leave if you like."

"What good would that do?" asked Larisa.

"It might reveal how ordinary your life with him would've been if I'd allowed you to carry on."

Who gave you the right? she thought. But then she looked at him. He'd removed his mask and was looking toward the church with his eyebrows drawn tight into the bridge of his nose, creating a wrinkle she almost reached up to smooth away with her finger. It wasn't an expression Larisa had expected, but she recognized it immediately.

"He got to you, didn't he?" She almost laughed at the irony.

"That's irrelevant. He's a determined ignoramus and as cold-blooded as a reptile. Why would you want someone who can't be moved by art?"

"The more important question is why do you want someone who doesn't want you?" she asked softly.

He looked at her then and Larisa knew she'd made a mistake. The edges of her vision blurred as his gaze focused on her, all seeing, all knowing, so hypnotic everything beyond it was erased from her awareness. "Are you sure you don't want me, Larisa?"

Her name in his voice rippled through her like an echo jarring loose the small stones on a mountainside, the whispered trigger of an avalanche. He moved closer.

"You still wish we were together."

Yes, she thought. But then she shook herself. "You're right. I do wish we were together like we were in the beginning, before I knew all your secrets. Before gunmen broke into your house, before CIA agents knocked on Hannah's door, before people died because I loved you."

"That's still possible."

"It's not." She shook free of his grasp and shoved her hands in her pockets. Her right hand dug down until she found the panic button buried in the folds. Once she pressed it, Agent Osna and his team would know where she was. They'd rush in and take Lucas away from her forever.

"It is."

She glared at him. Tears were forming in her eyes, and she didn't quite know why. Because she knew he believed what he was saying as equally as she wanted to believe it. Because he still didn't understand. He was like a boy who had grown up but still believed everything he wanted was always possible if he just reached for it hard enough. And she was the heartless woman ready to crush his dreams.

Red flag thoughts, Dr. Bade would say.

"I want you to give up on me," said Larisa. "No more texts, no more spying."

"You're not going to choose him over me."

"No. I'm choosing me over you." Larisa took a breath, closed her fist around the button. If she could get Lucas to agree, she wouldn't push it. She'd let him leave. Maybe she owed him that much. Prison would kill him. And where he was going probably wasn't even a real prison, but a black site somewhere.

Lucas crunched up his face in an incredulous expression, part disbelief, part mocking. "You're choosing to be alone?"

"I'm choosing to be without you. The rest doesn't matter." She took another breath. "If you really love me, you'll honor that."

"Absolutely not."

"Why not?"

"Because it's absurd. You're not thinking. No, you know what? You're in denial. What life do you think is going to be better than the one you had with me? We're perfect for each other."

Somewhere deep inside, a small voice whispered, *Nothing will ever be like what you had with him.*

Some part of that thought must have reflected in her face because Lucas's gaze softened. "Come on. Let's go back to Winter's place. We'll have dinner. If you still feel like you want to be alone forever, fine." He opened his mouth as though to say something else, but then stopped. She heard a vibration, then a sharp beep.

Lucas took out his phone as he smiled to himself. "I knew he wouldn't make it. I had Quinn wear a gag with a sensor on it so if he removed it before midnight I would know."

"Those weren't the rules."

"Each of us had our own rules," said Lucas. "He must think he's found you."

"I have." Quinn stood in the lawn just up the path, Kahleah beside him, the other sisters behind her, and—*oh God*—Larisa's mother just over Quinn's left shoulder. He'd removed his mask and hat and stood, strangely elegant in that dress that showed so much skin his nerves were probably fried from the exposure. She wanted to give him her coat, to button it up all the way to his neck.

"You're too late," said Lucas. "We're leaving now. Do what you want, you'll never hear from me again."

"Not even when she's gone?" Quinn crossed the lawn and

stood before them. Larisa was suddenly aware of how close she'd been standing to Lucas. From the outside, it probably hadn't looked like she was casting him away.

"What?"

"You won't tell me when she's dead?" Quinn's voice trembled.

Larisa expected Lucas to let out an exasperated sigh and berate Quinn for being hysterical. Instead, he'd gone quiet. He was staring at Quinn like he was the person Lucas most hated and loved in the world.

"This was never about love," said Quinn as he took another step closer. "It's about respect. Is she going to be safer with you or without you?"

Larisa watched the corners of Lucas's jaw clench and release as he stared at Quinn. She'd never seen him like this, at a loss for a sharp answer, shrinking beneath Quinn's gaze.

"Did you ask her how she felt last week when she heard about the explosion?"

"I told her we were fine."

"Did you ask her how she felt?" Quinn's voice rasped through what sounded like a dry riverbed in his throat. Rosa stepped hesitantly forward with a water bottle, but he ignored it. "Or we could ask her now."

"Unnecessary," snapped Lucas. "You've made your point."

"Have I?" Quinn's eyes took on a feverish light. "Because she has plans and a very long list of things she wants to do with her life. None of them are going to kill her as quickly as you will." Quinn coughed. "So, why don't you ask her to dinner again? And this time, you can explain why you think being with her is more important than all the other things she wants for her life." Quinn stepped back, waved his hand as though to give Lucas permission to move. He didn't. For a moment, Larisa thought he couldn't bring himself to look at her.

And then, just when it appeared he would have said something, the shrubbery parted, the swing behind her crashed into its arbor and people in tactical gear flowed forward to surround him.

Krissy screamed. Larisa thought she heard her mother utter a damning, "It's about fucking time." Then Lucas was being led away, arms cuffed, a hood over his head. Osna's team melted back into the shadows as quickly as they'd come.

"That was way less exciting than in the movies," said Krissy.

"Yeah, but we didn't hear his answer," said Jaden. "I mean, what if—"

"Nuh uh," said Rosa. "Don't even say it."

"I need a drink," said Suzette. "We'll meet you at the front door, darling," she called over her shoulder as she herded the sisters back into the church.

Quinn was coughing.

"What's wrong?" Larisa reached out to him, then let her arm fall short of its goal. She wasn't sure how to touch him. He almost felt like a stranger.

"I'm fine."

She smiled at that familiar dismissive tone. The particular way he always said it when he was not nearly fine, but he wanted to ignore the problem. "That was a good speech."

"Yeah? I'm not sure it would've been enough if the cavalry hadn't arrived."

"I don't think anything was going to be enough." She hooked her pointer finger around his pointer finger and led him to one of the swings. "Sit with me."

The giant skirts of their respective dresses took up a lot of space, but they managed to fit. She struggled out of her jacket and put it around his shoulders, dug the toe of her shoe into the ground to start them rocking. After a moment, Quinn leaned over and rested his head against her shoulder.

"Where did you find my bracelet?" he asked.

"In the old purse I was using during the shoot."

"Old?"

"Well, you know. Last season's bag." Larisa smiled.

From somewhere in the shadows to their left, a high-pitched giggle, a man's grunting.

"It doesn't feel over," said Quinn.

"It might not be. But I think you reached him better than I ever have."

"He was never going to be able to admit what you were giving up until something happened. Then it would've been too late."

She pulled his hand into her lap and laced her fingers through his.

"How do you feel?" he asked. The way he said it, she knew what he was asking. But she didn't want to answer, so she said brightly, "Well, I'm incredibly angry with you, and if you weren't so clearly in need of my attention, I'd make you sit by yourself all the way home."

"Larisa, no more hiding."

No more hiding. Be selfish.

"I suppose you won't be surprised to hear I was hanging on to him."

Quinn made a disbelieving click with his tongue.

"I know, I know, but it surprised me, okay? There were lots of good reasons for what I did. Obviously. I always have good reasons. But I never flat out told him no. I couldn't bring myself to ever completely close the door on him."

"He wouldn't have let you."

"Yes, but that was also an excuse. I liked that he would text me when I got caught by the tabloids. I think, maybe sometimes I even exposed myself to them so I'd hear from him. It was this game we were playing. Here are all the guys I'm messing with and they're all disposable. And the implication was always that when the timing was better, I'd go back to him. The weekend of Jaden's wedding, when you went off to have lunch with Parish, I think I even comforted myself with some glib thought that if I was really heartbroken and felt I couldn't live without you, I'd just pack up and go to Italy."

"But tonight, you told him. You called in the CIA. He knows now that you're done."

Larisa nodded. Yes, that was mostly true. But she hadn't called in the CIA. The panic button had never been activated. Osna and his team had come to her on their own.

"So how do you feel?" Quinn asked again.

"I feel terrible. I've ruined his life. And your life. And I really don't want to get on that plane tonight because who knows what my mother will say after witnessing that spectacle. And its just—" A sob rose up her throat. "It's just—I'm not sure I deserve you. And I'm so sorry for not telling you about Parish's baby, but—"

"You're pretty sure you'll do it again."

"I don't know how to trust someone. I've always been the strong one. I have the answers, I make the plans. I see a problem and I mark it off with a solution. No one has ever been able to do the same for me. And heaven help the person who thinks they're going to be with me and refuse my help." She took a breath. "But I want to get better."

"Maybe we can be gentle with each other and see how it goes?"

"You still want to be with me?"

"I absolutely still want to be with you."

"But are you sure?"

Quinn stood, gently pulled her up beside him and pushed back the brim of her hat. "Larisa, I love you."

Another sob. "That's the first time—"

"Second, I think. I told you in a voicemail when I was panicking."

"I didn't get it. My phone was smashed."

"Then let me say it again so you know for sure. I love you."

"You should kiss me then and prove it."

6 Months Later

Each day Quinn woke up and watched the sun rise over the Aegean Sea seemed more beautiful than the one before. The shooting schedule he'd settled on with FilmStreams packed the maximum union-allowed working hours into every day. He was so tired he fell asleep in the car on the way back to the hotel every night. But he'd promised himself, and his therapist, to claim the first hour of every day for himself even if it meant less sleep.

The hotel room had a balcony with a small table and chairs. The breakfast basket was delivered to the room's door half an hour before sunrise. So he sat, watching light slowly slide across the sea and ate with his left hand while he held his pen in his right, leaving space for whatever words came. Sometimes there were no words, just a feeling of gratitude, a sense of a long-clenched hand being slowly unfurled. Sometimes the words welled up and poured out of him until his cramping hand or the alarm on his phone told him he had to stop.

Sometimes the words were scenes, fragments of story, lines of dialogue, an image, a shot. Sometimes he wrote down things he wanted Larisa to know but couldn't say to her face. And then he'd mark the page with his pen and leave it there for her to find when she woke up and took her turn for breakfast at the little table.

On this particular morning, the day he was going to ask Steve

Helston to reach into himself and find some of the gravitas Quinn hoped was hidden beneath his cartoonish public persona and finally give Poseidon the humanity his fans had been waiting three movies to see, Quinn wrote:

> *I feel that I understand a little better why it was so hard to leave him. I keep telling myself he's incapable of truly caring for another person. But then I think how good it felt to have his attention. Every moment I was with him I was terrified, but I was also living to see what would happen next. Maybe it's like the way people lean forward during roller coasters. He makes violation feel like love.*

For her breakfast, Larisa ordered coffee from the café next to the hotel and paid the hotelier's son to bring it up to her no earlier than nine, and if he was late, that was fine. She slept late, sometimes went to bed early, often took an afternoon nap on days she didn't go to the set. She wasn't working this production as a consultant, but she'd discovered that she enjoyed showing herself off as Quinn's partner. And she knew how to handle Steve's ego in ways Quinn did not.

They were once again a team and it felt like the best way to ease into their recovery. LA felt full of ghosts, a feeling she hoped would pass, or something that would be easier to confront once they'd fallen into step together.

Every morning Quinn left something for her to read, she cried. Dr. Bade hadn't been enthusiastic about their choice to put the hard things on paper instead of speaking to each other. But they were both so tired, so fragile, so full of instincts to leave things unsaid.

She picked up the pen and wrote back to him.

> When you first came to my office for those sessions Eddie made you do, you said some terrible things to me. I think you felt bad about it, but you were angry at being trapped. You expected me to lash out. But I didn't. I don't even remember being bothered by them because I thought they were reasonable things to say to me. My only serious relationship had been with Lucas. He was always telling me that I didn't know enough, that I was silly, and emotional, and needed to expand my mind. Everything he said, I just took in as true. Not just true, but justified in a way that if I got upset about it, then that was on me. I let my parents do the same thing, and my cousin. I thought my greatest value to people was letting them say whatever they wanted about me. I see now that thinking like that only benefited him. Made it possible for him to mold me and twist me into what he wanted. I thanked him for it because he made me feel valuable.

A knock sounded on the door. Larisa ignored it.

She wiped away her tears and looked down at what she'd written. There was almost always more to say, but she felt small portions were easier to absorb. She thought, *Today is that big scene.* She pulled out her phone and texted Steve.

> Larisa: Don't be an ass today.

> S'Wonderful: I'm doing my speech today. It's gonna be awesome. You coming to watch?

> Larisa: Be flexible.

> S'Wonderful: I can touch my toes.

Larisa rolled her eyes. She would shower and dress and go to set. Part of her thought Quinn needed space to do things on his own. But she also thought, he'd want her there today even if all she did was glare at Steve when he stepped out of line.

Her phone rang.

"Miss Larisa, there's a man here asking for you."

The peace of the morning shattered on that sentence like a small rock dropped onto a glass table. She lurched to her feet and fled into the room as though someone had been spying on her. "Who is it?"

"Lawyer from Geneva. Do you want me to send him up?"

"No. I'm coming down. Fifteen minutes. Don't let him out of your sight." She regretted this last thought as she hung up. Much too dramatic. No need to worry the hotel staff. And if it was Lucas, she didn't want them to get involved.

She dressed quickly and hurried down.

It won't be Lucas.

Knowing the CIA, it could very well be Lucas.

But he promised.

The man waiting for her was a stranger dressed in a business suit of European tailoring. He carried a locked briefcase.

"Larisa de France-Kahn?"

"Yes."

"May I see some identification, please?"

Larisa glanced toward the hotel's front desk where the hotelier's wife and son stood behind the counter watching as Larisa pulled out her wallet.

"Thank you very much." The man sat down at one of the lobby's rattan chairs. After a moment of hesitation, Larisa sat down across from him. The man opened the briefcase and began pulling out folders.

"I hope I am not the first bearer of bad news. Lucas Onslow has passed on from this life."

Just hearing his name made Larisa's heart beat too fast. She pressed her hand against her chest and remembered the world thought Lucas had died in Orvieto in the explosion. But just to be sure something real hadn't happened, she asked, "Recently?"

"In February I'm afraid. I am Letto, the executor of his holdings. Apologies for taking so long to reach you. There was some contestation from the family and a few legal technicalities. But now, everything has been settled and I just need you to sign some documents demonstrating I have carried out my office and you understand your tax obligations."

Larisa picked up the first document, scanned it, set it down. "Oh fuck."

"Something is amiss?"

"No, I just. I wasn't expecting to receive anything from the estate."

Lotto chuckled. "Sometimes there is a silver lining to the loss of a loved one. You're based out of Los Angeles, correct?"

"Yes."

"And have you ever owned property internationally?"

"No."

"Conducted international banking?"

Larisa shook her head.

"Well, then. I will give you a brief tutorial of your next steps. Obviously, if you want to work with a firm in the States, that is understandable. I've prepared a list of those who have experience managing the variable portfolio that is now in your name."

"I'm sorry. Could we pause for a second?"

Lotto gave her a winning smile and patiently steepled his fingers.

"When was the will last updated?"

"Just a few days before his death. This was one of the reasons why it was contested."

"Can you tell me what it previously said?"

"Previously, you were to receive one half the value of stocks and bonds and the Italian villa, along with the sale values of smaller items. The other half would have gone to the family in London."

"And now?"

"Now, if we're simplifying for total value of assets, the family is receiving twenty percent, you're receiving forty percent, and a third beneficiary is also receiving forty percent. I hope this does not trouble you given the entire result is a surprise."

"Who is the other beneficiary?"

"I'm not at liberty—"

"Is it Rifat?" As soon as she said it, Larisa knew that wouldn't be it. Lucas was still alive, he wouldn't draw attention to his best helper by giving him his money. They would've set up a fund separately. She shook her head. There was only one answer. It hardly seemed possible.

He planned to let us go, she thought.

The lawyer was talking again, fee structures, taxes, things that were already automated, things she had the option to automate. Her three new Swiss bank accounts. But they weren't new apparently. They'd been in her name for five years and been sitting untouched, which explained why they hadn't been seized by the CIA.

Lucas had lived his life close to the margins, but apparently his legitimate work and his family money had been kept separate. None of the people he owed money to knew it existed. The CIA didn't know. Most likely, none of it had ever come from an arms sale. It was a small fortune, but it would be enough to buy a new car, put a down payment on a house, maybe rent an office. And

Quinn, as the third named beneficiary, would be receiving the same amount.

If he accepts it.

Larisa tried to imagine his reaction. He wouldn't like it, but he wouldn't turn it down when it would vault him so much closer to the life he wanted.

He gave us our future and he let us go.

Larisa stood and walked across the lobby to the deck at the back of the hotel that sat on the cliffs overlooking the sea. Down below, the narrow streets of Athens wound down to the water between rows of white stucco buildings and spindly trees. There were few people out walking as it was a cool day and not tourist season. But still, her eyes examined every face she saw until she reached so far down that all she could see were anonymous heads with dark hair. She felt she was being watched, a feeling she often had now that she knew how closely Lucas had kept tabs on her. But, for the first time since Milan, it didn't bother her.

The day passed without Larisa's notice. Her worries about Quinn managing Steve and the big scene were forgotten, surrendered to fate as she drifted through thoughts so fluid they couldn't be distinguished one from another. And yet, when Quinn returned, she was surprised to find the day gone, the sun long hidden by the sea. She was laying on the bed in their room mesmerized by the gauzy curtains of the canopy bed puffing in and out with the balcony breeze.

"Like they're breathing," she said. "The bed's alive."

Quinn lay down beside her. They weren't quite comfortable with each other yet, their bodies strangers, but not in a way that felt wrong. Together, they were working on becoming comfortable as individuals.

"Thanks," said Quinn. "I'll have nightmares about that tonight."

"How was it?"

"The scene? Passible."

"Steve?" she asked.

"Also passable. I might've overstepped. He might be a little afraid of me."

She reached for his hand and twined their arms together before linking fingers. This was touch Quinn was comfortable with. He'd promised her the rest would come when he couldn't feel Lucas on his skin anymore. Secretly, Larisa thought that moment might not ever come, but she was prepared to wait.

"Did the lawyer find you?" he asked.

She nodded.

"I almost refused it."

"I thought you would."

"Did you know?"

"No. I mean, he talked about it years ago, but I never thought he'd do it."

"It's more money than I've ever had." He left the second part of the thought unspoken. The, *But it's his.*

"It makes us free to build the life we want," said Larisa.

"It feels like we're accepting a loan he'll call in someday."

"I feel like that already," she said.

Quinn shifted in the bed, trying to get comfortable with whatever was in his mind. Finally he said, "Maybe it's wrong to think he's something we're going to move past. Maybe he's just always going to be part of us."

At first glance, Larisa hated the thought. But then, she saw the truth of it. Or at least its practicality.

"I don't want us to lie to each other when we're thinking about him," said Quinn. "So let's just make space for him. You and me and everything that comes with Lucas."

"I hate him."

"I think I love him."

Larisa lifted Quinn's hand to her mouth and kissed the ridge of his knuckles. "That too," she whispered.

"We'll build a house."

"With a secret dungeon?" she asked.

"Nicer than his."

"We'll host dinners full of food our friends have never heard of."

"And convert them into opera fans."

Quinn made a face. "We'll be so unpopular."

"But you'll be a famous director, so they'll still come and pretend to like it."

"And you'll make everything run," he said as he turned onto his side to gaze at her. "I'm with you until the end."

Larisa turned to face him. "I'm with you until the end," she said.

Please Leave a Review

So glad this book found you! If you enjoyed reading it, please leave a review. Please also tell people about this book. Books are sold by people talking about them.

Cheers, Jaye

You're welcome to post about Homme Fatale all you want on your own socials, but if you want a dedicated place to discuss this, and my other books, with your fellow readers, join my private, member-only reader group on Facebook.

Sign up for my mailing list to receive early offers, announcements, and bonus content.

Acknowledgements

Land Acknowledgement

Homme Fatale was written on the ancestral land and traditional territories of the Omaha, Oto, and Pawnee Nations. They are the original custodians of the land on which I have lived and worked while writing this novel.

I knew Casta Diva would be split into two books when I was listening to the Fates Mates podcast the summer of 2023 and Sarah and Jen were discussing dueling and masquerades in historical romance and bemoaning their absence in contemporary. To me, it felt like a challenge, how can a contemporary romance have a masquerade with true stakes in it? I wrote the climatic final scene of Homme Fatale before I knew there would be an entire book to support it, because obviously masquerades are amazing and we should have them in everything.

Special thanks to my intrepid beta readers Hannah Gage, Heather Leighson, and Emma V, who all agreed on several important things that caused me to rewrite a large portion of this book.

Thanks to Sarah McGuire my editor who fixed all the commas and also caught several continuity errors, to Damonza Designs for the great cover, and to Clara at Author Tree for taking my Word doc and making it look like a book.

About the Author

Jaye Viner lives on what used to be the plains of eastern Nebraska with a tall human and three fur bombs. She knows just enough about a wide variety of things to embarrass herself at parties she never attends. Her short fiction has been published in Drabblecast, Everyday Fiction, The Rumpus, and Others. She is the author of *Jane of Battery Park* and the *Elaborate Lives* Series. Find her on Instagram @Jaye_Viner or her website JayeViner.com

Social media links for ebook
https://twitter.com/JayeViner
https://www.instagram.com/jaye_viner/
https://www.facebook.com/JayeViner
www.jayeviner.com
https://www.goodreads.com/author/show/7107386.Jaye_Viner